SUB-ZERO

MATT JAMES

SEVERED PRESS
HOBART TASMANIA

SUB-ZERO

WWW.SEVEREDPRESS.COM

ISBN: 978-1-922323-06-4 11.95

For Greig Beck

Thank you for your support and friendship

ALSO BY MATT JAMES

DEAD MOON SERIES
Nightmares are Born
Home Sweet Hell
Song of Sorrow
In Memoriam (Coming Soon)

DEAD MOON SHORT STORIES
Nightmare at the Museum
Scared to Death

STAND-ALONE TITLES
The Dragon
Broken Glass
The Cursed Pharaoh
Dark Island
Sub-Zero

DANE MADDOCK ADVENTURES w/David Wood
Berserk
Skin and Bones
Venom

HANK BOYD ADVENTURES
Blood and Sand
Mayan Darkness
Babel Found
Elixir of Life

LOGAN REED THRILLERS
Plague
Evolve

PROLOGUE

McMurdo Station, Antarctica
Eleven Years Ago

Bleary-eyed, Gavin Kirk stared at his monitor, dazed, hoping and praying that it was time for his shift to be over. Being a radar technician inside an Antarctic research station was easy work because nothing ever showed up on his screen. Ever. But if a green blip did appear, it usually represented something they were expecting, like a supply ship dropping off and/or picking up cargo containers, or an incoming aircraft doing the same.

Checking his watch, Kirk sighed.

Still an hour left, he thought, rubbing his face.

He'd been at his station for eleven hours already and was deeply regretting his decision to cover for one of his fellow operators. Reflexively, his eyes flicked down to his wrist again, and he groaned in response. His shift was never going to end...

One more hour, Gavin. He thought. *Come on, dude. You can do this.*

At the moment, it was only Kirk and two of his CO's on duty. The late-night, graveyard shift was the worst McMurdo could throw at you. Literally, nothing appeared on their radars since deliveries were never scheduled to arrive overnight when the weather was at its worst.

The sun was still up, and knowing it was so close to Christmas, it wouldn't be setting for a long time, not until March. That's how it was in the southern hemisphere. It was summer in December—the sun had risen in September and would be up until the end of February.

Antarctic summers were something to behold and something to loathe. The all dark winters were too. It wouldn't have mattered much except that most of the people stationed here were Americans and they were used to the northern hemispheric life; Kirk included.

Leaning back in his worn, poorly padded office chair, Kirk yawned, blinking his eyes. For a second, they almost closed for good—but then, something caught his attention as it flashed across his monitor.

"Huh?" he said, getting the attention of one of his superiors from across the room.

"What is it, Kirk?" Commander Fredricks asked.

"I'm not sure, sir," he replied, yawning again. "I think I saw something."

"You *think* you saw something?"

"Well—"

"Either you saw it, or you didn't. There is no 'think.'"

Kirk rolled his eyes. *Says the man who hasn't had an original thought in years.*

Fredricks was a hard ass, mostly because he hated his command. Only scientific type gurus were really interested in being at McMurdo. Men like Kirk and Fredricks didn't belong here. They weren't even scientists. They were a part of the security detail for the station.

He looked up at his CO. "I definitely saw something."

"You sure?"

Kirk ground his teeth, hating the game Fredricks was playing. He returned his eyes to his monitor, mostly because he didn't want Fredricks to see how annoyed he was. "Yes, sir." The man loved having his ego stroked.

Fredricks stepped up beside him. "What was it?"

Kirk did the math and knew it could be only one thing. The blip hadn't come from the sea, its trajectory had originated from the sky.

"I believe it was a meteor splashing down off our coast."

Fredricks laughed hysterically. "A meteor? Really? That's what has your panties in a bunch?"

As mundane as it sounded, the relatively uneventful detection still needed to be recorded per McMurdo protocol. Kirk pulled a red binder out of his desk drawer but was stopped by the commander.

"Don't bother with that," Fredricks said. "It's just a meteor. I seriously doubt anyone back home is going to care about another damned rock falling from space."

"But, sir—"

"Look," Fredricks interrupted, waving his hand dismissively, "if it'll make you feel better, you can at least jot down the thing's splashdown coordinates, but please, for the love of God, don't file an entire report." He turned and headed off. "I don't have the time, or patience, for something as trivial as that."

Southern Ocean
Present Day

"So, what exactly am I looking for, Doc?"

Dr. Seth Donovan rubbed his forehead, wanting nothing more than to reach through his microphone and strangle the man on the other end. Donovan despised having to work so closely with "the help." Those within his science division hadn't gotten along with the Endeavor's crew since the day they set sail for the Antarctic.

As the head of the team, Donovan kept his squad of forty moving toward one, unified goal: scientific advancement. They never stopped pushing forward. He had been told multiple times that his ambitions were unobtainable. The first time was while he was studying for the multiple degrees he had eventually earned. Then, he was reminded about it while applying for the Antarctic operation. Now, near the end of his detail aboard the Endeavor, it was being brought to the forefront again.

In return, he told them all to "kiss his ass."

People didn't like Seth Donovan very much—but nor did he truly care what others thought of him. He was quickly moving up the DARPA ladder, specifically in the field of genetics. His desires were the same as the people cutting his lucrative paycheck: Keep the country safe by providing them the means to do so.

Donovan, however, had a higher purpose. More than anything, he wanted the glory that came with success.

His guaranteed promotion, which he deserved, would finally earn him the respect from all of the people that had mocked him over the years. Even if it was fake admiration, he'd be in a position for people to have to actually kiss his ass.

Blinking away visions of himself winning awards and collecting monetary bonuses, Donovan turned his attention back to the sailor in the ADS.

The Atmospheric Diving Suit resembled a bulbous suit of armor. The men aboard the Endeavor called this particular variation, "Stay Puft." Like the giant marshmallow man from the original *Ghostbusters*, the modified Newtsuit was mostly white and made its wearer look pudgy and clumsy.

The same could be said for a few of the captain's men.

Donovan tapped his wrist-mounted computer and keyed up his microphone, speaking his instructions through a clenched jaw and gritted teeth. "You are looking for an ultra-rare species of octopus, one that emits low levels of light via natural bioluminescence—one that didn't exist in this area until the last decade or so."

3

"Uh…" the man muttered back. "So, let me get this straight. I'm snagging a glowing squid?"

Glowing squid… Donovan thought, closing his eyes. *How on earth did I get saddled with these assholes?* Even before boarding the ship, he knew the seamen were going to be a nuisance.

And yet, they're so much worse.

"It's not a squid," he corrected, "it's the highly venomous cousin of the deadly blue-ringed octopus."

Donovan allowed himself the pleasure of a smile when the diver went silent. That made him feel in control. He didn't give away that his statement, from a technical perspective, was false. Yes, the animal they were looking for now was exceptionally dangerous, but no, it wasn't a relative of its infamous, blue-ringed cousin.

But really, just like humans are all related to one another, theoretically, ALL of these things are related too.

"Right…" the diver said, breathing more comfortably, "well, let's get this show on the road, shall we?"

Donovan was coordinating the descent beneath the ocean remotely from inside one of his four labs, safely aboard the Endeavor. To his right was the pilot of a Remotely Operated Vehicle, and the man seated on his left was responsible for the ROV's cameras, among other internal systems.

The four-foot-long, hot dog-shaped, unmanned submersible floated alongside the sailor in the ADS. Cameras mounted to eight different locations along the ROV would catch everything on video, documenting the groundbreaking event for all to see. Unfortunately, it could also document their failure—his failure—if they came away empty-handed and all of those in charge would see.

Can't let that happen, Donovan thought, squeezing the table-mounted microphone stand harder. *I won't allow it to happen.*

As the second technician powered on the cameras, the world beneath the waters of Antarctica bloomed to life. Even for a man as cold and as calculating as Donovan, he couldn't help but hold his breath in awe. The lighting wasn't enough though—he wanted more—but it was going to be an issue for everyone because they were so deep below the surface. As a result, the unmanned submersible was forced to use the lowest level of light, just enough for the cameras to see by.

The creatures living down here would likely scatter. The lowest level of light to us would be considered blazing to them—they'd never been out of the dark. It was going to be a slow process. To top it off, the weather outside was worsening. They needed to proceed with caution. Donovan and the rest of the Endeavor's crew had just a day to finish what they started. Winter was nearing and their time in Antarctica was up.

"Um," the diver said, "I think I've got something."

Donovan's right eyebrow raised in confusion. He had just checked the depth gauge and saw that they hadn't yet touched bottom. Octopuses weren't like their squid relatives. The former preferred to hide in whatever rocky crevasses they could squeeze themselves into. Squids were the exact opposite and loved the freedom of the open ocean.

"That can't be..."

Donovan's voice trailed off when he saw a pulse of light emanating from directly beneath the diver's feet. He had a wealth of cameras attached to his suit's hard casing. And right now, they were pointed straight down.

"Move back a little," Donovan ordered, "don't come down on top of it."

"Roger that," the diver replied. "Don't squish the squid."

Donovan ignored the smattering of laughter around him and focused his attention to the image on the screen. The octopus they were looking for was, indeed, bioluminescent, but it didn't use it in a way like this.

The rapid succession of pulses he witnessed now almost reminded him of Morse code. Donovan knew that the species was intelligent—smarter than most life on Earth. He recalled researchers describing the animal's DNA to be "alien-like" compared to the rest of the creatures. Their genetic profile didn't resemble any other living thing that called this planet home.

Truthfully unique, he thought, leaning closer to the screen array.

Each camera had its own display, and all of them were currently trained on the happenings beneath the booted feet of the diver— and each showed the magical light show. One of the many advantages they had aboard the Endeavor was government funding when it came to anything military. Donovan knew for a fact that their "budget" didn't actually exist. Yes, the ship's purpose being out at sea was public, but the exact costs involved were hidden.

Even as the head of the science division, Donovan wasn't privy to that information.

Neither is the captain, for that matter...

"Sir?" the ROV's pilot asked, his voice laced with concern.

Donovan saw it, and he didn't like what he was seeing.

As the diver moved away from the dome-shaped, rocky outcrop—and their prize—the creature's incredible display softened, and it began a low canine-like growl. It wasn't prepared to attack but warning them to stay back.

"How far is he from it?" Donovan asked, glancing over his shoulder.

"Thirty feet, sir," a woman, whose name Donovan never bothered to learn, replied.

He keyed his microphone. "Move in closer."

"Say the magic word..." the diver sarcastically responded, earning yet another chortle from the gathering mass of people.

The crowd was a mix of his people and the captain's crew. While not one to back down from anybody, Donovan understood rule number one on board the Endeavor. Don't piss off Captain House. So, he kept his mouth shut.

"Moving in another ten feet," the diver announced, instantly silencing the room.

The room, Lab 4, was, in reality, one enormous space split up into several large areas. The Endeavor was a recently decommissioned T-3 naval oil tanker. Soon after it was retired from active service, the US Navy and DARPA, the Defense Advanced Research Projects Agency, signed an agreement to build the floating research station.

Unfortunately, Donovan had to share his personal space with the ROV and ADS operators. Having them close by was imperative to the success of their mission here in the Antarctic. It was the only reason he allowed the sailors access to 'his' space.

Otherwise, I wouldn't let the Saltines in.

It's what he called the captain's men. If for no other purpose, it made Donovan feel better about being there and more in control. He *hated* the open ocean with a passion—everything about it irked him. But his own goals superseded his discomforts.

The cramped living quarters.

The food.

The people.

Donovan preferred the company of his laboratory equipment to that of living things. People, for the most part, were awful to be around. Some called him a "douchebag," but his like-minded colleagues thought of him as a genius.

The ADS was slow-moving, and when the diver finally got into position, the first thing out of his mouth was, "Uh oh, I think I made it mad."

The electric-blue flashes turned into a deeper shade of the same color. Donovan was shocked at what he saw. Whatever they had here was displaying its feelings like a mood ring on steroids.

A soft chime in Donovan's ear caused him to growl. The only person that could override his communications was Captain House.

"We have a situation above deck," House said.

Now, what...?

"What is it?" Donovan asked, aggravated.

Likewise, House sounded irritated too, grumbling something incoherently. What he said next boiled Donovan's blood.

"Bring our boy up ASAP. Our storm is rolling in fast and ahead of schedule."

"What!" Donovan shouted, turning all heads toward him.

"Now, Seth," House ordered, "or I'll come down there and do it myself."

Donovan walked away from his post. "You can't do this, Sebastian! Not after all we've been through. Not when we're *this* close."

"The hell I can't!" House replied. "This is my boat, Seth. If you don't bring my sailor back up—immediately—I'll arrest you for negligence. I am in sole command when it comes to the safety of everyone on this ship—not you!"

Donovan winced. He may have just broken rule number one.

Without answering the incensed captain, Donovan logged off and begrudgingly relayed the man's order. There was no way in hell that he'd transmit the message as his own.

"We're aborting," he announced. "Sorry, everyone, Captain's orders. Bring up the diver. Storm is coming in fast."

"Uh, Dr. Donovan?" the ROV's pilot said. "We have contact."

Contact? He thought it was a strange way to word a simple sighting.

Donovan turned and looked up at the main screen which was attached to the forward wall. There, floating ten feet away from their diver was an octopus no bigger than one you'd find inside someone's home aquarium. But it wasn't the creature's size, or even its shape, that caught everyone's eye...it was the animal's vibrant, cracking blue veins that pulsated beneath its inky-black skin.

Usually, things at this depth would evolve some type of translucency in their pigment, not requiring it in the darker depths of the world's ocean. And yet, the one hovering before them had the dark skin.

"What do I do?" the diver asked.

Before Donovan, or anyone else could reply, the animal shot forward at an incredible speed, latching itself onto the sailor's protective helmet. After years of studying the species, Donovan had never seen one act so aggressively to something so much bigger than it. All it had to do was retreat back into its hiding spot, and it would've been safe. Instead, it went out of its way to drive the diver away.

It attacked him! Donovan thought, smiling. *This one will be a treat to exam...*

"Fire harpoon!" Donovan shouted

He was happy to see the ROV pilot react immediately and depress the trigger of his fighter jet-like flight stick without skipping a beat. The controls were connected to the sub's net-loaded, hull-mounted harpoon gun. Instantly, both the diver and the creature were incased in the inescapable snare.

Inbetween flashes of light, cheers of joy, and the diver's frightened shrieks, Donovan turned to the closest technician. "Bring them up—now!"

1

The Southern Ocean contains some of the coldest water on Earth. Also known as the Antarctic Ocean, its sea temperatures range from fifty degrees Fahrenheit to an astonishingly low thirty degrees Fahrenheit. Not only is the ocean itself deadly, but so are the winds that steer it. Antarctica carries with it the strongest average wind speed of any place on the planet.

And the Endeavor research vessel has been sailing those very waters for almost three months now.

Retrofitted back into service from a decommissioned tanker and named after renowned explorer Captain Cook's ship—just not spelled the same—the *Endeavor* was deployed by two factions with a long history of working together within the United States military. The Navy and DARPA.

DARPA was responsible for the latest and greatest technologies in use by every branch of the military, and with their partnership here, they hoped to supply the soldiers fighting on the front lines with a newfound gift: Invulnerability of pain. To extend a soldier's effectiveness in combat, they intended to block the debilitating effects of pain.

Expensive pain blockers, the captain thought, rolling his eyes.

He thought the very idea of hiding someone's pain was ludicrous. How on God's green Earth could someone learn from their mistakes without pain in their lives? He believed that people were being babied enough as it was, even within the military.

Now, they're taking away, not only mental pain, but physical pain as well.

Yet, here he was, back on a naval ship. While, technically, it belonged to both the Navy *and* DARPA, he still would've never thought, not in a million years, that he'd be back at sea with an American flag on his shoulder.

Captain Sebastian House had been a sailor under Uncle Sam for twenty-five years before his beloved wife, Karen, was killed in a traffic accident at the hands of an intoxicated driver five years earlier. While his wife's death was hard on him, it was even harder on their only child, their daughter, Gianna.

Like her mother, "G" was a looker. Not only was she beautiful with skin that was a mix from her parents, black and white, she also possessed a genius-level IQ. It, like her father's intimidating demeanor, turned most people off, especially the men that she had dated. They were *terrified* of her brain...and of her dad's brawn.

Being a good bit smarter than your boyfriend didn't sit well with them. The constant rejection, combined with the emotional trauma sustained by her mother's death, drove Gianna to rely on something other than her father's unwavering love and support.

It drove her to habitual drug use.

One night, House got the phone call every parent dreaded to receive. His twenty-two-year-old daughter had been arrested for theft and assault. And worse yet, her arrest led to losing her high paying job with DARPA. She had been the youngest woman hired by DARPA in decades and accomplished the feat without any help from her father's friends within the organization.

At the time of her hire, House couldn't have been prouder of his little girl.

Three years later, and one lengthy stay in rehab for Gianna, they were *both* on board the Endeavor. She served as the ship's electronics guru, while House acted as the vessel's overseer, its captain, and she was his responsibility, per his contract with DARPA. No one, not even the one person that House answered to aboard his boat wanted her. She had burned one too many bridges—especially inside the company that had fired her.

And now I owe Damon a lifetime of favors, he thought, sighing.

Damon Becker was the onboard liaison for both the Navy and DARPA, serving as a direct line of communication to each within the Endeavor. He reported back to the states every two days, precisely, to update the chain of command with any and all details.

I'd have rather shot myself than taken that gig, House thought, shaking his head.

While House ran everything physically related to the tanker, another man—a dictator of sorts—had his fingers in all that pertained to the work they did in the name of scientific advancement.

Dr. Seth Donovan.

What an egotistical brat.

House was an old-school seadog. He believed that you earned your keep with hard work and the right attitude—which in today's world *didn't* include respect for your elders.

Donovan was twenty-six years younger than House, and it drove him mad to think that such a pompous asshat had already been given the position he had at twenty-eight. Theoretically, he and Donovan were equals while aboard the Endeavor, but House knew all he had to do was breathe differently and he could force the little shit into whatever he wanted.

Donovan was as spineless as the creature they sought.

House couldn't care less about the *squid*, as the men called it. The only reason they continued to call it a squid was because of how Donovan reacted to the name. But House wasn't going to force his will on any of his men, Donovan included. He'd been in his men's shoes before—for over two decades. Each and every person House ever served under had come off as a bureaucratic fuckfish.

He grinned. Yes, that's what they called the over-the-top, by-the-book commanders when he was enlisted, a *fuckfish*.

House wasn't what you would call a "typical Navy man." He didn't think or speak like most seafarers. Originally from Albany, Georgia, he thought and talked like those from the same area. Simple and without bullshit. Purely put, House got straight to the point and didn't hold back.

Gianna was the same way too. No one would've guessed that she was as smart as she was if you were judging by her looks and slight southern drawl. Plus, they both had issues in specific social circles because of their darker skin color. Gianna had it worse, though, because she was often referred to as a "half-breed."

House hated that they were both judged by their skin color. It was the twenty-first century, and people still gave them funny looks when they found out who they were, and what they did for a living. Whenever he told people he was going to be the captain of a state-of-the-art Naval research vessel, the person's reaction was always the same—it was like clockwork.

They were surprised.

Being in his fifties, House was accustomed to it.

Only being in her twenties, Gianna was still getting used to it.

"Neanderthals," he said when she was younger.

"All of them?" she asked with tears in her eyes.

He shrugged. "Not all of them... Those are the ones you don't let go. Be nice to everyone, and the people who are friendly back... They're the keepers."

House smiled at the memory until one of his men rushed forward with the incoming weather report. The nasty storm they were expecting had shifted...and sped up. Now, it would hit them even sooner. The current trip down to the bottom of the Southern Ocean was to be their last, but they were supposed to have at least another twelve hours.

House's eyes opened wide, calculating their time frame.

It'll be close, he told himself. But he knew better. House always leaned toward the side of caution. No one would ever berate him for looking out for his people's lives ahead of the mission. He shook his head. *Can't chance it.*

His verbal threat to Donovan, while genuine, meant very little if the man took it up with Becker. House held no real power over the scientist, just the ability to spook him into submission. Like most people who wielded power without earning it, Donovan rolled over every single time he sniffed a fight. Men like that had never fought for what they received and would gladly give it up to preserve themselves.

House would've gone down swinging if it were him.

In his prior stint aboard a military vessel, back with the Navy, House was the Executive Officer aboard the *USS Harry S. Truman.* His only regret before retiring was never commanding his own boat.

Being in charge was second nature for House. It was easy for him because of the way he saw his job. If he respected the people around him, they, in turn, would return the favor. If they didn't respect him back, they weren't going to be on his ship for long.

It made House smile when he recalled the "boys" that thought it would be wise to cross him. Usually, it only took him a few days to get them to see things more clearly. Sanitizing toilets for days on end could change someone's perspective in a hurry.

Lifting his left hand, House activated his comms unit via his new WiMP system, overriding and interrupting Donovan's own system below deck. The Wrist-Mounted Personal Computer was more of a mobile command console than anything else. It could literally do anything. The screen was four inches wide by two inches tall and had an incredibly responsive touchscreen. Those who held their own command aboard the Endeavor, including House's number two aboard the ship, was recently given one to test for DARPA.

He tapped the "All Call" button, knowing full well that Donovan was going to go nuts because of it. The man was a creature of habit and precision. House lived his life by flying by the seat of his pants, living life like every day was his last. That didn't mean he was reckless, though.

House was quite the opposite, actually.

When he was younger, House had been "advised" to look into the SEAL program. An on-leave admiral once witnessed him take down three drunkards at a local watering hole and was impressed when House came away from the kerfuffle completely unscathed. He should've gotten in trouble that night as well, but the high-ranking officer had vouched for him.

House loved being one of the guys, a sailor of the seven seas. There was something about it that he couldn't quite explain. He had lived the life of an average sailor for a few years already, so he thanked the admiral for his suggestions and ultimately refused to give it up. And he never became a SEAL, however, if he had, he probably would have been on a carrier, like the Truman, at some point.

House wasn't the "average sailor" either.

He was cunning and had the knack to see a situation unfold in advance of it happening. He was also dangerous and finished most of the SEAL training on his own. He was particularly skilled in hand-to-hand combat.

Growing up where he did, had its benefits.

House grew up a brawler, fending for himself on the streets of a town most people had never heard of. A good kid, for the most part, he never went around looking for fights, they just always seemed to find him. Then again, his fuse was as short as they came. Anything could set him off when he was in his younger years. Now, he channeled that energy into his mentoring of others and his workout regime.

He was what you would call a "workout warrior."

If House had a phone to throw, he would've after getting off the line with Donovan. Like the Special Forces units out in the field, the crew above the Endeavor had some pretty neat toys at their disposal.

Connected to his WiMP unit was a sub-vocal throat mic. The only thing House didn't appreciate was the computer-chipped sticker he had to wear on his neck. The only other piece of hardware within the crew's usual comms unit was a non-descript earpiece tethered to the back of their shirt collar. Everything else was run in house by the ship's Communications Team.

Including his daughter.

Gianna had her fingers in every high-tech system aboard his boat, which meant he knew he was about to get a call from her any second.

His earpiece chimed.

Speak of the Devil...

"Dad?"

"Not now, G," House replied, quickly ending the call.

The only reason she was calling was because of the diver in the ADS. He, Cole Triplett, had taken a liking to Gianna on their second day at sea. Typically, House would've ended the fraternization, but with his daughter's history of depression, he wanted her to be at her best mentally—for everyone's sake.

Plus, House and Gianna didn't work for the Navy. They were employed by DARPA. If he wanted an excuse, that was the one he'd use. There were no such rules for not dating another co-worker, at least, not that he knew of.

But if things ended poorly with "Trip" while still on the water, the incoming storm wasn't the only thing the crew of the Endeavor would have to endure. They'd be forced to weather another violent maelstrom.

Hell hath no fury like Gianna scorned.

2

Gianna tried to call him three separate times while he was en route to the ship's launch bay to confront Donovan and make sure he followed his orders. At first, he was going to stay in the bridge but didn't trust the scientist to promptly follow through.

Each time his daughter tried to reach him, he declined her call. House was the only person aboard the Endeavor that wielded such power during work hours. The other crew members could deny each other, but *no one* could block House from calling them.

Not even Donovan.

That made House smile the most. It was one of only a handful of things that he had over the man. Because he was officially in charge of everyone's wellbeing aboard the boat, House thought it a good idea to have the ability to contact anyone at any time.

Donovan saw it as a way to "control" people.

House shook his head and placed his hand on the air-tight door. Beyond it was the launch bay, consisting of a sealable pool down into the frigid waters of the Antarctic. The thick sleeves of his winter jacket felt cumbersome, especially inside of the comfortable, temperature-controlled ship. But with the extreme cold invading the boat on the other side of the hatch, House agreed that it was for the best.

It really was that cold.

With a hiss and a *whoosh* of icy air, House stepped into mayhem. Of the eight people stationed inside the launch bay, every single one of them was panicked, frantically running around and shouting at one another. But House could barely see any of them. Something at the center of the room was blinding him with a blue, pulsating light.

One of the boys' new toys?

The DARPA engineers aboard his boat were always coming up with new tech to try out on the open ocean. Without being able to see the light's origin, House assumed it was one of their inventions gone awry. He figured that someone had gotten over their skis and triggered God-knows-what.

But then he heard Trip's voice hollering through the bay's loudspeaker and realized that it wasn't something DARPA was responsible for. Something had definitely gone wrong, and it was no laughing matter.

His suit?

Shielding his face against the intense light, House descended the stairs in the room, carefully taking them one at a time. He wanted nothing more than to rush inside with his fists and his jaw clenched tight. Plus, Trip was a good sailor, incredibly well-disciplined while under duress—even more so when he was underwater and in trouble. The fact that the man was screaming like he was worried House immensely.

The stairs switchbacked to the left and then headed back in the other direction. When House got to the landing between sets, he snuck a quick peek at the scene before him amid the flashes.

Trip was, as he thought, still inside the ADS. Everyone who wasn't manning a terminal or rushing for a piece of random equipment had gathered around the launch pool at the floor of the Endeavor. Whatever was happening, it was occurring in, or around, the pool.

The pool itself had two heated, retractable sets of doors. The inner doors give the diver access into the ship. When the outer doors opened, the ocean swarmed in. The space in between was what they called Purgatory.

The Endeavor was Heaven.

The ocean was Hell.

Until he knew for sure what was going on, House needed to treat the situation before him as if it were life-threatening. So, he vaulted the last four steps and sprinted straight for the center of the room. Just as he was about to shout an order, one of the men jabbed at Trip's helmet with a long, metal pole.

What the hell? House thought, still not being able to take in the entire scene. But as soon as the pole touched the light's origin, it immediately began to dim, and once it did, House finally got a look at their catch.

"You're kidding me, right?" he asked, glancing at the sailor with the pole. "Did you just tranquilize an octopus?"

The man, a crew member he knew as Seaman Jordan, responded with just a shrug. Like House, he was obviously confused and couldn't formulate a proper answer. As far as the creature was concerned, it let loose a final series of rhythmic pulsations before falling harmlessly to the bay floor.

For a moment, no one moved.

Not until a voice, that House dreaded hearing in person, spoke up from the room's hatch above and behind him.

"Contain the specimen and transport it to my examination lab above decks, immediately!"

Seth Donovan.

House stepped aside as people from Donovan's team came rushing in with a bevy of gear. They seemed to be carrying some type of mobile fish tank. One guy dropped a hose into the water to House's left, while a woman flipped a handful of switches before depressing a large red button.

It seemed that whatever sedative they gave the octopus wasn't meant to last very long. The tank resembled an upside-down fishbowl with three tubes protruding from its crown. The base was straightforward and rectangular and locked into place once the creature was moved into position. When secure, freezing Antarctic water instantly started to pour inside of it.

House heard a hiss, and then...

"What the hell was that, sir?"

He turned his attention to the sailor in the helmetless ADS, Cole Triplett. Trip looked more suited for the science team with his lean build and thick, black-rimmed glasses, but his knowledge of the ADS' systems made him the best man for the job when it needed to get wet. Trip had helped design some of the upgrades long before they set sail and logged an insane amount of hours inside of it.

Similar to Gianna, Trip was intellectually gifted, but like House, he preferred the independence the open ocean offered him to, say, an office setting or a laboratory. The younger man would've excelled in both environments, advancing further than most at his age.

He has both here, House thought, smiling a little. Trip excelled on the Endeavor, impressing House in a variety of fields, specifically dive tech and mechanical engineering.

"Next time," Trip said, struggling out of the suit, "I'm strapping a harpoon to Stay Puft's arm, and I'm going fishing!"

House crossed his arms and grinned, getting a confused look out of Trip.

"You going to keep complaining, or are you going to get out of that suit and tell me what happened?"

"You weren't watching?"

House shook his head. "I was a little busy, you know, being a captain and all."

Trip smiled and seconds later, a sound resembling an oversized deadbolt unlocking filled the air. Next, the chest and upper back sections separated, allowing Trip to shimmy out of the one-of-a-kind Atmospheric Diving Suit. There wasn't another piece of equipment like it in the U.S. Navy.

The back and legs each had thrusters attached to them, allowing the *pilot*, Trip, to navigate through the water effortlessly, and all without a separate propulsion system—an underwater jetpack. Steering it wasn't as easy as Trip made it look either. House attempted to pilot the suit once—*once*—on a bet from the *Endeavor's* head engineer and failed miserably in front of the entire crew.

Damn you, Buddy.

Chief Engineer Marcus "Buddy" Malone was an even older seadog than House. He was in his early seventies but ran laps around those forty years younger than him. House brought the man in to be his head of engineering because of their days together aboard the *Harry S. Truman.* Buddy held the same title on the carrier before retiring over a decade ago, and House didn't trust anyone more than him with machines. Plus, it didn't hurt that they were both Georgia natives and die-hard Bulldogs fans.

Go Dawgs!

A technician to House's right operated the winch holding the ADS aloft, and while he carefully guided it, and Trip, over to the suit's docking station near the pool, the diver recounted what had happened to him.

"Seriously, Captain, that thing—whatever it is—is no joke! There I was, hovering just above the seafloor, when *BAM*, it reached out for me and latched onto my helmet."

House laughed softly.

Trip had an imagination like no other. Loved over-the-top fiction stories—movies, books, graphic novels...

"So," House said, eyebrow raised, "the squid wanted a kiss? That's what's got you all hot and bothered?"

Trip's eyes widened. "The hell it did, sir! Look what that thing did to my helmet!"

House watched the man for a few seconds and realized that Trip was wide-eyed scared, well, maybe a little, but he was also having trouble seeing. He wasn't going to say anything yet. If Trip were really having sight issues the next time House saw him, then he'd order him to the medical bay to see the ship's doctor.

Shifting his attention from the spooked diver to the ADS' helmet, House was stunned at what he saw. The octopus had apparently used its beaked mouth to carve grooves into the suit's usually stout, machined armor. In all his years at sea, House had never seen anything like it before.

He needed to find out what, exactly, had just boarded his ship.

"Run diagnostics on the ADS and report back to me ASAP... If you're up to it?"

Trip looked offended. "Just because I got a little...startled..." he blinked hard, "doesn't mean I can't do my job, Captain."

House loved the sailor's attitude, but on the inside, he was worried about him. He was fond of Trip, and the more he came to like the young man, the more he approved of his daughter taking a liking to him.

Turning away from the scene, House looked for Donovan and his team, growling in anger when he couldn't find any of them. They had totally abandoned a crewman in need, all for the "sake of science." The first thing House would do when he found Donovan was to threaten to shove a broken test tube up his ass. Everyone on his boat looked after one another. The sea was judge, jury, and in some cases, the executioner of them all. They were entirely at her mercy, like a flea on a dog's back.

He snarled. "Donovan..."

* * *

Forced to climb the stairs the whole way up, House wasn't happy. Donovan's team had entered the launch bay via the freight elevator. It was how they moved most of their bulky, or weighty, gear about the Endeavor. Unfortunately, the next closest lift was toward the forward section of the ship.

The launch bay sat near the rear of the boat and was on the bottom level, built just in front of the engine room. Donovan's core lab had been built on the top deck, per his instructions, and was connected to other pods within a network of corridors. The above deck workspaces were constructed to make use of the, otherwise, empty expanse of nothing. From above, they resembled a honeycomb of steel-framed boxes.

It was an easy way for the crew to get from Point A to Point B without having to brave the frigid outdoor air. Everything inside the Endeavor was temperature controlled. House didn't mind being comfortable. His people performed better when under less stress.

Warmth definitely made an Antarctic mission seem less terrible.

And with the extra workspace up top, each crewmember was, in turn, given more accommodating quarters below deck. *Everything* within the belly of the Endeavor had been stripped down and redone. House whistled when he had first gotten a look at where he'd be living for the next three months.

House wasn't going anywhere anytime soon—Gianna either. Neither of them had anything to go home to with Karen gone. Both had signed a short-term contract with DARPA with the hopes of it being extended.

The thought of being back out at sea full-time—and with his daughter by his side—made House smile.

What didn't make him smile was the fact that Donovan was ignoring him. He had phoned the man three times already and he never picked up. Either the Endeavor's state-of-the-art communications array was down, or the scientist had taken his earpiece out.

House knew it was the latter. Gianna told him several times that their array was unkillable. Along with some of her friends from home, Gianna had personally seen to it. Those *friends*, House was assured, would make their system infallible. He just wished that they were legitimate programmers and not underground hackers.

Gianna was a master of both.

* * *

Donovan and his team drained the seawater from the pill-shaped containment unit, letting its remnants spill out onto the floor without care. The drains at their feet would take care of any flooding problem if there were ever enough water to constitute a *flood*.

Laser-focused on this task, Donovan wasn't concerned about anything else. The specimen wasn't exactly what they were looking for. Still, it no doubt carried the same potent neurotoxin that its cousins did. Regardless of what this octopus really was, it would serve its purpose: Advancement.

With rubberized gloves and aprons, they carefully laid the octopus out on the examination table, strapping down its limbs one-by-one. They needed to gain access to its salivary gland and extract the tetrodotoxin within. If this creature was as closely related to the dangerous blue-ringed variety, then its venom was some of the deadliest on the planet and would need to be handled with extreme care.

Donovan looked over his scalpel. Then, with a steady hand, he got to work.

3

Pounding up the stairs, House was about to try Donovan again, but instead, got a call from Damon Becker. Rolling his eyes, House knew it was wrong not to inform the government liaison about the current goings-on.

He tapped the WiMP's corresponding icon, keying his comms unit. "House here."

Becker got right to it. "What do I hear about a killer sea monster coming aboard our boat?"

House knew that Becker understood what pushed his buttons and calling it "our boat" instead of the "government's boat," or worse, "my boat," was the perfect way to avoid House's wrath. Becker wasn't the captain. He was.

"Talk to Trip, did you?" House asked. Trip was the only one that would've called the smallish creature a "killer sea monster."

"Since he was the only one to answer the damned phone, yes! Also said he was fighting through a migraine or something."

House cringed for both Becker and Trip.

He hadn't known that Becker was trying to reach him, or that Trip's *condition* was as bad as it sounded. Since everything had happened, House hadn't gotten a chance to check his messages. He had no excuse though because their system provided easy access to them, just in case a team member was out of pocket.

Or, the thing still has a few bugs that Gianna has yet to fix.

The comms system wasn't perfect, ever-changing as DARPA deemed, putting them in a position to be testing new updates all the time. The Endeavor was an experimental research station after all. That's what they did here, experiment, and research. They lived by trial and error.

"Sorry about that, Damon." He really was. The last thing House wanted to do was piss off the people that paid the bills and gave him his ship.

"Yes, well, what about this animal, Captain?"

Breathing hard, House wasn't sure what to tell him. "Honestly," he said, entering the outer door to the topside lab, "I have no idea. The one thing I do know is..."

House's voice trailed off when he stepped into the room. The next set of doors led into the lab itself. From where he was, House could already see Donovan and three others leaning over an operating table. He knew the scientist didn't screw around, but this was insane! There was no way that they could've prepped the octopus for dissection unless...

Damn you, Seth, House thought, knowing Donovan wanted the specimen as fresh as possible. *He's going to put it under and cut it open while it's still alive.*

House wasn't a doctor, but he knew that there was no way to tell how the animal would react under such conditions. He could picture it waking up halfway through the procedure with its guts hanging out and going ballistic.

House kind of hoped that's what was going to happen.

Grabbing the door handle, he pulled, intent on testing the strength of the hinges. But nothing happened. He, the captain of the Endeavor, had been locked out. He quickly slid his keycard through the lock. It answered him with a buzz and a red light.

He grabbed the handle again, this time with both of his powerful hands, and yelled at the top of his lungs. "Donovan!"

House. Was. Livid.

Never—not since boarding this ship—had someone defied him like Donovan just did. After House's keycard didn't work, he knew, for a fact, that he'd been purposely locked out, and it wasn't some random anomaly. There was no door on board the Endeavor he wasn't allowed access to, per the ship's safety protocols.

He called the only person that could help him.

"Hey, Daddy-O, what's up?"

His daughter's leisurely way of addressing him threw him off for a moment, but then, House watched as Donovan cut into the unconscious specimen.

As the scalpel blade connected with soft tissue, the room bloomed to life with a crackling, electric-blue explosion of light. The octopus was unconsciously reacting to the procedure.

The light show got House's brain back on track.

"Get me into the topside lab, now!"

"Oh...Okay," Gianna replied, caught off guard by her father's outburst. "Give me a second to override the locking mechanism."

She didn't say anything more. He was glad too. He wasn't in the mood for explanations. Sometimes, his daughter was just another body on this ship. He hated to think of his little girl like that, but unfortunately, in the end, it was the truth. Yes, he was her father, and he loved her more than anything, but he was also her superior.

She hung up, and House's comms went off again immediately with another incoming call.

"Captain?" It was Trip. "Sorry to bother you, but I'm not feeling too good down here. Gonna go lie down for a few, okay?"

"No problem, son," House replied, trying to calm down. It wasn't Trip's fault that Donovan was going rogue. House needed to focus his rage on the scientist and not Trip. "Get some rest." Before they disconnected, House threw in, "Good job down there today."

Trip laughed. "Never a dull moment around you, sir."

Hanging up, House sighed as another call came in.

Ugh, why me? But he knew why... He was the man in charge. *Comes with the title.*

He answered. "Go for House."

"Sir?"

Sam Ferguson was the Endeavor's Executive Officer, House's right-hand man. But more than anything, right now, he was tracking the incoming storm and plotting alternate routes back to McMurdo.

"Fergie," as some liked to call the freckled redhead behind his back, was a straight shooter. House didn't think the man had a funny bone in his body, nor had House ever seen him smile or laugh. Sam's specialty? Being a damn fine sailor. House knew Sam would be moving up the ranks within the Navy soon after their job in the Antarctic was done and that Sam's time as his XO was soon going to be over.

Still unable to gain entry in the lab, House relaxed and gave his number two his full attention. Sam wouldn't be contacting House mid-warpath unless it was urgent.

"What do you have, Sam?"

"The storm, sir."

"What about it?"

Sam took a breath. "We miscalculated its speed and intensity."

Shit, House thought, rubbing his salt-and-pepper, stubbled chin.

"How much time do we have?" he asked, already knowing he wasn't going to like the answer. No one ever miscalculated something and had it be in their favor. Ever. Whenever something got screwed up, it was *always* for the worse. House took it as a good sign, usually, since his crew rarely ever "screwed the pooch."

Buddy loved saying that.

The ship tilted slightly beneath House's feet, startling him.

"Now," Sam simply said. "Right now—and it's projected to be one of the worst storms in years."

The boat shuddered violently.

House grumbled another curse. "Any chance it was miscalculated a second time?" House was hopeful...slightly.

"No, sir. This is going to be really bad."

House nodded, thinking. "Alright, then. Sound the alarm and make the necessary preparations."

"What about you, sir?"

House took a deep breath. "I'm gonna do my best to try and not kill Seth."

Before Sam could reply, House ended the call.

He was left in peace for a grand total of nine seconds before Gianna rang him back.

"Almost there, Dad. How you doin' up there?"

The wind was howling around House now, making it difficult for him to hear her words. The lab was built into the top deck, which meant it was taking the brunt of the force. The lab was also situated at the front of the ship. House and the others within it were taking the storm head-on. The Endeavor was pointed back at the mainland, heading for McMurdo Station. Everyone inside was in the worst possible spot for what was coming.

What's already here.

"So far so good, G," House replied, lying.

The United States Antarctic Research Center was built on the southern tip of Ross Island, just off the coast of continental Antarctica. In a joint partnership with New Zealand, McMurdo Station was the most-populated community in all of Antarctica, housing a *whopping* 1,200-plus residents during the warmer *winter* months.

It was also the Endeavor's port during their time in the Southern Ocean. Now, House wasn't so sure they'd be able to complete an entire docking sequence and get ashore. They'd more than likely have to wait out the storm on board which meant lots of sick men and women. Even House's iron stomach could only handle so much.

Probably should've asked Sam about an exact timeframe, House thought, shrugging it off. It didn't matter right then. He needed to put a stop to Donovan's tunnel-visioned, inhumane madness. Typically, they'd do nothing more than put the animal under and extract a bit of its venom—but not this time. Donovan was intent on tearing the thing to ribbons if it meant getting what he wanted.

The ship tilted again, spilling one of Donovan's assistants to the floor. House was still latched onto the door handles, keeping himself upright with the best of his ability. The team member that went down fell facing House, and quickly got to her feet and relayed his presence to Donovan.

House growled in anger.

The fact that she didn't immediately open the doors told him that no one in that room held any loyalty to their captain—just Donovan.

Now, he was beyond livid, wanting nothing more than to rip the doors from their hinges and beat Donovan to death with them.

Calm down, Sebastian. Easy...

Donovan barely gave him a look, only nonchalantly glancing over his shoulder. House raised his fist to put it through the shatterproof, glass door. He didn't, of course, knowing his hand would more-than-likely break. The lab, along with the other topside pods, were specially constructed to absorb Mother Nature's fury. Just another of DARPA's experiments aboard the Endeavor. House's anger was something to behold, worthy of a pay-per-view billing, but he was not nearly as strong as a *planet*, so he laid off the glass and waited for his daughter to do her thing.

"G!" House roared, his typically patient demeanor running on empty. He could hear her speaking to someone in low whispers off-mic. "Any time now!"

"Working on it!" she shouted back—the storm was right on top of them now, getting there in what had to be record time. He could barely hear her over the rumble of the elements around him. The pods should survive the storm—*should*—without a hitch, but as far as those within them...he wasn't sure.

As soon as the thought crossed his mind, House was thrown backward, tossed like a ragdoll. Everyone except Donovan was cast aside, as well. Rubbing the back of his head, House sat up and noticed that the scientist was gripping the table with both hands, leaning over it when everyone else went down.

Then, the lights within the surgical suite burst and showered the center of the room, Donovan and octopus included, in sparks.

4

The next thing that happened was nothing House could've predicted. As soon as the first spark hit the fileted specimen, it detonated into a bright blue fireball. What was just as shocking was that Donovan didn't flinch. The scientist would've definitely lost the hair on his head if the man had any. He kept it smooth, completely clean shaven. Still, there was no possible way he could have avoided getting burned.

Idiot!

"Argh!" Donovan howled as he was showered in the steaming blue liquid.

His hands went to his eyes, covering them as he screamed louder. He tried desperately to wipe the plasma away but he couldn't. His gloved hands were slathered in the stuff, and for his effort, all he did was spread it in deeper.

By now, House was already back on his feet and at the doors, yanking on them anew. The power within the pod flickered again, causing Gianna to shout a curse in his ear.

"Shit! Come on, you twitchy bitch!"

Something at the back of the lab caught fire.

"What's wrong?" House asked, trying to get a better look at the advancing blaze. "I need to get in there now!" As much as House despised Donovan, he needed to get inside and get the man to safety. The others in the room seemed to have been totally unaffected, having been tossed away from the scene before the explosion.

Gianna growled, sounding exactly like her father. "Every time the power surges, I lose connection to the door locks. This ship is completely unique. The guts were installed before I got involved, remember? I'm still working out the kinks. Too much to do—not enough time in the day to do it. Sound familiar?" House agreed and had said the same thing several times over the last few months since he'd been aboard.

She snarled. "Bastards should've hired me from the get-go! We wouldn't be in this fucking mess if they had!"

Even with everything going on, House couldn't help but smile.

A chorus of shrieks brought his attention back to the situation at hand and off of his brilliant, yet, foulmouthed child. Now, Donovan had his hands clutched around his skull and was bellowing at the ceiling above. In response to his cries, the three other people in the lab scurried away, huddling together and screaming in fright.

Donovan was in agony.

The room was alight, and the scientist's people were terrified of what might be happening to their boss. Then, they scattered to the corners of the room when the overhead, non-water fire suppression system let loose with its gaseous payload.

The compound worked quicker than water and was infinitely safer to deploy around electronics. It was also a lot easier to clean up afterward. Large amounts of water inside of a ship was never a good thing in any form, even with the Endeavor's impressive drainage configuration.

The foggy gas buffeted everything within the room, and the lights went out. Still clutching the door handles, House waited for them to turn back on, or, at least, for the red emergency lights to kick in. It was the emergency lights that bloomed to life, and when they did, House leaped away from the double doors, shocked at what he witnessed.

Donovan was there, standing on the other side, still as the dead. The only thing that moved was his head, tilting back and forth as if he was a predator studying its prey. The last thing House saw before Donovan collapsed to the floor was the scientist's eyes. They quickly flashed blue, looking eerily similar to the color the octopus had produced. Then, the irregularity was gone, and Donovan's dark-brown eyes rolled into the back of his head, and he went down like a sack of potatoes.

Must've been my imagination, House thought, shaking his head.

CLICK.

House's right eyebrow raised, confused. He knew it was the doors unlocking, but he wasn't sure why, or how, it happened. Gianna radioed him back and told him.

"That was me, Dad. You should be all clear now."

"Uh," he replied, throwing open the double doors, "thanks. How—"

"I killed the power to the lab. When the system rebooted, the door locks disengaged."

"Huh..." he said, once again impressed, "smart girl."

"Technically, I'm a genius." She laughed. "Good luck, Dad. I'm gonna go check on Trip, okay?"

"Sure," he replied, "let me know how he's doing." House knelt next to Donovan. "He didn't sound so good a couple of minutes ago."

Donovan was unconscious, and parts of his face and head were swollen and welted from the flames. House checked for a pulse and found the scientist's skin to be ice cold. His pulse, however, was steady, a little fast maybe, but solid, nevertheless. With the help of one of the science team members, House hauled Donovan to his feet and dragged him out of the ruined lab and back toward the medical bay.

"What...the hell...happened in there?" House asked, grunting.

"I'm not sure, sir," Donovan's assistant replied. "We did everything by the book up until the flash and fire."

Sir... 'Now' they show me respect.

Backseating his anger at everyone involved, House and the other man pushed through the lab's outer doors. As they moved, they continued into the corridor connecting the lab's pod to the Endeavor's greenhouse. While the other pods had solid walls and roofs, the greenhouse was encased in thick, impact glass. They used the greenhouse as an experiment to see if sailors could grow their own food while at sea.

House knew the brass back home wanted nothing more than to cut costs. It stunned him that their food supply was on the list of potential cuts.

"Speaking of what happened... The creature's reaction?" House said, eyeing the technician.

He shrugged. "No idea. I've never seen anything like it."

Neither had House, and that's what worried him the most. He'd seen everything the ocean could throw at you, even a storm as bad as the one they were trying to survive—just not one of the Antarctic varieties.

Navigating the rest of the corridors and subsequent pods went well. Only twice did they drop Donovan. It was mostly the other person's fault, though. House had a firm grip on the scientist's belt and had his left arm under Donovan's right armpit.

The other, smaller man couldn't have gone toe-to-toe with Gianna for more than three seconds before tapping out. His daughter wasn't big—far from it, actually. What she lacked in size and strength, she more than made up for in tenacity.

Halfway to the next pod, two medics came rushing toward them. Gratefully, one held a collapsible gurney. House and the science assistant were relieved of Donovan's dead weight, and the Chief Scientist was rushed back the way the medics had come.

Two floors down, and in the center of the ship, was the medical bay. It, like everything else aboard the Endeavor, was state-of-the-art and experimental in design.

"Sir?" the subordinate asked. "What about the lab?"

House faced him. "Lock it down for now. We'll worry about clean up after the storm subsides. No one goes in or out without my say-so. With Dr. Donovan out of commission, his team will now be reporting directly to XO Ferguson or me."

The shaken man nodded and headed back toward the front of the ship. House, left alone in the corridor between the greenhouse and the elevator, stopped and leaned against the closest wall. There, in the still air, he took a series of deep inhalations and calmed his nerves. But as soon as he started to feel better, the lights above his head flickered and the ship was, once more, cast into darkness and buffeted by Mother Nature's unmatchable, brute strength.

No time for breaks, Sebastian, he thought.

He took a step and paused as the lights came back to life, then winked on and off several more times before finally settling into the *on* position.

If they lost power in a storm like this, it wouldn't be Hell on Earth for everyone, it'd be Hell on Ship, including him. Comms would go down first because they were tied into the ship's built-in Wi-Fi array. It needed power, of course, and the generators below decks could only pump out so much juice. One-by-one, they'd lose one system after the other until there was nothing left.

Bypassing the elevator, House headed for the rear of the boat. There sat the bridge, and his station, the wheelhouse. It was House's command center, his home away from his onboard home—his room—while also being away from his stateside home.

He spent more time in the wheelhouse than anywhere else. House loved this ship—his command too—and he needed to get back to work and help his crew guide it, and whoever was within her womb, to safety.

But can we make it to McMurdo?

That was one of a hundred questions House needed answers to.

5

Eradication.

This was a horrifying dream, for sure.

"Eradication?" He shook with fear. "Why—who?"

Devastation.

"Stop," he muttered, thrashing in his sleep. "Please, stop." He sobbed. "Please..."

Seth Donovan saw the world through another's eyes—through warbling, tinted lenses of sapphire. Acts of chaos, death, and destruction—the worst kind of atrocities—flashed across his mind like a highlight reel from the abyss. While he knew what the voice in his head was saying and showing him was wrong...it felt right.

The horrible images were easily translated, but the words weren't. Yet, Donovan understood their meaning with ease. His mind was working on autopilot, deciphering the unfamiliar language all by itself—without the aid of a learned linguist.

Annihilation.

Getting to his feet, and killing everything in front of him, felt like the right thing to do—the only thing to do.

Extermination.

The only thing to do...

The strangest occurrence, though, was that the voice in his head didn't belong to some demon from another world. The entity speaking to him from deep within his own human heart was his. The words were being uttered by his voice—his own subconscious. They harmonized with another's too.

He had experienced some awful nightmares in the past, but nothing like the one he was being put through now. He was fully aware of what he was "dreaming" this time. In normal dreams, he'd lose most, if not all, recollection of what had actually happened while he was asleep.

Eradication.

"N-no."

Devastation. The words repeated over and over again.

"Hello?"

Annihilation.

"Who...who are you?" Donovan was terrified by what he was being told to do—even more so because he could actually see himself slitting someone's throat. He could feel his victim's warm blood running over his hands, reveling in their gurgled gasps.

Sebastian House's blood.

Extermination!

His eyes snapped open, and he sucked in a deep breath, shaking. His skin broke out in goosebumps. Very little in the world could terrorize him, but the voice—his voice—the imagery—had done it.

What the hell was that? he asked himself.

His hand went to his forehead, and he rubbed it hard, trying desperately to knead away the intense throbbing behind his eyes. It felt like he'd been struck with Thor's hammer and given a lightning-induced concussion. However, he didn't remember hitting his head recently. Donovan carefully sat up, instantly being overcome with nausea. The discomfort forced him to pause his ascent.

Feeling the acidic bile rise, he grabbed a nearby garbage pail and vomited. As soon as the vitriol left his stomach, throat, and mouth, Donovan laid back and took in several deep breaths. He'd definitely sustained some sort of horrible head injury. There was no other explanation.

What...what happened to me?

Donovan recalled the overhead lights in the lab flickering and then bursting from an energy surge. He also remembered the ship rocking from the torrent outside. He could still feel it now, telling him that his state of unconsciousness had been brief.

Head trauma was bad enough, but add in the power of an Antarctic storm against the hull of their boat and—he retched into the pail again, wiping his mouth with his bare hand. Through dazed, tear-filled eyes, he saw something odd on the back of his right hand. Where he expected to see trace amounts of vomit, he saw something else mixed in with it.

Something blue.

His hand shivered. The only thing he'd seen that color in the last, well, ever, was the pulsating plasma within the octopus back in his containment lab. It seemed that both its blood *and* its venom strobed the color, not one or the other.

They're one and the same, he thought. *Its blood IS its venom!*

It was fascinating to think about, but at the moment, Donovan was still frozen in abject terror. He could do nothing else but struggle to breathe and stare at the back of his tainted hand.

A knock on the door was the blissful interruption he needed, a real Godsend for the comatose scientist. It woke him out of his funk and got him moving...sort of. Donovan was too woozy to do much else except hide his stained skin beneath the wool sheet of the uncomfortable hospital bed.

"Come in," he rasped, not recognizing his own voice. The fright he felt over his own health was still present, mostly on the inside— but he was afraid it showed on the outside too. He couldn't let anyone know what was "possibly" happening, whether or not he was infected with some sort of previously undocumented contagion.

The last person on the planet that he wanted a visit from opened the door and entered.

Captain House.

"Sebastian?" Donovan said, caught off guard. He and House would use their first names whenever they were together in private, or while talking one on one through their comms. Donovan didn't like to, though. He didn't want to be friendly with a man who enjoyed throwing his weight around.

"How are you, Seth? You've been out for over an hour."

Is he actually concerned?

With everything happening, Donovan decided to play the civil game. Plus, he wasn't in the right frame of mind, or physical state, to put up a fight.

"Okay, I guess." He really didn't know if he was. Besides the headache and the blue-tinted liquid inside his body, Donovan felt fine. "Honestly," he laughed, "I have no idea how I feel." He groaned, his stomach in knots. "How's the storm?"

The boat shook, and both men cringed because of it.

"Bad," House replied, laughing softly. "Real bad. Luckily, she's a solid boat."

"Yeah, sure..." Donovan said, having trouble concentrating on both House and what was happening to him.

"Quite the display of fireworks up there, huh?" House asked.

Eradication.

Donovan shook his head. "Fireworks?"

Devastation.

House squinted at him. "The lab, I mean."

Donovan sat up, much to the chagrin of his aching body. "What happened to my laboratory?"

House looked confused. "You don't remember, do you?"

"Obviously not, Sebastian. Stop fucking around with me and tell me what happened to my lab!"

House sat on the bed next to Donovan. "It's gone, Seth."

"Gone?"

Donovan heaved into the wastebasket again. As he retched, he saw more and more of the blue plasma exit his body. When he was finished, he slid the pail under his bed and wiped his mouth with the inside of his thick blanket.

No one could find out about his condition yet, especially House. The captain would pull the "Safety Card" and quarantine him for the remainder of their voyage. Donovan wasn't sure he had that kind of time, and there wasn't anyone on board he trusted to find the answers more than himself. His specialty was genetics, after all. He'd put his years of schooling to the test.

Once you leave, he thought, looking back up at House.

"What do you mean, 'gone?'" He tried to picture it transpiring but couldn't, not even a little. Donovan started hyperventilating, unable to breathe. "There were...millions of dollars...in equipment in there...and ten-times that in valuable research. It can't be gone!"

The stress was too much, and Donovan's eyes danced. He flopped back onto his bed and covered his tear-filled eyes with his left arm. He shook again. This time, it was because his tears were not normal, they were ice cold, instead of that of his body temperature. Something awful was definitely going on inside of him.

"Gone..." he repeated, his voice trailing off.

"Are you—"

"Go away, Sebastian. Leave me alone." Donovan was distraught, yes, but he also needed House to leave.

The captain growled but stood and headed for the door. "Just so you know, it wasn't one of your lackeys that pulled you from that burning room—it was me."

What? Donovan thought. He knew he should've thanked House for saving his life, but he needed to be alone more. House had to get out.

Annihilation.

"I," he winced, hearing the terrible words repeat again, "would've rather died with my work than go home empty-handed."

Without another rebuttal, House left, slamming the door on his way out. The force of the door banging into its frame rocked Donovan's already abused mind. Biting his lip, he launched to his feet, stumbling for a few before gaining a shred of equilibrium. He immediately started gathering all the evidence of his "infection," trying desperately to ignore the words booming in his mind.

Reaching for the door handle, he dropped to one knee, when the last word stabbed his brain with a mental icepick. The pain was so intense that he almost lost consciousness for a second time.

Extermination.

* * *

Gianna held onto the walls of the narrow hallway to keep herself upright. After hanging up with her father, she'd done what she said she was going to do and headed straight for Trip's room below deck.

Like her dad, she spent most of her time inside the bridge, whereas Trip, being a part of the ADS exploratory team, spent most of his days deep in the bowels of the Endeavor. Compared to all of those on board, they worked as far away from one another as was possible.

Whenever they could, they stole away in either's quarters. Their relationship was much further along than her father knew, too. And she was going to break the big news to him once they were safely docked at McMurdo.

Gianna House was eight weeks pregnant.

The only people that knew were herself, Trip, and the ship's medical specialist, Dr. Lisa Bowen, who was sworn to secrecy, just as long as Gianna agreed to tell her dad by the time they made port. If not, Bowen would do it herself and hang Gianna out to dry.

That can't happen, she thought, biting her lower lip.

If Bowen told her father, instead of Gianna doing it herself, it would break his heart. House didn't deserve to have his heart ripped out of his chest again. She'd done enough of that when she was younger. Their relationship was currently in a great place— better than it had been since before her mom died, and the last thing Gianna wanted to do was drive a wedge in between the two of them. She refused to let her child—his first grandchild—be that wedge.

She'd already embarrassed him once when she had been fired from her job with DARPA, a position she only held for two years. Now, his reputation was at stake for bringing her back into the fold. If she fouled up in any way, he'd pay the price this time, not her. There was nothing that could be worse than her father being reprimanded for a screw up of hers.

Three levels beneath the top deck, she turned right and headed towards the front half of the ship. Trip's room was the third door on the left. Hers was across the hall. Everyone, including Donovan and his science team, had rooms in this section. They were all created equal here. No one had a better living arrangement than the other. Usually, the "Captain's Quarters" were a good bit larger than anyone else's, but not here.

It was all her father's doing too. He believed that they were all the same—all crew members aboard the same research vessel with an identical endgame.

"We just get there in different ways," House had said once.

Carefully, Gianna knocked on Trip's door with two soft *thumps*. Five heartbeats later, he opened the door for her. She smiled at him—at the fact that he was wearing his prescription sunglasses indoors. He looked terrible, but better than he did before.

Trip stepped aside, allowed Gianna to enter, then gently shut the door behind her.

"They, uh," he said, motioning to his headgear, "help with the headaches."

"Dampeners against the light," she said, figuring as much.

He smiled and kissed her hard. "I do what I must so I can see this beautiful face without flinching."

Gianna laughed and playfully raised a fist to punch him. He mockingly cowered back and held out his hands in front of him.

"You wouldn't harm the father of your first-born son, would you?"

She sneered and stepped in close. "Of our *daughter*, no?"

At first, Gianna was scared to divulge that she was pregnant, especially with them going ashore so soon. She was afraid that Trip would reject the thought of being her child's father and abandon them like so many of her friends' dads had over the years.

Obviously, Gianna didn't take rejection well. Her past proved as much.

"Do you love me?" she asked, flatly laying it out on the table.

No pressure, she thought. *The worst thing that can happen is for him to say no and ruin my life.*

Trip's eyes opened wide, but from her perspective, she could only see his eyebrows raise. He tapped his chin and grinned like an idiot before answering her.

"Hmmm, let me think... A drop-dead gorgeous, sexy-as-hell nerd that willingly crawled into the sheets with me? Hmmm. Could I ever love a woman such as that?"

Gianna dove on him, tackling him to the bed. For a few seconds, they playfully wrestled with one another, pinching and poking at the other's ticklish spots. Next, their lips locked, and their hands went from harmless playtime to *spirited investigation*.

Passion wasn't an issue between Trip and her. Finding the courage to tell her dad how far that passion had gotten them was.

They'd initially met in the launch bay. It was one of their first nights at sea. Gianna didn't initially notice Trip that night but did recall that a young man with thick glasses was polite to her and well-spoken. Two weeks, and a handful of private calls later, they met for a drink in her cabin. She smuggled some good scotch on board.

After three light pours, Trip was toast.

After three light pours, Gianna was ready to go.

Alcohol did wonders for her sex drive.

Since then, they had spent more nights together than apart. Once they were finished for the night, they'd sneak back into their own rooms before anyone else had woken up.

Until her father caught her one morning.

She'd thrown open Trip's door, only to find her dad about to knock on hers. Hearing the commotion behind him, he spun to see her in only a loose-fitting Dr. Dre "2001" t-shirt and her panties. Gianna had impulsively beaten down Trip's door that night, uncaring that she was half-naked. Right then and there, for anyone that happened to be strolling down the hall, she had nothing to tell her father except the truth.

She and Trip were an item.

Surprisingly, he wasn't furious. It made her more uncomfortable with the whole situation than it did Trip. House thought that someone of Trip's ilk would be good for her. He was polite, honest, and well-educated.

"How can *you* be nervous?" Trip asked the next morning. "You're not the one banging his boss' daughter!"

As she and Trip ripped each other's clothes off, Gianna tuned out the memory and focused on the present. It was much easier to do *it* without thinking about what her "daddy" would say if he found out.

She smiled, biting Trip's lower lip as they kissed.

He already knows.

6

The storm seemed to have settled for the moment, but that didn't make Donovan's trek to his room any simpler. As the ship continued to sway side to side, the long, utilitarian corridors appeared as if they were a slithering snake. He thought about using the elevator to make it easier on himself but knew he'd have less of a chance of running into anyone if he took the stairs instead.

Only an idiot would be using the stairs now...

Sub-zero venom, he thought.

It's precisely the substance he sought here. Every specimen he'd examined so far, all thirteen of them, would prove useful once he got back on dry land. While impressive, the lab aboard the Endeavor was nowhere near as sophisticated as the one he required to properly process his research.

He felt his stomach lurch with the next wave, bringing with it another round of bile. Stopping, he gripped onto the railing of the last staircase before his room and forced the goo back down. It was disgusting and did very little to calm his shaking nerves and weak stomach.

This wasn't just a toxic substance coursing its way through his system. There was something else at work here. He'd read enough science fiction novels, and watched enough movies, to understand that a farfetched, yet, factual change was taking place inside him. You didn't have to be a believer in the stuff to agree with the assessment that he was in serious trouble.

Stepping onto his room's level, Donovan gasped for air and turned the corner. His cabin was up ahead, directly across the hall from House's. Because of their importance to the Endeavor, they lived near one another as a safety precaution. If it was late, and their comms system was down, they'd be easy to summon.

Or, House just wants to keep an eye on me. It's what he alleged from the beginning.

Donovan's eyes felt like they were about to pop. The pressure building up behind them was excruciating. He needed to discover exactly what was going on, but more than anything, he needed to rest. If he passed out on the floor of a high-traffic hallway such as this, someone was bound to stumble over him. Then, House would quarantine him for sure.

Successfully making it to his room, Donovan placed his hand on the handle and froze when a door near his creaked open. Nervous, he fumbled with the knob but was regrettably spotted.

"Dr. Donovan?"

He looked over his shoulder and found Gianna House staring at him. But that wasn't her room. It was Triplett's, the diver from earlier. Donovan had heard that the two were close but had never seen them interact with one another with more than their eyes.

He turned and faced her.

"You look terrible..." she said, looking worried.

Eradication.

There was the whispered voice again.

Donovan grinned, something coming over him. "No worse than you." His grin turned into a full-fledged smile. He cackled like a lunatic. "Tell me again, how did you get this job, Ms. House?"

Gianna crossed her arms and stared daggers into him, looking very much like her father. Donovan had never said something so harsh and straightforward to the girl before. It felt good to speak his mind, what he wanted when he wanted. He'd just experienced a sensation that he hadn't felt in some time.

Deep down, Seth Donovan felt confident.

The feeling only lasted momentarily as his ordinary thoughts about the beautiful woman came flooding back. Who didn't love to gawk at her? He looked her up and down and, once more, grinned.

Devastation.

Donovan stepped toward Gianna but stopped when Triplett joined her at the door. His predatory thoughts and stance shrank back, and he fled into his room and locked the door. He had no idea what that was all about. Donovan had dreamt about Gianna many times, imagining her naked and on top of him in bed. This had been entirely different, though.

He wanted to cause the young woman harm.

Annihilation.

"What the fuck?" he muttered, grabbing his head with both hands. "Shut up..."

The queasiness suddenly returned, and Donovan couldn't hold it down this time. He rushed to his quaint, private restroom, nearly ripping the lid off the toilet as he heaved into it. Instead of there being vomit and blue plasma, there was only the foreign substance.

Extermination.

The viscous liquid flowed freely, but it also choked him to the point that he saw spots. As a result, the pressure behind his eyes built to a crescendo. When he was finished, he stood and took a much-needed breath, free of the agony in his eye sockets.

Next, Donavon stumbled to the toilet that was next to the sink and rinsed out his mouth. Satisfied that he had gotten most of the gunk out, he looked up into the mirror above the sink and froze. His dark-brown eyes had changed to the same electric blue of the plasma flowing through the octopus.

Falling away from the sink, he collided with the wall behind him. There, only feet away from the mirror, he remained motionless and stared, hand to chest, hyperventilating. It wasn't just the irises that had begun to change, it was the blood vessels within his eyes too. His bloodshot eyes weren't filled with red veins, the white sclera, and his black pupils like he would've expected to see. The veins were blue. So far, his pupils and whites were unaffected.

So far.

The burns on his face and head seemed to be rapidly healing as well, an impossible feat. The blistered skin was already scabbing. He should've looked quite the opposite with the injuries being so fresh.

Running back into his room, he ripped off his soiled clothing and stuffed them deep into his clothes hamper. Like the linens from the medical bay, Donovan would take care of them for good later. Before heading downstairs, he had stuffed the bedsheets and garbage bag into a hatch leading directly to the ship's trash compactor.

Now totally nude, Donovan stopped and stared down at his body. *Oh, god.* The veins nearest to the skin were becoming tinted with the same azure color. The spreading infection—that had to be it—it appeared to be moving quickly through his body via his pumping heart! The vessels surrounding his chest cavity were currently the darkest of them all.

And with every thump of his human heart, the inhuman *stuff* coursing its way through his body pulsed too.

Just like the specimen.

He swiftly dressed and slid on a pair of sunglasses to hide his eyes. Taking a couple of deep breaths, the queasiness in his stomach lessened. Even the swaying of the ship didn't seem to bother him. Regardless if he felt *better* or not, he wanted answers, and he knew there was only one place to get them.

Donovan needed to return to his lab.

* * *

House didn't mean to aggressively throw open the door to the wheelhouse, but he did it anyway...with a little help of a monster swell. He and the rest of the ship tipped forward, and House let go of the door handle to brace himself against its frame. The outcome was a loud *boom* inside the normally quiet upper level of the bridge. All eyes stationed there turned on him as a result.

He cleared his throat. "Sorry about that." He stepped in and straightened his shirt. "Back to work..."

The name "wheelhouse" was more of a tongue-in-cheek joke than anything else. The official name for the level was *Command*. The wheelhouse did, in fact, have a classic ship wheel. No one ever used it, though. Technology piloted the Endeavor, not man. House was nothing more than a bored supervisor on most days. Most weeks, actually. The events of tonight were the most exciting he'd seen since setting sail.

On any typical day, XO Sam Ferguson would be overseeing the controls while House managed the matters of everything else on board his boat. To put it plainly, House tried desperately to *not* be cooped up in the bridge all day...every day. Unfortunately, he was needed here more than he wanted to be and since he was the man in charge, he didn't openly complain.

There were literally hundreds of men that would kill for a gig like his. His job was reasonably cushy, and he had more freedom than any other ship commander in the Navy—not that he was a member of the Navy. The thing that concerned him most was the future. What would happen when this mission was through? Would he still be the captain on the Endeavor with another assignment? Would there be another destination for him? He thought of this vessel as his—he was the skipper until he decided otherwise.

Why else bring me in if only to let me go so soon?

House sat in his designated chair and eyed his second-in-command. "Any updates, Sam?"

The sailor turned toward him with a look of trepidation.

"What?"

"McMurdo, sir. They, uh, confirmed that they're closing up shop for twenty-four hours to wait out the storm."

Just marvelous. Their ninety-day cruise had just been turned into a ninety-*one*-day venture.

"We've been ordered to stay idle once we've reached a half-a-mile out, just in case."

"Just in case of what?" House asked, genuinely confused.

"The storm is getting worse."

House stood. "Worse?"

"Yes, sir," Sam replied, "I suggested that we turn around and move farther out to sea, but—"

"We'd be on our own if something happened," House finished. "At a half-mile out, they could come to us if it was a life or death emergency."

"Correct, sir. That's what McMurdo said too."

As House knew they would. Safety was the top priority in these parts. A lot could go wrong in as remote a place as the Southern Ocean. A lot. Like losing the Endeavor and all of its crew in the blink of an eye.

"Do what they want, but keep us pointed directly at the storm. I don't want us getting sideswiped and capsize."

Bill Johnston, one of the two pilots, turned around. "But, sir, we're almost six-hundred-feet bow to stern. Can that really happen?"

House faced the man. "Until it doesn't, we go about it as if it can."

"Sir?" Johnston asked.

"Anything can happen," Sam replied, nodding his agreement. "Do as the captain says and stay on course accordingly."

Johnston turned. "Aye aye, sir."

House headed left, toward one of the two staircases that descended into the heart of the bridge. The wheelhouse was actually more of a loft above the second floor of the three-story-tall bridge. It gave House, Sam, and the pilots an eagle-eye view of the water through the thirty-foot-tall pane of impact glass at the front of the structure.

Before he headed down, House gripped the railing in front of him and looked out over the rest of his command center as it rocked beneath him. Directly below his perch was *Navigation*, and thanks to their one-of-a-kind comms system, they weren't required to be at the captain's side twenty-four-seven like they had been in the past.

Dominik Lucas was the boat's chief navigational officer. He was supposedly the best in the southern hemisphere and was hired purely on Sam's recommendation. They had been friends from their days at the Naval Academy.

House descended the first banking staircase, feeling like he was an iconic movie star when he stepped off of it. The banking stairs hugged the outer glass wall of the open-air room and deposited him near the front of the men on the second floor. Like clockwork, everyone stopped and looked up at him like he was more than just their boss. He laughed at how something as simple as stairs could draw the attention of six sets of eyes.

House didn't pay the onlookers any attention, though. Instead, he just continued forward and took the next staircase to the bridge's first floor, *Engineering*. It's where his old friend, Buddy Malone, was stationed.

Technically, the Endeavor had three elevators, but only two of them were used daily by the majority of the crew. The third lift had only two destinations and was used solely by Buddy's coverall-wearing engineer team. It was a one-way trip from the bridge, to the engine room beneath their feet. And since the day they set sail, Buddy had done nothing but bitch about being too far away from his beloved machines.

"Everything is automated from here," House had said during Buddy's tour. Buddy had already agreed to join him aboard the research vessel, but the old coot had wanted an early look at his new workstation and was stunned to see it inside the bridge and not the engine room. That was six months before they set sail. To House, it seemed like an eternity ago.

"Automated don't mean better, boy," Buddy retorted.

"That's *Captain*, Buddy," House slyly corrected. "You know better."

"Oh, right, sorry... *Captain* Boy."

Buddy reminded House of his father. His "Pops" had grown up in the same era as Buddy did—a very racist Georgia. Most of the country was at odds with race in the fifties.

Still is now.

House knew there had been rumblings about him being re-hired simply because he was black. That didn't stop him from hiring a nucleus of African American crewmen, though. It wasn't at all intentional on his part. If someone had dark skin and didn't qualify for the job, House didn't hire him. Plain and simple.

House applied the same reasoning to his hiring of women. He believed there were plenty that deserved a job, like one of the many on the Endeavor. Bottom line, he didn't discriminate and didn't go out of his way to bring in minorities.

At the end of the day, House wanted the best people on board his boat. Period. If that meant hiring an old black engineer along with his "mutt" daughter, then House was happy to do so.

He loved his crew.

House had even approved Donovan's hire, though the scientist didn't know it. The captain had never met the headstrong man before. He'd only heard of him through the grapevine. Gianna had talked him up, initially saying that he was ballsy and hated playing the bureaucratic game. It wasn't until after they began working together that House regretted signing off on him. Gianna was embarrassed for ever believing in him.

What a pain in the ass!

Halfway down the second set of banking staircases, House paused mid-step when he heard, "Hey, boy! Been a while, huh?"

House waved and mumbled under his breath. "Speaking of a pain in the ass."

7

Now feeling much better, Donovan made his way to the sealed doors of his laboratory. He knew they were locked because he was the one who had written the guidelines of what to do if something like this happened. Well, not just him. He and House devised them together as the people in charge of their respective teams.

Thankfully, Donovan quieted the voice in his head—the one that was telling him to do wicked things. Like brutally murder Gianna House and everyone else on board the Endeavor.

He could even envision himself doing it too, something that had never crossed his mind...until now. Even in his angriest of mindsets, Donovan would've never ended another person's life in cold blood. The more he thought about it, the more he was convinced that it was the damned octopus that was responsible for the demented visions. The alterations weren't only physical, they were mental too. So far, the only thing he absolutely knew was that something inside of the animal had infected him and was turning him into...

What exactly? he asked himself, unsuccessfully coming up with anything.

That was the question Donovan was hoping to answer soon.

He was buried beneath his winter gear so that the only part of his body that was visible was the lower half of his face. Twice someone had stopped him and asked why he was dressed to be outdoors while still inside the comfortable settings of the ship.

"Ever since the accident, I haven't felt well," he said both times. "I c—can't seem to get warm."

It was quite the opposite, however. Donovan was truthfully burning up beneath his layers. It felt like summer to him, and he wanted nothing more than to disrobe and take a stroll in the storm with nothing on except his own skin. It made no sense since he was still ice cold to the touch.

Donovan, an Arizona native, was continually acclimating more and more to the chilled climate. He craved it, actually. Back home in Flagstaff, he enjoyed the crisp nights as much as the next person, but now...

"How?" he asked aloud.

It was one of a thousand questions he had for his little friend. Reaching out for the locked door handles like he'd done countless times before, he instinctively pulled the sealed entrance apart with a shout of pain. The deadbolts snapped like twigs, as did his arms. Donovan pulled with such force that he broke metal and bone.

"Grrr," he growled, amazed when the pain instantly subsided. "Huh?" In response, his body shook uncontrollably.

As quickly as the bones had snapped, he could feel them mending themselves back together. The breaks itched like crazy. But all Donovan could do was stare at his trembling hands with wonder. He was definitely changing—becoming something else. He was mutating into something inhuman.

Buried within an octopus' DNA was the ability to heal from devastating injuries. They could even grow back limbs if needed. Besides being incredibly intelligent, they were quite strong, considering the way they were designed. Donovan didn't feel like a marvel of nature. He felt more like a freak from beyond the stars.

The lab was a disaster, covered in a dusty film as a result of the waterless fire extinguishers above his head. The middle of the space was mostly cleared of all debris. The four examination tables that usually took up the center of the room had also been shoved aside. Everything about the disarray bothered Donovan.

Sitting on a nearby table, back in its flooded containment unit, were the remains of the creature that had altered his life forever. *Alter,* he thought, looking back down at his hands. It, the octopus, floated in crystal-clear water, suspended as if it were inside a stasis pod on its way to some distant planet. It had done more than *alter* his life...

Yes, a voice whispered.

Donovan shook his head, blinking hard. The voice was, once more, his—but not his. He didn't say "yes," yet, he heard it in his own voice. Something was definitely speaking to him, or...he was losing his mind.

"Eradication," Donovan said, wincing at the word.

Holding his breath, he lifted his foot to step into the lab but stopped midstride. Something about it didn't sit right with him— besides the state of the room. However, something deep inside Donovan urged him forward regardless of how he thought he felt.

"The voice?"

It, the voice murmuring in his head, could also just be a figment of his fractured mind, a newly formed psychosis caused by the trauma he sustained. In his delirium, Donovan could, realistically, see himself talking to himself like he figured he was doing now. It wasn't that much of a stretch. He regularly spoke to himself while working, verbally solving formulas.

So, he decided to conduct an experiment, here and now. He

would attempt to contact the other voice. Closing his eyes, he pictured himself sitting at a table, and directly across from him was an empty seat. Concentrating, he willed the other Donovan to show his face. Unfortunately, his focus waned, shattered by an onrush of nausea.

Gasping for oxygen, he opened his eyes and was relieved when the feeling dwindled to nothing.

So, he took in the room again while he caught his breath.

The only piece of equipment left powered on was the containment tank. It softly shined with the light of the LED cluster built into its base. The result was that the specimen shined from below, casting the ceiling in a series of horrifying, undulating shadows.

The quadripus was missing four of its limbs, and the fact that it wasn't excitedly strobing as he approached told Donovan that it was dead. His heart ached as he came to that realization. He felt as if a family member's life had been wrongly snuffed out, filling him with an equal feeling of rage.

Lifting his shaking arms out in front of him, he gently placed his gloved hands on the glass, swiftly retracting them and yanking the coverings off. The shallower veins in the top of his hands pumped and strobed, faintly displaying the same shades of blue the octopus had only hours ago. Soon, Donovan wouldn't be able to hide the alterations—the transformation. Whatever it really was, would be easily noted by all. He couldn't go around forever with his entire body covered. Someone was bound to notice, and when they did...

I can't let that happen, he thought. *I won't let it happen.*

He closed his eyes and imagined what he'd do to ensure his freedom. Would he play it safe and hide until they docked at McMurdo? If he did, then what? If he decided to go with that, he'd be stuck on Antarctica, quarantined in a lab as someone else's specimen with no way home.

Arizona didn't seem right anymore, either. He didn't want to go somewhere warm and sunny. No, Donovan wanted to go somewhere cold year-round, like here, but somewhere with infinitely more possibilities for—

"Devastation," he finished.

Donovan stumbled back, his eyes opening wide. The voice had come to him again, this time speaking aloud through his own mouth. He needed to figure out how, and why, it—he—whoever—was doing it. He needed to try and communicate with it again, and he needed to see if there was a way to reverse what was happening to him.

"A cure."

Slowly, he reached for the pill-shaped tank a second time, trembling with anticipation. "Woah!" he shouted, feeling his body lunge forward. He didn't tell it to do that.

Something else took control and moved him closer.

He tried to fight the unseen force but failed, his hands reflexively squeezing the glass almost to the point of breaking. He now knew for a fact that there was a second consciousness within him. Even though he was still freaked out, he steadied himself and slowly allowed the other "existence" to take over. "It" dipped Donovan's head, and shut his eyes.

"Annihilation," he whispered.

Donovan started to panic until—*boom*—he saw a sea of blue crackle to life behind his closed eyelids. Everything was in shades of it, but it swirled and shifted as if it were liquid, almost like he was underwater. Whatever the plasma was that was rippling through the specimen's body, and now imbued in his, it wasn't some potent form of venom—quite the opposite, actually.

It wasn't designed to *take* life as poison did.

It was designed to *give* or improve it.

It was something conscious—and it was something not of this world.

He couldn't explain it, but he understood it, what it sought, what it was. It wanted what every living thing desired. Survival. And, for that to ensue, it needed to multiply and grow stronger.

But how? Donovan thought, piecing together a plan.

The first thing he'd need to do was take over the ship, starting with the bridge and its captain. The thought had come to him immediately, and it came with absolute conviction.

The problem with doing that was that Donovan didn't know the first thing about seafaring, or in this case, the navigation systems and mechanisms that controlled the Endeavor. He was a scientist, not a sailor. Plus, he was just one being. Donovan wasn't a normal man anymore. He didn't know what he was, only that he wasn't the same as before.

He flexed his arms, chest, and back. Accepting his fate instead of worrying about it felt good. His grandfather died of terminal cancer and was so at peace with his fate. He told Donovan that coming to terms with his fate made him the happiest he'd been in years. His grandfather was also a man of faith and literally couldn't wait to see his wife and parents again in Heaven.

"I'm not the same as before," Donovan said, teeth clenched.

He grinned and replied. "No, Seth, we are better than before."

This time, his speaking voice was soft and soothing.

"Yes," he agreed with himself, "so much better…"

But he—they—needed to know more about what was happening. If he could tap into his newfound gift and understand it for what it truly was, he might be able to use it to its full potential. There had to be more than what was already revealed.

"We are strong," his gentle voice assured, washing his nervousness away.

"Yes…" they said together, the audibly spoken voices harmonizing perfectly, one higher than the other. He smiled wide. "Yes, we are." Then, the last of the four terrible words that had been replaying in his head over and over again left his lips.

"Extermination."

Seth Donovan smiled.

* * *

House's earpiece chimed, warning him of an incoming call. Following the soft *bing* was the caller's name: Gianna House. Never had he been more thankful for an interruption than now. Buddy began chewing him out as soon as he stepped foot into the engineer's "office," going on and on about House not coming down to "his level" anymore unless he needed a favor.

"I don't ask for favors, Bud. I'm the captain, remember?"

Buddy laughed. "Not to me, you ain't! To me, you'll always be my 'Baby Black Seabass.'"

House rubbed the sleep from his face, failing in the attempt. "You know that's horribly racist, right?"

Buddy shrugged and grinned, amused with himself. "Good cookin' either way."

That's when Gianna's call saved his sanity.

"Oh, sorry," House said, turning and waving, "I have to take this." He hurried away. "Later, Bud."

House scampered back up the first flight of stairs. The entire time he climbed, all he could hear was Gianna's worried voice, and Buddy hollering after him. House was starting to wonder if the fumes were finally getting to the old codger.

"Dad," Gianna said, "I think there's something wrong with Seth."

That sobered House up some. He had only been half listening while he was trying to make out whatever it was that Buddy was hollering. By now, House had left Engineering in the dust and was starting his climb back to Command, quickly bypassing Navigation before anyone could ask him what had gotten Buddy all riled up.

"What happened?" he asked.

"Well," she replied, "I went to check on Trip, remember?"

Oh, he remembered all right, and he wasn't happy that it had been over half an hour since she had left to go check on him. He had expected a call back right away. *She's twenty-five, Sebastian. Give her a break!* He shut up whatever controlled his inner monologue and turned his attention back to his daughter.

"He seemed...off...more than usual, I mean. I think he wanted to hurt me."

House stopped dead, pausing his climb at the middle of the stairs between levels, the only private place the bridge offered.

What?

"How do you mean?" he asked, looking out to sea, away from prying eyes and ears. "What did he do exactly?"

"Nothing, really, but he wasn't acting the same—said some hurtful things out of the blue and then stepped toward me like he wanted a go."

House wasn't sure if Gianna meant sex or a fight. Either way, it wasn't good for either of them. Both warranted a sit-down with the seemingly distraught scientist. Only then would House know whether or not he'd have to beat the man to death with his own shoes.

"Trip can vouch for me...if you don't believe me."

Ouch.

"And why wouldn't I believe you?" Gianna got awfully silent. "G?" Nothing... "G, you there?"

"Sorry, Dad, lost you there for a second."

Lost me? he thought. That wasn't possible when one of the two connections were topside. *What's going on with her?*

"What the hell was that!" someone shouted.

He turned and saw what the commotion was all about. Through the swirling storm outside was a blue flash, out toward the bow of the ship—toward Donovan's wrecked surgical lab.

"Hang on, baby."

House vaulted the remaining stairs two at a time, yelling, "Sam!"

The XO came rushing over. "Already on it, sir. I have two ESD agents checking it out now."

House patted Sam on the shoulder, happy to hear that two of the four members of the Endeavor Security Detail were already en route. He stepped away from Sam and returned to his call. "You still there?"

"Sounds like you've got your hands full."

He smiled. "You know me." He frowned. House wanted to be with her. "Need me to come down and put my size twelves in Seth's ass?"

"No, no, no, Dad, I'm good. I'm gonna spend the night with Trip, if the storm permits—just in case Seth shows up and still isn't acting right."

"Oh," he replied, "okay…"

Gianna laughed. "We'll be fine, Dad. I promise. You should try and get some rest too."

8

The Endeavor Security Detail (ESD) was the definition of distrust. Both House and Donovan were equally uncomfortable with them being on board. The four members of the special outfit worked directly for Damon Becker, and him alone. Becker, along with his superiors in Washington, had placed the team on the research vessel to ensure that House and Donovan were being forthcoming with their findings, and not withholding vital information.

What made matters worse, especially for House, was that his authority over them was limited to deeming their participation as either counterproductive or unsafe for the current mission and the people involved. So far, they had stayed out of the way with an occasional entanglement here and there.

The ESD members chosen to investigate the disturbance at the recently quarantined laboratory were agents Rick Abbott and Jennifer Grigson—and neither were happy about it. While both were ex-military, having each served multiple tours in the Middle East, Abbott and Grigson had, so far, enjoyed getting paid well to do next-to-nothing. They preferred to keep it that way too.

Both agents carried holstered 9mm pistols on their hips, but they didn't bother drawing them...ever. Their detail aboard the "Nerd Boat," as they called it, rarely gave them a reason to do so.

"Whattaya think we got here?" Abbott asked, speaking through a gritted jaw and a toothpick. He rarely went anywhere without both.

"Not sure," Grigson replied, running a hand through her short black hair, "probably just one of Donovan's machines going haywire."

Abbott wasn't so sure. "I thought they powered-down all of the doc's gizmos?"

Grigson shrugged. "They could've missed one." She smiled. "What, you scared of the Bogeyman?"

"*Pffft*," Abbott snorted, "only if he's got an IED strapped to his chest."

They stopped just outside of the external lab doors and immediately saw that there was more than just a nonessential disturbance. Against her better judgment, Grigson didn't bother to relay the findings to Captain House. For all she and Abbott knew, something could've simply gotten triggered as it tipped over, what with the onslaught of the storm and all. In the three months of being aboard, they had yet to see someone disobey orders—the captain's or otherwise.

The straightest crew I've ever seen, Grigson thought, mildly impressed.

Even though this was a glorified lab on water, she reckoned there'd be at least one rough-and-tough sailor-type. *Nope.* She figured House would've told Becker to go fuck himself at some point, but so far, House had played by the rules, and everyone had gotten along fine. Publicly, anyway. She doubted it was as civil as it seemed when they got behind closed doors. It was plain to see that House and Donovan didn't like one another.

Abbott opened the door and stepped in first. Grigson followed close behind, acting like an owl and keeping her head on a swivel. Usually, there was a second set of doors that led into Donovan's topside containment lab. Their job was to contain whatever was inside of them after all. The doors were still there, but had been ripped from their hinges and tossed aside as if they were made of balsa wood. She didn't draw her sidearm, but she did rest her right palm atop it.

"What coulda done this?" Abbott asked, not playing around. His pistol was drawn and pointed into the opening of the lab.

Grigson shrugged. "Your guess is as good as—"

The sound of breaking glass startled them both. It had come from the rear of the thirty-by-thirty room. She should've been able to see what it was, but the emergency lights didn't seem to reach all the way to the back of the space.

Silently pulling her gun free, Grigson announced their presence to the intruder. "ESD," she said. "Come out and explain yourself."

Grigson twitched when a second unseen object crashed to the floor.

"This area is off-limits," Abbott said, steadying his aim at the source of the noise. "Only Captain House and Dr. Donovan are permitted here."

"Donovan..." a voice muttered, snickering at the name.

The ESD agents glanced at one another. The speaker's voice sounded familiar, but it also sounded off. Regardless of the fact if they knew the person or not, he or she was violating the captain's orders and, therefore, they were also violating the ESD's.

"Yes, that's right," Grigson replied, "Captain House and Dr. Donovan. The captain just gave everyone strict orders not to—"

"Donovan..."

She lowered her gun, pointing it nonthreateningly at the floor. She knew that voice. "Doctor?"

Grigson was answered by another raspy laugh, but unlike the first one, this voice was softer and of a higher pitch.

She glanced at Abbot and held up two fingers, silently asking him what she was thinking. *Are there two people in here with us?* He could only shrug. Abbott was as confused as she was.

Stepping heel-to-toe, the agents rounded the central examination area, the spot that had taken the brunt of the destruction in the accident. She went right. Abbott went left. The floor was still slick with powdery residue as was the entire room, for that matter.

Where's the thing? Grigson thought, looking for the octopus' remains.

She had been on hand when the science team recovered it from somewhere on the ocean floor. From what she figured, it should've been floating in its tank on the back counter of the lab.

Is that what broke?

Halfway to the back of the room, a figure stood, still cloaked in darkness. The ESD agents froze and took aim, waiting for the stranger to identify him or herself. Clicking on her small LED flashlight, Grigson relaxed when she aimed it at the back of the man's bald head.

"Doctor?" she asked, holstering her weapon. "You okay?"

The man turned, filling the agents with dread.

"Yes, *we* are fine."

"Good God..." Abbott muttered.

Grigson took a step back, garnering the full attention of the nightmare before them. Slowly, she redrew her sidearm, but kept it low, next to her right thigh.

Seth Donovan's eyes were unlike anything she had ever seen. They were entirely blue, containing none of their usual whites, irises, or pupils. Instead, they shined bright with a rolling, liquid plasma of some kind. In the darker section of the lab, the agents witnessed his veins pulse with electricity—the same as that of the creature.

Grigson's thoughts went immediately to the octopus. It had similar *blood*—if that's what that stuff was.

"We?" Abbott asked, likewise stepping away.

Donovan turned his cold stare on Abbott and explained.

"Yes, we are Seth Donovan. Together, we are better."

"Who else is in there with you?" Grigson asked, fingering her still-lowered weapon's trigger.

He smiled. "We are one. There is no Seth Donovan." His eyes began flashing, exactly like the specimen. "Not anymore."

The scientist leaped over two examination tables, covering twenty feet of distance in the blink of an eye. When he landed, he did so atop Abbott who fell to the ground without getting a shot off. Grigson snapped up her pistol and swung it around but was too late. Her partner's horrifying shrieks were quickly cut off by a sickening crack and a wet gurgle.

"Uh, Rick?" she asked, her voice quivering. "Donovan?"

Neither one answered her.

The scientist had gone crazy and killed a man. She let that sink in. Donovan just murdered someone in cold blood—someone that was armed and had military training. But Grigson also had both at her disposal.

Keeping her gun trained on Abbott's last location, Grigson cautiously sidestepped her way back toward the ruined inner doors. She made it two-thirds of the way there before Donovan showed himself again. He was still where Grigson thought he'd be, and she swiftly pumped two rounds into his chest.

Donovan screeched into the air and quickly slunk back down—out of sight. She could hear him scurrying around on all fours, zigging and zagging back deeper into the room. With him on the move, she turned and ran for the intact outer doors, ready to shoulder through them and not stop until she reached the bridge. She'd notify House while making her way to him.

Right when she was about to shove through the exit, she was yanked off her feet and slammed into a nearby wall.

"Oof!"

Grigson felt something crack in her left side. With the single attack, at least one of her ribs had broken. She'd been injured in combat in the past, but never as quick and effective as this.

The agent tried to raise her left hand to activate her comms unit in her ear but couldn't move her arm away from her ribs. The pain in her side was too much. The only other option was to holster her weapon and use her right hand—and that sure as hell wasn't going to happen! So, she decided to take care of things here first. Shaking, she aimed the pistol back into the empty void.

"Where the hell...did he go?" she whispered, grunting out the words. She couldn't catch her breath.

The typically unshakeable Jennifer Grigson shrieked in fright when a figure dropped from the ceiling directly above her. Reacting with the same lightning-fast reaction time that made her an exceptional soldier, she pulled the trigger of her gun twice more. Both of the rounds penetrated Donovan's stomach, just above his belly button.

Shockingly, the scientist took the bullets with no adverse response. Stunned, Grigson was able to pull her sidearm's trigger one more time before he was upon her.

With a hand around her throat, Donovan lifted Grigson into the air as if she weighed nothing. She knew for a fact that he wasn't strong enough to do such a thing. As far as Grigson knew, the man had never been inside of a gym a day in his life.

"Guh," she gagged, choking on her saliva. His grip was firm, but he wasn't trying to crush her windpipe.

The slightly taller man leaned in close and smiled. His breath smelled of rotting fish, making Grigson gag even more.

"We, Agent Grigson, are better together."

With a sickening pop, Donovan's lower jaw dislocated away from the rest of his skull in the same way a snake did before engulfing its prey. Grigson struggled for her next breath of air, losing it when she saw something terrible emerge from the scientist's throat.

It wasn't his tongue, either.

The wriggling *addition* pulsed with the same blue energy that his eyes did. It appeared to pulse in time with his eyes, actually. The thing also looked as if it acted independently of him, darting back and forth like an agitated cat's tail.

It's...alive?

He leaned in closer, his face only inches from hers.

The glowing appendage shot forward, like a frog's tongue, but instead of it latching onto her face as she expected, it forcibly entered Grigson's agape mouth, stifling her petrified screams. The only sound she could emit was a pathetic whimper as the growth squirmed its way deeper and deeper into her body until it stopped in her stomach.

Then, as if someone turned on a garden hose, it spewed a searing-hot, acidic liquid into her gut, enveloping her entire body in agony. It was the smell that had made her gag earlier. It wasn't rotting sea life she'd caught a whiff of moments ago, it was the creature's payload.

With each passing second, Grigson felt herself slipping closer and closer into blissful unconsciousness. There wasn't pain there. This feeling was like the one she had when she tried to escape the mental pain after she had gotten out of the military and turned to alcohol. It numbed everything.

Her eyes snapped open. She still held her gun.

At this point, Grigson wasn't sure what Donovan's intentions were. Was he going to kill her like he did Abbott? His eyes, while swirling with blue plasma, looked maniacal—crazed. Either way, she was going to put up a fight like her life depended on it because currently, it did.

With a quaking, heavy hand, she jammed the pistol's muzzle into Donovan's upper abdomen and, at point-blank range, emptied the entirety of her gun's magazine. With clouded vision, she couldn't tell if it did a damn thing. Nothing, not even a terrorist on bath salts, should've been able to stand up to that type of barrage.

The last thing she remembered, before blacking out, was seeing the appendage slither from her mouth back into his. Then, his lower jaw locked back into place with a quick snap of mending sinew.

*   *   *

Donovan dropped her inert form to the floor and smiled proudly like a father would to his daughter. He had seen House behold Gianna in the same way. Now, it was his time to mentor a new creation, as the captain once did.

"We, Agent Grigson," he said, feeling something inside him stir, "are better together."

As soon as he uttered the words, Grigson shot to her feet and stumbled away from the monster. Her empty gun clattered to the tile floor, and she clawed like mad at her skull. Donovan knew she was trying to silence the voice that had, at first, frightened him— but not now. And after a few seconds, she wouldn't want them to go away. And after a minute, she'd gladly welcome them with open arms—their company, their guidance.

He observed Grigson's behavior, studying her hard, watching her calm down and lower her hands away from her temples. Slowly, she stood up straight and faced him. She smiled at Donovan, showing off her own glowing eyes. Strangely, her transformation went much smoother than his. He supposed it was because he had direct contact with the substance.

"We really are better together," she said, looking up at him with understanding.

Donovan's mind was instantly invaded by a chorus of voices— memories too. It was the first time he'd occupied someone else's mind, an act he did without thought. It felt like the ordinary thing to do. With that single feat, he was given snippets into Grigson's life, including her deepest, darkest fears and desires, but more importantly, he was given her knowledge.

A scientist by trade, Donovan now contained all of the

Endeavor's security protocols, its communication passcodes, and the combination to the ESD vault—where the detachment stored its munitions. If he could acquire more knowledge like this…

"We are better together," he said in multiple voices, speaking as one.

Donovan's words didn't come from his mouth this time, though—they had come from his mind—his thoughts. Grigson confirmed that she'd heard him and replied in the same extrasensory manner.

Yes, Seth, she agreed, mouth unmoving, flashing eyes locked onto his, *we are.*

9

Fifteen minutes had passed since the two ESD agents had entered the quarantined laboratory. Both Captain House and XO Ferguson each tried to raise the pair but were unsuccessful. Sam offered to go have a look, but House swiftly rejected his proposal.

"I need you here, Sam," he said, patting the younger man's shoulder. "Keep me updated and continue to try and hail the agents."

House was a man of action. He hated protocol—especially when it meant he'd be sitting on his ass waiting for others to do a job he could've just as easily done. Until he figured out what was going on aboard his boat, it would be the last time he'd send glorified security guards to check on something so important.

He spun and headed for the door. "I'll do it myself," he grumbled, annoyed that the ESD couldn't do what they were being paid to do.

This was the exact opposite of what House looked for in his crew. Unlike the majority of those on board, the actions, and overall purpose, of the ESD were disloyal, and they were lousy at their jobs. The proof was the fact that he had to go check on them.

"Aye, sir," Sam replied, relaying the orders he was given without argument. He did have one question, though. "What about the other ESD agents? What should I tell them if they call?"

House stopped and glanced over his shoulder. "Tell them the truth—that we're still waiting to hear back from Abbott and Grigson." He gave the XO a hard stare. "Just don't tell them that I'm the one snooping around..."

Sam gave him a curt nod and went back to his duties.

The real problem with House "doing it himself" wasn't that he shouldn't have been doing it, it was what would happen if he did, indeed, find trouble. There weren't any weapons available, not unless he joined ranks with the ESD overnight. And since their team's inception was built around distrust, House doubted he could convince them to supply him with anything more dangerous than a stapler and a box of paperclips.

He wasn't completely defenseless, however. House had his hands and his head. Not only could he punch his way out of a shitty situation, but he could also think his way out of it *while* he did the punching. Before leaving Command, he lifted the lid of a glass box attached to the inner wall, shrugging when he grasped the handle of the fire axe.

Better than nothing, I suppose.

Casually carrying the improvised weapon on his right shoulder, House reached for the handle and was startled when it swung open, revealing his daughter and Trip. Gianna must've been the only person to witness him stumbling back because she was the only one who laughed. Or, it could've been that she was the only person aboard the Endeavor with big enough balls to do so while in his presence, and at his expense. At second glance, Trip didn't seem to notice what had transpired, glancing back the way they'd come.

The only other person with a large enough set was Buddy. House was lucky the engineer wasn't around. Buddy would've never let him hear the end of it, even though, in the end, it wasn't that big of a deal.

Buddy would know how to make it one.

"Oh," she said, snorting in between words, "sorry." Then, she noticed the axe. "What are you doing with that?"

House didn't want her knowing. "There's a, uh, problem that needs fixing."

Gianna defiantly crossed her arms, looking very much like him. "And an axe can fix this...*problem*...of yours? Don't they usually destroy things?" She continued. "Now, if you wanted to fix something, I'd go with a hammer or a screwdri—"

House swiftly stepped through the door and shut it, cutting her off. Knowing he wasn't going to be able to hide what he was about to do, he decided to come clean with her. House looked up and down the hall, making sure no one was within earshot of what he was about to say.

"Okay, look," he said, sighing, "since I know you're not going to let this go, I'll tell you—but only if you swear to keep it under wraps until we find out what, exactly, is going on."

She grinned. "On penalty of death?"

House's eyes narrowed. "I'll throw you off this boat...for good."

Gianna's face fell. Never had House spoken to her like that. But he needed her to understand that he wasn't joking when it came to the potential severity of the situation. Unfortunately, he knew he didn't have it in him to abandon her at McMurdo. Still, he held his ground, gripping the handle of his axe tightly.

"Oh," she replied, "okay. I see..."

"Are we clear?" he asked, standing tall.

Gianna nodded, but Trip raised his hand like he was still in grammar school.

"Question..." he said nervously. "If one of us doesn't want to know, is it too late for him, or her, to leave?"

Gianna latched onto his arm. "Nope. Sorry, but you're staying."

Obviously unhappy about being shanghaied into service, Trip could only shrug and wait for House to explain.

"We have a problem back at the lab."

Gianna and Trip glanced at one another, then settled their eyes back on House. He, once more, looked up and down the corridor, wanting nothing more than for someone to appear and delay what he was about to reveal. The chances of that taking place were remote since the only doors visible led to either the wheelhouse or the stairs, and everyone that belonged back in Command, besides himself, were on duty.

"There was an incident inside the lab a few minutes ago, and we sent two ESD agents to have a look and—"

"Neither of them was heard from again," Trip finished.

House and Gianna stared at him.

"Trip..." Gianna said, shaking her head. "This isn't one of your crappy movies."

House's reaction was very different, though. "Who told you?"

Gianna's facial expression went from one of embarrassment to one of shock. "Wait... That really happened?"

House stepped forward, threatening Trip.

"No one told me anything!" he yelped, getting shushed by both Houses. He calmed and explained himself. "Every cheesy horror movie says that."

House wiped his sweaty brow and stepped away from the cowering man. Regardless of the situation, he needed to stay in control until he completed his investigation and found everything out.

Before setting off down the stairs, House tapped his WiMP's screen, activating his comms unit.

"Captain?" Sam asked.

"Any luck?"

"No, sir," he replied, "but we'll keep at it."

"Copy that," House said, ending the call.

He turned left and took a deep breath. He wouldn't verbally admit it, but he was happy to have two more sets of eyes with him. "Okay, this is how it's going to go." He pointed at Trip. "Stay behind me." Then, he turned to Gianna. "You're bringing up the rear."

Gianna was about to protest her position in line but was silenced by his raised palm.

"I need someone I trust to watch our asses." He glanced at Trip. "No offense."

Trip shrugged. "None taken. She is your kid, after all."

Since that was taken care of, House had to ask... "What's with the shades?"

"They help with the headaches."

"Still that bad?" House asked, heading off, genuinely concerned with his well-being.

Trip nodded. "Yea, like an SOB."

"Has Dr. Bowen taken a look at you?"

"Not yet," Trip replied. "Honestly, I'd rather have the base physician do it."

"Why not Lisa?" Gianna asked. "Is it because she's a woman?"

Trip snorted. "No way, I love women!" The Houses stopped and looked at him. Trip shrank back under their gaze and quickly clarified what he intended to say. "What I meant was... I prefer the doctor at McMurdo because he's a friend of the family."

House didn't know that.

"That's why you're stationed here?"

Trip nodded. "He said with the lack of interest in McMurdo as a whole, that I'd move up the ladder quickly. My parents agreed with the move, and well, here I am!" He frowned. "Come to think of it, base command recommended me for my job here—acted like they couldn't wait to get rid of me."

House nodded, understanding why a move to McMurdo made sense, professionally speaking.

There'd be less competition for promotions down here than almost anywhere else on planet Earth. Still... The freezing cold temperatures, the isolation, the lack of overall freedom to do just about anything... But he didn't get to comment about Trip's family situation. Gianna slammed home the period at the end of the sentence—only—she did it in a brasher way than House had intended to do.

He wanted to let the young man down gently and tell him that the people around him didn't seem to care for him very much. Gianna, on the other hand, didn't do anything gently, especially use her words.

She lovingly clutched Trip's left elbow, laid her head on his shoulder, and laughed. "Kinda sounds like your family hates you."

10

House led the pair down three flights of stairs and stopped at the outer door that led into the top deck's honeycomb of corridors and pods. Instead of the uppermost level being outside and at the mercy of the elements, as it was on most container ships and oil tankers, the Endeavor had an artificial ceiling constructed that resembled a gigantic inflated, yet ultra-durable, Kevlar-reinforced balloon.

Split into three rows of three, the nine pods were used in a variety of different capacities, ninety percent of which was run by the science division. A smart man in his own right, House didn't bother asking about most of it, knowing even he wouldn't understand the "nerd speak" being slung his way.

The inflatable also contained steel-framed walls to divide it into airtight compartments and usable hallways and was a revolutionary design—another thing being tested aboard his ship. A heated gel within the one-of-a-kind Temperature Controlled Bladder's (TCB) lining kept it from freezing and cracking like a building-sized eggshell.

Onward, House thought, stepping through the door.

The pod nearest the bridge contained a variety of equipment, mostly "overstock" for the other pods between the bridge and the forward-most pod, Donovan's lab. Both House and Donovan agreed that having it where it was located was best for everyone. Regrettably, they found nothing inside the room to use as a better weapon than his axe, and they quickly moved on.

Next was the greenhouse.

This was one of House's favorite places to kill time and veg. Literally. He came here daily and picked at the various fruits and vegetables grown within the groundbreaking conservatory. A similar version was already in development aboard a top-secret carrier. Very little was known about that particular ship, but House had been told that *his* boat's greenhouse had been marveled at and quickly copied.

That made him proud.

He punched his personal access code into the control pad to the right of the greenhouse's automatic doors, one of the only rooms to have them, and he and the others were met with an onrush of warm, humid air. The conservatory was self-sustained and was kept at a higher temperature than the rest of the ship. Like he had countless times before, he snagged a Granny Smith apple from the tree directly to the left of the entrance, and took one enormous bite, relishing in the delicious juices that followed.

"Really?"

Mid-chew, he stopped and looked at Gianna. "What?"

"You're eating at a time like this?"

House's eyes found Trip's who quickly looked away so as to keep out of the feud that was brewing between House and Gianna. He faced his daughter again and swallowed.

He shrugged. "I missed lunch and," he took another bite, "we don't even know if there's anything to worry about." House finished two-thirds of the apple and tossed it into the Endeavor's miniature compost bin situated at the other side of the enclosure.

"Seriously, this ship has everything!" That's what Gianna had said after taking her first tour of the vessel. It blew House's mind that the engineers that originally designed the ship seven years ago decided to include, of all things, an onboard compost container.

It didn't surprise him once he realized how many different experiments were going on at the same time. Not everyone within Donovan's team was solely dedicated to their octopus hunt. Only about a third of the forty-or-so scientists were dedicated to the deep-sea mission.

Three were heading the greenhouse alone. Two of them were famous botanists, whom which, naturally, House had never heard of before.

Two other non-octopus scientists worked hand-in-hand with Trip and his team in the launch bay. The Endeavor's ADS suit contained several modifications within it, and the engineers were closely monitoring it while it was in use—also while it was being stored. Trip was the best pilot they had on staff—also the most willing of anyone to man it in the open water.

Another of the scientists worked with Buddy on the engines, attempting to improve their output. She'd even talked about eventually converting the entire system to electric.

Yet another worked with Chief Lucas, up in Navigation, who was also trying to expand the system's capabilities.

In reality, the entire Endeavor was one massive, military-funded laboratory.

The only department on the Endeavor that didn't have a member of Donovan's team working side-by-side with them was House and his wheelhouse crew. They were left alone per the captain's orders.

"Just let us do our jobs," House had said when he was

approached by the government liaison. Becker was about to argue, but House had cut him off with a raised hand. "Let us. Do our. Jobs." His face said something like, "We're going to do our jobs the way we want to whether you like it or not, so back off!"

The Endeavor was the first of its kind and was meant to be reproduced, but it would take this ship's success to warrant the enormous expense. Even though another tanker was already being retrofitted for service, it wouldn't get the full go-ahead unless the Antarctic voyage passed with flying colors.

House wanted everything to go swimmingly.

He also wanted to keep his boat.

Punching the button to the greenhouse's exit, House paused and turned. Facing Gianna and Trip, he simply said, "Keep your eyes peeled and stay behind me." They nodded and slid closer to one another, Gianna going as far as interlacing the fingers of her right hand in Trip's left.

He hit the button and blinked against the surge of cool, dry air. But it wasn't just the colder air that caused him to flinch, it was the coppery smell of blood. House didn't recall anyone besides Donovan being injured in the incident, nor did he remember the man bleeding very much at all.

Shit, he thought, picturing the stacks of reports he'd have to sign-off on. More than that, though, another person had been hurt, and he needed to find them before anything worse occurred. They'd had no incidents until now—less than a day away from docking.

Figures...

Gripping the axe hard with both hands, he held it out in front of him, blade forward, and quietly walked heel-to-toe, attempting to hide his approach. Thankfully, Gianna and Trip were smart enough to see what he was doing and walked in the same manner. The lab's outer doors were ajar, and House could also see that the lab's inner doors were too.

"What happened?" Gianna whispered.

House peered over his shoulder and gave his daughter a look that could instantly curdle non-dairy milk. She shrank back a little but kept silent. He didn't mean to frighten her, but he'd never forgive himself if something happened to her.

Reluctantly, he quietly answered her. "Nothing good."

The short walk from the greenhouse to the lab was a chilling one, and it had nothing to do with the physical temperature.

Inside the corridor, like most of the ship, it was a comfortable sixty-seven degrees. They kept it on the cool side, so those that were working hard weren't uncomfortable. Those that didn't do a lot of heavy lifting usually wore a light jacket or a sweater to make up for it.

The outer doors were wedged open, the hinges on both bent beyond repair. The inner doors weren't wedged open at all. Instead, they'd been completely torn away and tossed aside with a feat of brute, Herculean strength. No one, not even the handful of gym rats on board could've done this.

Not even George Novacek, House thought.

Affectionately nicknamed Nova, George was a man of hulking mass. A person of few words, you'd know when Buddy's assistant was angry when he went "SuperNova" and destroyed something. He'd been in the Navy at one point but had been discharged because of an incident involving a superior officer's jaw being broken.

Buddy said he wasn't taking the job unless Nova came along. And like how House's ass was on the line for Gianna, so was Buddy's for Nova if he did something nasty. So far, the big man had only wrecked a couple pieces of gym equipment, no people.

The lab was dark except for a single, red emergency light at the rear of the room. House waited a beat before entering, listening for something that didn't belong.

Like, anything at all.

Theoretically, no one besides the ESD agents should've been inside. With them MIA, any, and all movement would be seen as a potential threat to House. Carefully, he stepped through the demolished entrance, and once more, stopped dead. The scent of blood was stronger here. Whoever, or whatever died, was definitely in this room.

He looked at his daughter. "Can you bring up the lights?"

She nodded and pulled her tablet out of the bag that was on her shoulder. She never went anywhere without it. The screen lit up after a series of numbers and letters that House knew would be impossible to crack. He had prodded her more than once about it and could never glean much information. He knew it was eighteen characters long and that none of them repeated. It dawned on House that she could be lying to throw anyone off if they tried to hack her system. It could've been all zeros, for all he knew.

He respected that. She had a job to do too, one that was pivotal to their mission. If it were him in her shoes, he'd have done the same exact thing.

Smart girl.

He went right, and Gianna and Trip went left. So far, there was nothing except the smell of blood to worry about. Ten seconds later, whichever of the light fixtures that still worked blinked to life, and when they did, Gianna screamed.

11

Gripping the axe firmly in his right hand, House planted his left hand on the nearest examination table and vaulted over it. Timing his landing perfectly, House used his body's downward momentum to aid the axe head's descending arc...right into the forehead of Gianna's unidentified assailant. But before the blade struck, House jerked it back up, pausing the killer blow just inches above the man's mangled skull.

What he'd initially thought to be his daughter's attacker, ended up being someone on the receiving end of his own violent assault. Whoever killed the man, they, obviously, didn't care about making an easily traceable mess—and it was quite the mess.

He wasn't a detective, by any means, but it didn't take a rocket scientist to figure out that leaving a scene as untidy as this wasn't the best way to get away with a murder. He knelt next to the ravaged ESD agent and read his name tag aloud.

"Abbott."

Rick Abbott was someone, like the other three ESD agents, House knew very little about. But no matter who he was, no one deserved to die as brutally as he did. It was a method he'd never heard of, let alone seen. Then again, House had spent a lifetime sailing the seas, not investigating murders.

Abbott's mouth was wrenched open, beyond any human's capability. His lower jaw was hanging to the left, dislocated, possibly even broken. Without touching him, House leaned over the body, holding a hand over his nose and mouth as he did. It took everything for him not to retch at the sight.

The back of Abbott's head was missing, blown out by way of his gaping mouth. Something thick and cylindrical seemed to have been forced into his mouth and had been driven in so hard, that it burst through bone and brain matter.

Dammit... House turned away from the gruesome scene.

Gianna's face was buried into Trip's chest, and she was bawling her eyes out. Trip wasn't looking at the body or Gianna. He was staring at something on the ground to his left. House decided to leave the dead man be and see what had Trip's attention.

As his eyes scanned past another examination table, House saw it. The specimen, the one that attacked Trip beneath the surface, was pinned to the floor, cut open, as if on display for further studying and research.

Is Abbott's killer a scientist?

House's revelation that the murderer was a scientist did little else to help solve the case. House still had no idea what was going on. He had to give credence to the fact that the killer might be a scientist, after all, the death did occur in the lab. House was also stunned that someone aboard the Endeavor had the capacity to kill a man in this manner—a man that was a combat veteran, at that.

One of the few things House knew about the ESD agents was that they were all, indeed, former Special Forces soldiers. Becker mentioned as much in his initial briefing on the unit back in McMurdo.

The remains of the octopus had been dissected and inspected. House wasn't sure what the person could've been looking for. The glowing, flashing plasma within it was now a dull, blue-grey color.

"What were you looking for?" House asked himself, standing, visualizing the killer in action. He started with Abbott's brutal murder. Then, he moved his attention to the dismembered octopus.

Honestly, it didn't matter why. Regardless of the *why*, one of the Endeavor's crew was dead and the person, or persons involved, needed to be apprehended before they struck again.

"Who..." Gianna choked out, "who could've done such a thing?"

"Grigson," House replied, thinking aloud. "She should've been here. You gotta think that if Abbott was left here to find that she would've been left too."

"If she was murdered," Trip added, snapping out of his stupor.

House nodded. "She was sent along with him. They were supposed to do nothing else except investigate the scene of the disturbance and then report back to Becker and me with their findings. Why haven't we heard from her?"

He radioed Sam. "Anything yet?"

"No, sir. How about you?"

House's eyes flashed down to Abbott's corpse. "No... Nothing on my end either. I'll let you know if I find anything, though."

He ended the call and sighed. He hated lying to Sam. The XO was one of the most loyal men he had ever met, more so than his own flesh and blood.

House only knew about Gianna and Trip's relationship because of sheer luck and good/bad timing. The last thing he wanted to do was create a rift between him and Sam by not being forthcoming.

"Shit..." he muttered, calling the sailor back.

"Sir?"

"Leave the room," House ordered.

The XO didn't reply, but House could hear him moving about. "Done. What's wrong?"

House took a deep breath. "Abbott is dead."

"What!"

"We don't know how, and we don't need to freak out the rest of the crew."

"Understood. What about Agent Grigson?"

"MIA," House replied.

"Is she a suspect?"

House shook his head, even though Sam couldn't see it. "Maybe...but I'm not sure. The few times I've spoken with her, she didn't lend herself to having the temperament to kill a man so...disgustingly."

"That bad?" Sam asked.

"No, much worse than that. I can't even begin to explain..."

"Okay," Sam replied, swallowing hard, "let me know if anything changes. But, sir?"

"Yeah?"

"We're going to have to report this soon, you know that, right?"

House nodded in agreement and looked at his daughter. "I know, Sam. Just...just give me a little bit to look over everything. I'll radio it in myself."

"What about the body?" Sam asked.

House knew he couldn't leave Abbott in the lab. The last thing he needed was for someone to stumble upon it. He knew what he needed to do.

"Alert Dr. Bowen and have her people take care of it, *but*," House sternly added, "under no circumstances is she or her staff to report it."

"Yes, sir. Good luck."

The call ended, and House rubbed his face hard. What had he gotten himself into? He wasn't a homicide detective. He was a sailor of the world's oceans, but he was also the leader of the crew. It wasn't uncommon for a person in his position to have to shift responsibilities during a moment of crisis.

I'd say this qualifies, he thought, laughing on the inside—at the ridiculousness of it all. He shook his head in disbelief. *But murder, really?*

This was only the second time a sailor had been killed, in a non-combat situation, under his watch. The first time was during his third year as Executive Officer of the *USS Harry S. Truman*. Unlike what happened here, that was an accident. A pipe had burst below decks, and the debris struck one of his men in the neck. By the time the medics got to him, it was too late, and he had bled out.

House needed to apprehend Abbott's murderer before someone else accompanied him in death.

* * *

ESD Agent Jennifer Grigson no longer felt alone—quite the opposite, actually. She'd never been so connected to someone in her life. She knew everything about Seth Donovan, and he knew all about her. Their minds were one, linked, and she knew she'd never experience loss or sorrow ever again. He promised as much.

And I meant it, Donovan whispered from across the ship.

They communicated as if they were standing next to one another, but in actuality, they were hundreds of feet apart, through layer upon layer of steel. They each had a mission to accomplish before they could move on with their plan.

Multiply.

Their newfound group consciousness needed to grow more. They needed additional knowledge. They required more minds to join theirs.

Even though Grigson and Donovan shared one mind, it was Donovan who was in control. It was his world, and Grigson was invited into it. She had no idea how they were connected or what caused it. The last thing she remembered was waking up on the floor of the lab and hearing him whispering into her head.

Calm down, Jennifer, he said. *You are fine. We are better together.*

After leaving the lab, Grigson descended two levels and quickly made her way toward the middle section of the ship. Her destination was one she knew well, and one that Donovan was now very familiar with too.

The office of the Endeavor Security Detail.

Donovan reminded her that with Abbott dead that she was the only one of the two of them that could enter the office without being questioned. Her injuries would be noticed, however, and would more than likely cause an issue.

Her hand went to her mouth.

Somehow, Grigson had sustained a busted lower lip, and she could feel a knot atop her right cheekbone. She stopped and looked at her reflection in a nearby mirrored window. There were also a series of black and blue markings on her neck. Strangely, they looked as if they had come from someone's hand. She could distinctly see at least three fingers on one side of her neck and a thumbprint on the other.

Recently, someone violently grasped her by the neck and had done so with an incredible amount of force. She couldn't recall who, though.

As if she didn't recognize the human staring back at her, Grigson poked and prodded at her face. Oddly, the injuries didn't hurt to touch. Curious, she jammed her index finger into multiple parts of her exposed flesh—anywhere she could see. Her flesh didn't turn red with the pressure, nor did the open wounds bleed. Her skin was cold to the touch, too.

Ice-cold.

She quickly checked for a pulse, trying both her wrist and her neck and found nothing.

Jennifer Grigson was dead.

"Huh?" she said aloud, getting a reply.

What troubles you? It was Donovan.

"Am I dead, Seth?" Calling the scientist by his first name felt right. Family didn't call each other by their surnames like the professional world sometimes thought necessary.

Would it bother you if you were?

Grigson had to think about it but shook her head.

Good, Seth said, seeing her physical reply in the mirror, through her eyes.

"We are better together," Grigson said, smiling. Then, she frowned. "What about Rick?"

Agent Abbott? Seth asked. *He isn't with us.*

Grigson sniffed and held back tears she knew wouldn't fall. Dead people didn't cry. "But why?"

A feeling of comfort washed over her body as if Donovan just gave her the warmest of hugs. Like the merging of their minds, their physical connection was also indescribable. Grigson felt like she was in Donovan's body, and that he was in hers.

You were my first, Jennifer. Rick's death meant that you and I could be together.

Grigson beamed with pride. She had no idea that she was Donovan's first...joining.

Joining... Seth said. *I like that.* He smiled. *You are my joined.*

"And I won't be your last," she stated with confidence.

Good, Donovan said. *Do as I explained, and you will feel even more comfort.*

"And you?"

Now, it was Donovan's turn to grin. *I'm doing the same as you. Together, we will increase our footprint in this world.*

That made Grigson happy. Their duo was about to explode into something much grander. She was excited to see what more than two minds merged as one would feel like. She shook with anticipation.

"Grigson?"

She stopped in her tracks, unaware that she had entered the ESD office. Grigson was so absorbed in the possibility of furthering her and Donovan's "family" that she'd completely zoned out as she continued into the room.

It took her a second to remember the other agents' names.

Someone else helped her out.

They are Fields and Dansby.

"Abbott sent me back to give you guys a message," Grigson said, doing everything she could to hold back her smile.

"What did he say?" Ryan Fields asked, right eyebrow raised.

Grigson lifted her lowered eyes. Her *electric* blue eyes...

"He said you should avoid ending up like him."

Grigson tapped into a previously unknown reserve. She bent at the knees and sprang across the room, landing atop Fields. As soon as she hit him, she pinned his shoulders to the hard floor with newfound strength and forced her recently formed, tongue-like appendage down his throat. Just as she began pumping her life-giving plasma into Fields' body, Nick Dansby attacked her from behind.

His thick arms wrapped around her throat, but he was no match for her. Even with him on her back, Grigson leaned in closer to her victim and finished delivering her glorious payload. She watched as Fields' eyes rolled back into his head, and his skin paled as he suffocated to death.

Was this what she looked like when Donovan had joined with her? Did she also have the same look on her face before she died and was then resurrected with Donovan's blessing?

It's what Grigson believed.

Her admiration for Seth Donovan was like what some felt for their god. She worshiped his abilities, feeling that her existence wouldn't be capable without his permission. And she felt that she needed to prove herself by succeeding here and now.

Fields fell still, but then his eyes snapped open, and he balled his fist, striking Dansby hard in the face. The other agent was thrown back, accompanied by a crack of breaking bone. Fields had hit him so hard that Dansby's nose broke.

Grigson had never felt such pride. She'd just turned one of the toughest men she'd ever met. Ryan Fields was a hard ass. He didn't have any close relationships and frequently stated that he didn't need friends to be happy.

All he needed was money—a real mercenary type.

As one, and with a shared consciousness, the former-ESD agents, Grigson and Fields, stood and turned on their former colleague.

How are things, Jennifer? Donovan asked, checking in. *I feel something stirring within me.*

Grigson smiled like a Great White.

"Good," she replied aloud. She glanced at Fields who grinned. "Everything is good."

12

Donovan was very pleased with Grigson's progress—and her immediate success. She proved to be an excellent addition to his... He wasn't sure what to call their growing assemblage. They weren't a family in the ordinary sense, but they were closer than most households could ever be. He literally knew everything about those that he was connected to.

My Joined, he thought. They were joined to him, but they were also the "Joined," a new species.

Grigson, Fields, and eventually Dansby.

He knew all their wants and desires.

Next, Donovan wished to absorb knowledge in the world of medicine. He was somewhat versed in the subject, but nowhere near enough for his current drive. He *had* to have it. It drove him crazy that he didn't already own it. He required it to advance in his quest. He also hoped it would help him understand what he'd become.

It hadn't taken Donovan long before he knew what his goal was—his endgame. In fact, it had only taken a few minutes after he linked with Grigson before it all came to him.

He needed to be connected to everyone, which meant he'd need to kill every man, woman, and child on the planet to do so—maybe even the globe's animals too. The realization that he'd become the most effective mass murderer in history didn't faze him at all. He didn't want to be their overlord—their dictator—though.

Donovan wanted the whole world to be a part of him.

He, like the plasma coursing itself through his veins, was a virus. The only explanation he could come up with is that this thing was some type of undiscovered contagion.

At random intervals, since the transformation had begun, Donovan experienced visions of a liquidy blue world. He didn't think he had tapped into the octopus' memories since it was too dark at the bottom of the ocean to see such a blue world as this. No, the visions he experienced felt like they were coming from within his own body, or at least from within the fluid itself.

Do I have microbes living inside my body? Are they the cause of it all?

Donovan searched his memory and came up with a term coined "science fiction." He also knew that Mary Shelly was the Godmother of the genre. Then, he attempted to recall something else from his past, something that should've been easy to recollect. His mother's name, for instance.

After five seconds of pondering it and failing to come up with the seemingly easy answer, he gave up and marched on. It was as if the only knowledge he had retained from his previous life was the things that were important to his new, single goal.

"We are better together," he uttered, unsure of why the phrase was stuck in his head. "Assimilation is key."

No longer were the words eradication, devastation, annihilation, and extermination repeating themselves over and over again. Now, there was only one word.

Assimilation. It would bring with it the other four actions.

He'd still bring about eradication, devastation, annihilation, and extermination, but he'd do it through the process of assimilation— through the process of joining.

Donovan had fled and hid after he attacked Grigson and her partner. Having someone else inside his head was a new experience. When he had pounced on Grigson, he had no idea what the outcome would be. The physical changes had the same effect on him, and he'd become comfortable with the alterations pretty quickly, so it was only a matter of time.

So, for now, he'd wait and watch as his joined did the heavy lifting for him.

He'd wait and watch...and enjoy every minute of it.

* * *

Dr. Lisa Bowen quietly ushered four others into the dark laboratory. Before entering, she asked Gianna to kill the lights and return the room to its state of quarantine. Also being a professionally trained medical examiner, she wanted to see the scene as it was when Rick Abbott was murdered.

The first thing she did upon seeing the body was to check the time and begin recording her findings. It wasn't just for her records. Her report would be for DARPA as well. Abbott had been a government employee, after all. Bowen was going to do everything in her power to explain how someone's life had ended so horribly.

The fatal wound she saw now reminded her of a large caliber gunshot through the back of the head. However, it was plain to see that Abbott wasn't killed by those means. There was no evidence of him being shot at all, not that there wasn't any evidence of shots being fired.

She found a handful of spent casings near the front of the room. "Does Agent Abbott have his sidearm?"

One of her assistants, Daphne, nodded. "Yes, ma'am, he does." The female tech took a quick series of pictures before removing the still-holstered weapon with her gloved hands. Then, she ejected the magazine. "Still full, too."

Bowen bit her lip. *So, it was Grigson doing the shooting...* She looked up from the floor. *Who were you shooting at?*

She returned to Daphne, who was still with the body, and knelt beside the deceased. Clicking on her penlight, Bowen went about with her examination while ordering the others to perform tasks of their own. Daphne, however, stayed by her side.

"Goodrum, you and Santos check out the specimen that Donovan found earlier today." She looked up at the two men. "The captain said it had seen better days."

They both nodded and moved off.

"Nathan," she said, looking over her shoulder, "see if you can get a better idea of where the killer may have gone. Blood trail, additional bullets casings, what-have-you..."

John Nathan gave his boss a playful salute and headed back the way they had come, exiting the broken inner doors and ducking through the set of outer ones that were still ajar. Nathan was six-four and powerfully built. When first meeting the man, Bowen was surprised to hear that he'd quit playing college football to concentrate on medicine.

"Punched a hole straight through," Daphne commented, returning Bowen's attention to the body. "I have a couple of ideas of what could've caused a wound like this, but it isn't anything that would be found aboard a ship like this."

"I agree," Bowen replied. "Something odd happened here, for sure." She sighed. "Very disturbing."

While Bowen continued to examine Abbott, Daphne turned her attention to the ground directly around his body. From Bowen's angle, and with their limited light, she couldn't see what the hubbub was all about.

Not until Daphne wiped her gloved index finger through the liquid and raised it for Bowen to see. The doctor aimed her flashlight beam at the younger woman's extended finger and gasped.

It wasn't blood, well, some of it was, but it was mostly that of a blue-tinged sludge. Bowen immediately pointed her light straight into the wound and saw more of it pooled inside Abbott's head. The back of his cranium was suctioned to the floor, acting as a dam. The barrier kept the liquid from flowing more freely.

"The, uh, *stuff* seems to be fresher inside the wound," Bowen said, swallowing hard.

She'd seen a lot of awful things in her years, but even the most disgusting medical problem could usually be explained away by something simple. This was anything but that. She'd been the head of her class back in med-school and couldn't figure it out. Bowen doubted that even her professor, a man she admired greatly, could adequately diagnose what happened here.

She dove into her bag and swiftly procured a one-ounce glass vial and a thin, long-handled, metallic lab scoop. It was designed to gently obtain small portions of whatever she was collecting. In this case, she was after the ooze.

After filling the vial two-thirds of the way full, she sealed it and brought the small container up to her face. Next, Bowen raised her penlight. At first, she saw nothing out of the ordinary, minus the fact that the substance came from inside a dead man's head.

Bowen and Daphne both jumped to their feet when they heard Nathan shout for help somewhere outside the lab doors. It sounded like he was fighting for his life—and losing the battle. No one on her team carried anything that could be used as a weapon, except for Bowen. She had a set of razor-sharp scalpels in her bag, just in case. It was a part of her emergency surgical kit, something she carried with her everywhere she went while onboard the Endeavor. It was a crutch for her, similar to Gianna and her tablet.

Nathan's cries for help halted almost as soon as they started. The air within the dark room returned back to its former, quiet state.

No one moved.

Just then, the single overhead light flickered. When it blinked back to life, a figure was standing just inside the outer doors. He remained there, unmoving, cloaked in shadows.

Until the lights winked out again...

After a few seconds, the fluorescents relit, but the mysterious figure was gone. Bowen stepped into the center of the room and splayed her penlight around the space, not finding anything out of the ordinary. Daphne, Goodrum, and Santos, likewise, lifted their lights to join in on the search.

With a yelp and a flash of blinding, blue light, Santos disappeared from view behind one of the surgical tables. The attack was so close to Bowen and Daphne that it showered them in crimson. They were both slathered in Santos' blood, and they quickly clutched one another in fright.

A skittering sound picked up all around them, and it must have been too much for Daphne to handle. The younger girl squealed, shoved out of Bowen's arms, and took off racing toward the front doors.

The doctor's eyes found Goodrum's. Quietly, she reached a hand out but was likewise sprayed in his blood when he was ripped away from her, their fingertips touching one another's. She and Daphne were the last ones alive. Whatever killed Abbott had come back.

Daphne! Bowen thought, returning her attention to her frightened assistant.

Another figure stepped into the room, directly behind the backpedaling Daphne. Tripping, she banged into the tall, broad man's chest and cried out in fear. Turning quickly, she lashed out with her flashlight. The small, yet well-built Maglite, struck the newcomer in the temple.

"John?" Daphne asked, putting a trembling hand to her mouth. "Oh, my God, I'm so sorry! I—"

Bowen stumbled back when Nathan grabbed Daphne by the throat and plucked her off the ground with ease. He was much larger than the petite medical assistant, but no one should've been able to manhandle another human being with such ease—especially one that was thrashing as wildly as Daphne currently was.

"What are you doing?" Bowen shouted, diving into her bag.

She procured one of the scalpels, pulled off the blade's plastic guard, and charged in to help her friend. Halfway to Daphne, Bowen was yanked to a stop by something behind her. Frightened and running on pure adrenaline, she spun and buried the tip of the instrument into her attacker's shoulder.

"Seth?" she asked, stumbling backward.

Donovan was hanging upside-down. His clothes consisted of a pair of tattered pants, and nothing else—shirt, shoes, socks—all were missing. With his face impossibly close to hers, Bowen could do nothing else except stand as still as a stone, frozen in fear. Donovan wasn't himself anymore. Something had happened to him during the accident.

But I examined him, she thought, running through a hundred different possibilities.

"What happened?" Bowen asked, choking back a sob.

Donovan's malicious grin widened.

He replied in a chorus of harmonizing voices—Bowen's team's voices. "We were born."

*   *   *

With Bowen's scalpel embedded in the meat of his shoulder, and still hanging upside-down, Donovan gripped Bowen by the head and lifted her off the ground, his bare feet sticking to the ceiling without issue. Bowen's eyes opened wide when his lower jaw dislocated, and the appendage that took the place of his tongue shot forward. As before, it buried itself deep within his target's open mouth, and similarly, a gagging sound replaced that of the person's screams.

As he pumped the plasma into her body, the knowledge that he sought was swiftly transferred to him, transplanted into his brain by the shared consciousness of the organisms within his new blood. Those organisms were the ones that collected the data from within Lisa Bowen's mind. With every passing second, Donovan's hypothesis into the creatures, now living within him, became clearer and more apparent.

The octopus was infected with a type of super-bacterium. It was a completely natural mutation and more unique than anything on his homeworld. He didn't know how he knew that to be accurate, but it was. The conviction he felt, and the ease with which he believed it, confirmed as much.

Before dropping Bowen's lifeless body to the floor, Donovan came across a more recent memory, one that revolved around the captain's daughter.

"Interesting..." Donovan said, wiping his drooling mouth.

"Yes," Nathan, Santos, and Goodrum replied together, "very interesting..."

The only one that didn't speak was Daphne. She was dead. It saddened Donovan to know that she didn't survive her rebirth. Apparently, and regrettably, not everyone was meant to.

He released his hold on the ceiling and dropped, flipping in midair. He landed effortlessly, and without sound, on top of the nearest examination table. There, perched like a vulture, he beamed when Bowen stirred awake and stood.

They had the knowledge of the ESD agents and the use of their weapons, and now they had the experience of the ship's medical staff. There was only one thing left now that Donovan required to meet his goal—the Endeavor itself.

They needed to overthrow the bridge and join with House and the rest of the crew.

Then, they'd head for McMurdo Station.

Command. Navigation. Engineering. Donovan smiled wide. *Assimilation.*

13

With Grigson still missing, and Abbott dead, and with no other leads to follow, House was forced to put the Endeavor on high alert. He made the call himself, overriding everyone's comms unit to do so. Currently, House leaned on the rail that overlooked Navigation and Engineering. Just in case, he kept the fire axe handy, propping it up against a pole near his feet.

Their biggest issue, besides having a killer on the loose and another sailor missing, was that they couldn't dock yet. Sam was finishing up with a call to McMurdo now. House could've just as straightforwardly called them himself, but he didn't. He honestly didn't know what to tell them. Sam kept things professional and only stated the facts.

"Okay," the XO said, getting House's attention. "See you at 0600 hours."

House stood straight and turned but didn't remove himself from the railing. Solemnly, he folded his arms and sighed, waiting for Sam to inform him. But he already knew what the young man was going to say.

"As we expected, sir," Sam said.

"6 A.M., huh?"

Sam nodded. "I'm afraid so."

House met the XO's eyes, feeling tired. "They're getting whacked that hard?"

"I'm not sure," Sam replied, shrugging, "but I'd imagine it's worse than what we're experiencing." He blushed, realizing what he said. "The weather, I mean... But there's supposed to be a long enough break for us to make a successful approach. So, it's not all bad news."

House patted Sam on the shoulder, making sure he knew that he understood what he'd meant. Turning, he looked back out over the three-story-tall room. If he leaned out far enough, he'd be able to see Buddy's station directly beneath him, though House doubted he was actually there. The old mechanic preferred the engine room any day to his desk.

Blinking hard, House yawned as he spoke. "Any...word from the ESD office?"

"No, sir." Sam looked worried.

"What's the matter?"

The XO took a deep breath. "I can't raise any of them, sir."

Just wonderful, House thought, cracking his neck. He picked up his axe. *Better go have a look.*

"Need a hand?" Sam asked as he always did.

House shook his head. "No, I'm good. Besides, this place would fall apart without you looking after it." Sam rolled his eyes but smirked, nonetheless.

Together, Gianna and Trip had gone back to her room while House made his way up to the bridge. He would've preferred his daughter stay in the bridge, but at least she wasn't alone.

Gianna said she was feeling queasy after her experience, and honestly, House couldn't blame her. The hole in the back of Abbott's head, combined with the look on his face, was a hard thing to get over.

Or forget.

No, this time, House would go at it alone and visit the ESD office and demand to know why they were ignoring his calls. Even they, "Becker's Bunch," could get written up for dereliction of duty. What good was having a security detail on board if they couldn't be reached when in need? There were still two of them left—three if Grigson ever showed her face again.

Even if her profile didn't match that of a coldblooded killer, House didn't know much about Grigson to begin with, although she was his prime suspect. The only other person that wasn't acting like himself was Donovan. House almost laughed out loud at the notion of the sheepish scientist murdering someone with such ferocity. He was definitely the definition of "all bark and no bite."

House liked to think he possessed the perfect balance of both bark and bite. He might have to let that dog out soon too. If he found the other two ESD agents sitting on their asses doing nothing, House was going to go all Cujo on them and tear them a new one.

He'd never had a major run-in with any of the ESD agents, but House did get a sense that they knew he held no real authority over them, unless you counted the paperwork he could file against them. While everyone else gave House their full attention—even Donovan, whenever he was present—no one within the ESD did. Again, it had yet to cause an issue, even after three months out at sea.

My luck, House thought, shaking his head. *Now, out of all the days, they get ballsy and act like pricks.*

The ESD office wasn't far from the bridge, only a couple of minutes' walk if you weren't in a hurry, and since he'd been all over the ship in the last couple of hours, House was taking his damn time. His comms unit was wide open, and anyone could get a hold of him if he were needed.

His mind wandered, and he thought of his deceased wife, and his rebellious daughter. Gianna had straightened her life up, but that side of her was still there. House harbored the same edge, but he managed to contain it, having the wisdom to understand a time and place to release it upon the world.

Like now...

He stopped dead in his tracks.

The door to the ESD office was as open as his comms unit, something that *never* happened. They didn't want anyone in their business and kept the door locked at all times. Besides, they were aboard to keep an eye out for any subterfuge amongst House and Donovan's teams. He couldn't care less if they kept the doors locked.

With everything that had transpired since bringing that damned octopus on board, House decided it was time to let the dog out. Thankfully, this old dog still had a spring in his step and a little stealth up his sleeve. He used the latter to silently glide up to the agape entrance and snap his head in and out of the opening. In the millisecond it took him to do so, House got a look at the entire room.

The square space was void of life; there had definitely been a struggle recently. The "vault," as it was called, was wide open and empty. It wasn't actually a vault, that's just what the agents called their weapons locker. Regardless, it meant bad news. House had personally cataloged everything that was inside it, demanding that he at least know what was being brought on his ship. God forbid if something like a bomb got smuggled on board because one of the agents was a terrorist or something.

Each of the four ESD agents had a sidearm, but there were also four Tasers and eight pairs of handcuffs. Oddly, the restraints were the only thing still present. Apparently, whoever took the weapons didn't plan on detaining anyone.

They plan on hurting people.

Seemingly alone, House let his guard down and stepped inside. Passing across the threshold, he was bowled into with the force of a wrecking ball. He was thrown sideways, taken off his feet, straight into the left-hand wall. Whoever it was that hit him, they must've been incredibly stout to move him like that. House wasn't a giant like Nova, but he still stood six-one and weighed a hair over two-hundred pounds.

The axe clattered to the floor as he hit, but he kept his wits about him and quickly reacquired it. Shaking off the impact, he looked up at his attacker from one knee, stunned at who assaulted him.

"Agent Grigson?"

It was plain to see that she was well-built, but House easily outweighed her by more than sixty pounds. He slowly stood, towering over her by six inches. There was no way in hell that she should've been able to take him off his feet. Her sidearm was still holstered on her right hip, and she sported a sheathed combat knife on her left side next to one of the missing Tasers.

"You okay?" he asked, knowing she wasn't. "What's wrong with your eyes?"

They flashed and swirled with the same intensity he saw earlier down in the launch bay, only this time, it was confined to the woman's eye sockets. He wasn't aware of Grigson being involved in the creature's acquisition, nor how it could possibly relate to her eyes now, but it was the only thing he could think of.

"We are fine," Grigson replied, smiling wide. It wasn't a happy smile, either. It was one of a hungry predator. It looked as if she wanted to have House for lunch.

"We?" House asked, needing to keep her talking while he came up with a plan.

"Yes," Grigson said, "we..."

Without taking her focus off of him, she raised her right hand and pointed toward the weapons locker at the rear of the room. House took his eyes off the woman long enough to see something he had missed earlier. The back wall of the office was splattered with blood.

She stepped forward, her eyes pulsating furiously.

"I...I don't understand," House said, moving to his left, but keeping his shoulders square to her. He held the fire axe in both hands, keeping it between them. "Who is *we*?"

She smiled as if she was sharing a joke with someone not in the room. Her lips opened and closed. It took House a second to realize that she was inaudibly speaking to someone. Grigson wasn't wearing her earpiece either, so House had no idea who it could be, or how it was happening.

"We..." Grigson replied. "'We' is all of us."

What the hell does that mean?

House needed to come up with something fast! The office wasn't huge, maybe twenty-by-twenty in size and it was filled with the everyday office essentials. Desks, chairs, filing cabinets... He wouldn't have a lot of room to maneuver if he got into a brawl with the smaller, yet, seemingly powerful agent.

"Who gave you the drugs?" House asked, feeling foolish.

Grigson laughed, but it came out like a rasping hiss.

She launched at him, and he reacted by bringing the axe head skyward in a rising arch. The blade connected and slashed Grigson's flesh, catching across the left side of her face, jaw to cheek. Being unarmed, House couldn't believe that she attacked him like that.

Grigson hardly stumbled back, however. She didn't bleed either.

"What the fuck?" House mumbled, stepping back, dumbfounded.

Grigson fingered the wound, sticking her index finger through her face and into her mouth.

"Sorry, Captain," she hissed, laughing as she spoke, "but the dead don't bleed."

14

The dead? House thought, trying to put two and two together. He was concentrating so hard on what Grigson said that he didn't get his hands up in time to block her next attack.

Grigson was airborne, having leaped straight over a desk like an Olympic gymnast, striking House in the chest hard with her booted feet. Stumbling back, he tripped over something on the floor and fell.

"Not...possible!" he grunted, shoving the axe handle sideways across her chest. She'd gone airborne again as soon as he went down, pouncing on top of him with hooked fingers and her teeth bared. He watched in horror as her mouth opened wider, and then, with a pop, her lower jaw unhinged. Out slid the most revolting thing he'd ever seen.

"Oh, God!" he shouted, sneering in disgust.

Her tongue, at least he thought it was her tongue, like her eyes, strobed and swirled just beneath the surface. The texture reminded him of sandpaper but slathered in snot.

He put his prodigious upper-body strength to use and pushed against her slighter frame, bench-pressing her skyward. Locking out his elbows, House was able to get his feet between them and flipped the agent up-and-over his head. Grigson slammed into the rear wall head-first, denting the plaster with her forehead and shoulder.

House took the respite to get to his feet and collect himself. He turned to face Grigson but stumbled again on whatever had tripped him before. He looked down and found Agent Dansby staring back up at him. It wasn't the fact that he was dead that stunned House the most, it was how he had died.

Oh, shit...

House could see straight through the man's open mouth and spotted the floor through the back of his busted-out skull. Then it dawned on him... Whoever, or whatever, killed Dansby also ended Abbott's life.

"You killed Abbott and Dansby?"

Grigson didn't respond. She just yanked her shoulder out of the wall and spun on House. She closed her spread fingers into fists and looked ready to launch herself at him once more. If she did, House was going to be prepared for it.

Instead, the thing that now posed as her tongue backtracked into her mouth and her lower jaw snapped back into place. The sight and sound made House gag. She had to help her mandible at the end, twisting and pulling on it until it was back in place enough to speak.

"Danthby?" she replied with a slight lisp. "Yeth..." She opened and closed her mouth a couple times, and her speech returned to normal. "He didn't take to our joining. But, Abbott," she smiled, "no, that wasn't me."

House was done with the games.

"Who killed Abbott?" he roared, gripping the axe handle so hard he thought he'd break it.

What she said next both confused and shook House.

"Seth Donovan."

House's shoulders dropped, and his head swam at the mention of the scientist's name. Abbott was the first to die, which meant that Donovan started it all. Unfortunately, House couldn't reflect on what it truly meant. He needed to disable Grigson long enough to call for help, or at least warn the rest of the crew. If he tried to operate his WiMP now, he'd be leaving himself open to an attack.

"And your eyes?" House asked, wanting more information.

She smiled and pointed at the floor. "He found something amazing down there."

Grigson's legs bent and flexed. She left her feet, hands out in front of her, reaching for him, ready to try and *join* with him—whatever the hell that meant. It's what she had called it when he questioned her about Dansby's death.

We?

The way she said it was odd, as was the way she was seemingly talking to someone else whilst having no communicator on. House wasn't a fool not to see that he was dealing with something radically different here. He didn't know if the cause of her...mutation...was genetically engineered or alien, or both, nor did he honestly care.

Regardless of the ailment's origin, he needed to stop it.

Instead of meeting the airborne agent head-on, House did the smarter thing and ducked beneath her. Feeling her boot graze the side of his head, he spun on one knee and readied his axe, bringing it down on her left wrist as she landed. The never-before-used, factory-sharpened blade cut through the joint with ease.

At first, she shrieked at the sight of her missing hand, but House wasn't so sure if she felt any pain at all. Maybe whatever was left of the real Jennifer Grigson's mind saw the severed hand laying on the floor and couldn't process what had happened. Then, she calmed and inspected the stump, intrigued. Her lack of additional concern made House's stomach churn.

So did the lack of blood.

She really is dead, isn't she?

But it seemed like Jennifer was still in there somewhere, watching her body get mutilated at the hands of the ship's captain?

Completely out of his element, House wasn't sure what to think. So, he didn't, advancing on her instead. She surprised him again when she leaped at his face. Luckily, House got his hands up this time, but had the axe ripped from his grasp in the meantime. And, like she'd done several times now, she struck his much-larger body with an incredibly forceful blow.

Intertwined, both combatants exchanged fisticuffs, tumbling over one of the desks at the rear of the room. As they fought, House recognized that she was brawling with him more than using any specific technique. Whatever had happened to Grigson, it didn't give her a new, untapped fighting ability. She was more than capable, but House was better.

They landed hard on the floor and separated.

How do you kill something that's already dead?

He studied her and realized that she wasn't breathing. Choking her out wouldn't be an option. It would've been the easiest way to put her down. All he'd have to do was get his arms around her neck and use his height and weight advantages against her.

He still needed a way to finish her off, and it came to him moments later. "Cutting the cord" was always a winning move. The snake didn't survive without its head. But could he really remove another human being's head?

The thought made him sick to his stomach.

No choice, Sebastian. She isn't human anymore.

Breathing in deep, House let it out and went on the offensive this time, crashing into the zombified ESD agent. He needed to stay away from the thing in her mouth and figured that being behind her was the best way to do that. She swung wildly at his face. House ducked beneath it and used her momentum against her, grabbing her shirt and spinning her.

Now facing away from him, House bearhugged her from behind and wrapped his thick arms around her neck. He almost let go when he heard the sickening pop of her jaw opening again, shuddering at the awful sound.

Then, the *tentacle* emerged.

It slapped against his arms, pumping God-knows-what onto

them. The smell was as horrible as you'd think, and he quickly struggled to find a hold. The mucus-like ooze was acting as a lubricant against his grip, slick and disgusting.

Resetting his position, House slipped his right elbow underneath her chin and pulled back as hard as he could.

The maneuver didn't seem to do much, though. Needing to try anything that actually counted for something, he recalled that Grigson was armed with a gun, a knife, and a Taser. The third option was out since he was in contact with her. Zapping himself into unconsciousness didn't sound like a groovy idea.

With no other ideas, House released his right hand and groped her waist for a weapon, finding one after a few gut-wrenching seconds. Feeling the knife's hilt, he gripped it and pulled it free of its sheath, immediately plunging it into her neck, and hopefully, the creature within. Growling, he pushed harder, burying the blade up to the hilt.

Almost immediately, Grigson thrashed beneath his weight, trying desperately to get up and fight back. But even with her increased strength, she couldn't pry him off of her back. She too was slathered in the viscous liquid. Grigson attempted to shove off the floor but couldn't, and repeatedly slipped and crashed back down. Plus, she was missing her left hand.

The plasma was boiling hot, but oddly, stung House's skin like something that was unbelievably cold. It was strange...and horrifying. He still couldn't get over the fact that this stuff was the same as what was inside the octopus—the one Donovan was dissecting at the time of his injury.

Grigson's continuous flashing lessened in intensity with each passing moment. For good measure, House gripped the knife handle and twisted it back and forth until her light show was all but gone.

He leaned into her and whispered, "I'm sorry, Jennifer."

With one final gurgle, Grigson vomited a sea of blue, and the organism was forcibly ejected from her throat with a series of disgusting heaves.

House jumped to his feet and yanked the blade free. Still straddling Grigson's corpse, he lifted it high over his head, ready to strike again. He didn't need to finish *it* off, however. The serpent-like creature died on its own, ejecting azure liquid from the puncture wound in its side. Its tiny, toothless mouth opened and closed like a fish out of water, and then it flopped to the floor of the ESD office where it instantly shriveled up like a raisin and morphed into a dull, grey color in no time flat.

"Dad?"

House stumbled to his feet, blue gunk dripping from his elbows to his fingertips. Gianna was at the entrance to the room and had a terrified look on her face. Then, her horrified gaze turned away from him and found Grigson's feet.

Gianna's complexion paled some more before pitching over and puking.

"I didn't kill her," House said, rushing toward his daughter, trying to explain what happened. "Well, not exactly. I, uh..." Honestly, he was still trying to process what happened. So, instead of trying to bullshit his way through an explanation, he told her the truth.

"I think we're in trouble."

15

Donovan silently moved his people into position just outside of the bridge. Along the way, they joined with another six sailors, two he'd previously met, four he didn't know. Now, he knew all of them. Intimately. It's what made the experience of converging minds so intoxicating for him and the others.

Everyone felt like they belonged to something greater than themselves because they genuinely were. They'd never feel alone again—depressed, unwanted and unbelieved in. It was sad how so many had carried those feelings with them.

And with every new mind he added, Donovan yearned for another.

Assimilation, he whispered into their thoughts, *I must have more...*

Donovan and the others were spread across all three levels of the bridge, waiting quietly just outside of the three central entrances. Donovan and a handful of his joined would attack Command, while ESD Agent Fields and Medical Assistant Nathan's groups were arranged to bull rush Navigation and Engineering, respectively. It would be synchronized flawlessly, all direction and reaction communicated cerebrally, and with no delay or lag.

Imagine what I could do with a large-scale army?

The possibility of directing hordes of joined all around the globe made Donovan giddy which, in turn, made those attached to him experience the same level of eagerness. They wanted it as much as he did, and that made Donovan mad with anticipation. He reached for the door handle and internally counted down.

3... 2... 1... Now!

As one perfectly coordinated force, they burst through the doors to all three levels of the bridge, leaping atop the closest of the crew. Some were even members of Donovan's science division. It didn't bother him who was attacked. Everyone that wasn't already assimilated was fair game.

The first to go down was one of Chief Lucas' men in Navigation. Next to be attacked were a sailor in Command and a massive man in Engineering.

Nova, Donovan thought, knowing that particular individual wouldn't go down easy. *Double him—triple him!*

While his people took care of the rest, uniting or killing everyone they encountered, Donovan focused his own attack on

House's loyal second-in-command, Samuel Ferguson. The XO spun and watched in terror as Donovan's entity finished expelling its life-altering plasma into his quarry. Either the woman beneath him would become one of them, or the searing ooze would melt her insides and kill her.

He had learned to not push so hard anymore. He hadn't broken the back of a person's skull in a while.

A while... How long has it been?

Time was different to him now. Donovan couldn't recall exactly when he changed into who he was. His memories were chaotic, with the addition of everyone else's. He could feel his control slip away on occasion, when he was caught in the moment. When that happened, he went on autopilot and reacted instinctually. Like now, for example, he didn't remember leaping onto the female sailor.

The strength of the parasite residing within him was impressive, even having the ability to take over a being as powerful as him. Donovan believed he was capable of handling them, however. He refused to be another mind-controlled drone like the people he controlled.

Hmmm, parasite... Is that what you are?

He hoped he'd get an answer in return. The realization of what was inside of him—inside of all of them—had just come to him, like it was common knowledge. What was strange was it didn't bother him. If anything, the creatures freed Donovan, opening his eyes.

As it retracted back into his throat, he looked up and eyed Sam. The redhead was about to slam his fist down on what Donovan knew was an alarm.

"Hello, Sam."

"Donovan?" Sam asked, eyes wide with stunned realization.

Stop him.

Two of Donovan's joined bolted for the XO, chasing him away. Showing an agility and speed Donovan didn't know the man possessed, Sam leaped over the sailor that went low and spun away from the scientist that went high. Both of Donovan's people fell to the floor, quickly recovering and taking off in pursuit. But not before Sam pushed through the exit and disappeared from sight.

No!

The only person aboard the Endeavor that knew the ship better than Sam was House. If he made it to the lower levels, Donovan would never find him, with help from all the minds he now possessed.

The sound of crashing glass pulled Donovan back into the fight.

Down in Engineering, Nathan was struggling to subdue George Novacek. One of Nathan's partners on the medical team, a man named Goodrum, was already dead. His connection to Donovan had been severed after being thrown headfirst into a monitor. The electric jolt was strong enough to kill the entity within him.

Donovan now understood how delicate they were. It didn't take much to extinguish their existence. If he was to succeed, Donovan needed to continue to add more joined with the knowledge that he'd lose many in his conquest. This conquest would require sacrifices.

We are better together.

Donovan smiled.

They weren't only limited by their numbers, but also by their physical design. There was strength in numbers, however...if you had enough of them, that was. *I understand now!* The "we" wasn't him and the entity, it was all of them combined into one larger, more exceptional being.

We—more than one. That's what they are too!

The more time he spent bonded to the parasite—no, *parasites*—the better he comprehended their intentions. Information flooded in faster than he could process it.

Before they found him, they were trapped in the octopus deep beneath the freezing waters of the Southern Ocean, unable to reproduce because of the surrounding temperatures. They survived for years, keeping the octopus alive despite a shortage in food, waiting for something else to come along that they could infect.

The Endeavor's presence in Antarctica, and Triplett's dive helmet gave them that opportunity to rise from the depths and finally resume their task. They'd tried to increase their numbers inside of their prey but couldn't find anything large enough to sustain it. Its goal was simple—singular.

Multiply.

They were, in every way, a living, conscious virus. Unlike your typical disease, they were aware of their existence. They didn't have a name either. They didn't require one. Also, people gave things names, not nature.

The rest of the Command crew fell, including one death and two joinings. The same thing happened with the Navigation team, and Donovan was pleased to see that Chief Lucas survived the connection process and was already linked to the rest of them. Engineering was like the wheelhouse, in that, they missed an opportunity to add Buddy Malone into the fold.

Donovan grinned when he felt an immense presence force its

way into their shared consciousness. It literally shoved Donovan's physical body aside, nearly knocking him off his feet.

Hello, Nova, Donovan thought, unable to hide his excitement.

The feeling quickly faded, though. Without Sam or Buddy, Donovan wouldn't get too far. The other members of the wheelhouse and those of Buddy's crew did their jobs to the best of their abilities, but it was the two missing men that knew the ins and outs of the Endeavor's critical systems.

At least Donovan could take solace in the fact that he now held a third of the ship's crew under his influence, and if he couldn't get the Executive Officer and Chief Engineer, he'd get someone even better.

"Argh!"

Just then, he felt a searing hot poker jab itself in his chest. He looked down at his nude upper body but saw nothing out of the ordinary. His skin had further paled, showing off his pulsating veins even more, but besides that... Confused, Donovan reached out to his joined and panicked when he noticed there was one missing—his favorite—his first.

"Jennifer?" he asked, not being able to feel her.

She was dead...again.

Grigson had barely been able to show him her true potential before being snuffed out by Captain House. He wasn't sure how he knew that, but he did. Then again, Grigson would've known, so it was only natural that he would too, even if he didn't see it happen. What she saw, he saw—as a memory in this case.

Donovan tightened his fists in anger, projecting his disdain for House into every single one of the crewmen connected to him. He'd been so laser-focused on his own mission here that he'd neglected Grigson's solo assignment below decks.

He'd also underestimated the captain's abilities.

Grinding his teeth, Donovan confirmed his next target to everyone. Sebastian House was next on his list.

16

Sam Ferguson ran for his life, ducking down the first stairwell he could find. Then, he changed directions five times and floors four times before finding a place to hide and collect himself. Admittedly, Sam wasn't a fighter. He was an All-American collegiate athlete, a long-distance runner. It's what he did best, even better than his job as Captain House's XO.

Locking the door to the janitor's closet, Sam tapped the call icon on his WiMP with a shaking finger, activating his comms unit.

"Captain House," he said, telling the system who to dial. The command was followed by a soft *bing*, confirming that the call had been successfully placed. Sam took a deep breath and said, "Sir?" He desperately needed to contact House.

No answer.

"Cap—"

Voices picked up somewhere down the hall, tensing Sam's already rigid spine. He waited to try another call, stopping and listening carefully. However, the corridor on the other side was silent, once more. He breathed easier and called the one person that might know where the captain was.

"Gianna House," he said after initiating another call.

"Oh, my God, Sam!" She was panting, drawing deep gulps of air. She'd been running like him. "What the hell is going on?"

Sam slunk back against the wall, knocking a mop and bucket over as he did. The coiled tendrils of the mop head slapped the back of his neck, and he shot to his feet, rattled. Hand on his chest, Sam's thoughts went to the men and women inside the bridge, specifically Chief Lucas.

Dominik...

"Sam?" Gianna asked. "You okay?"

Not knowing the state of the bridge's crew, Sam said the only thing he could, something he thought he'd never have to say. "We've lost the Endeavor."

*   *   *

Before exiting the ESD office, House toweled off with a spare uniform shirt belonging to Agent Dansby. He attached the combat knife and sheath to his belt on his left side, also snagging Grigson's sidearm and a spare magazine. The gun stayed tucked in the back of his pants for emergencies only. He'd go with the fire axe, or knife, for now, unless he was provoked to draw the pistol and open fire.

After Gianna wiped the spittle off her face, she gladly accepted the Taser and tucked it into her bag.

The goo stunk worse than anything House had ever smelled, but it wasn't anything he couldn't handle. Gianna, on the other hand, was forced to keep her distance, putting a couple of feet between him and herself as they headed back to the bridge.

"The bridge?" Gianna asked. "You don't know, do you?"

House stopped and faced her. "Know what?"

It was then that House grabbed for his earpiece and realized that it had been knocked loose during the fisticuffs. He re-secured it and heard a familiar, soft tone. He had a message. Activating it, he told the system to "play messages."

House broke out in a cold sweat when he heard Sam shouting on the other end. Merged within the XO's cries for help, were other voices. Some were shouting. Even more were snarling.

The bridge had been overrun.

It was a mutiny driven by Donovan and the creatures that had infected him and Grigson. The agent mentioned that it was "all of us" when House had questioned her. He seriously doubted that it was just the two of them, though. "All of us," in that case, should've been "both of us" if she'd only been describing two individuals' involvements.

That reminded him...

"Any word from Dr. Bowen and her team?" he asked his daughter.

Gianna didn't reply. She just shook her head and bit her lip.

Dammit, House thought, rubbing his forehead.

Five people didn't simply disappear into thin air. Either they were forced to join Donovan's freakshow, or they were dead, like Abbott and Dansby and who knows who else. At this rate, House may have already lost more than half his crew without even knowing it.

"Any word from McMurdo?" House asked, pounding up the stairs.

"None," Gianna replied, "we can't get through."

House stopped again. "What?"

"The bridge," she said. "They locked us out. Someone inside is blocking all comms to the outside world." She patted his shoulder, instantly flaring her nostrils in disgust when her hand came away with something nasty and stringy. She gagged and turned away from her father.

"You feeling okay, G?"

She nodded, then shook her head, not verbally answering him.

"Right," he said, laughing at the absurdity of his question, "how can anyone be okay at a time like this?"

"I'm just..." she looked like she wanted to tell him something, but didn't, "I'm just not feeling well. The storm, the killings, the smell..."

She said the last part while looking at him.

House rolled his eyes and started back up the stairs. "Can you do anything from here?"

"About the smell, no," Gianna replied, smiling. House turned to her. "Kidding—kidding! And no, the only systems I have access to are the boat itself. I can't get a signal out any further than that."

"But you do have access to the rest of the Endeavor?" He needed to be sure.

"Yep," she replied, sounding annoyed. "Maybe if you dig some of the blue shit out of your ears you woulda heard me the first time I said it." She raised her voice and repeated herself. "I have access to the boat!"

House could only shake his head. Gianna definitely took after her mother with her sense of humor. Karen was the queen of not giving a damn what people thought. Gianna was the princess of that kingdom. House was the court jester. In his line of work, House absolutely cared what others thought about him.

He went to turn the corner and head up the next flight of stairs but was stopped by Gianna.

"No," she said, "not up there."

He eyed her, waiting for an explanation.

"The closer you get to the bridge, the more of them there'll be."

He crossed his arms. "And how do you know that?"

She shrugged. "Seems pretty obvious, when you think about it. Donovan just overtook the bridge, right? Do you really think he'd let it be ripped away from him so easily? I'm telling you, there'll be a blockade of Blue Bloods up there guarding him!"

"Blue Bloods?" he asked.

She shrugged again. "The name sorta just popped into my head."

House wasn't about to start calling them that, but nor did he have a better name. He doubted that even Donovan knew what "they" really were.

"Can they track our location through our comms?"

Gianna shook her head. "Not that I've found, no."

He nodded, laying out a plan in his head.

"What are you thinking, Dad?"

He placed a hand on her shoulder. "We need to get to a safe location, find everyone we can that isn't...infected, or whatever...and plan a counterattack."

"Counterattack?" She snorted. "You aren't a SEAL, Dad. Plus, you're kinda old."

Ignoring the last part of what she said, he pushed her back down the way they'd come. "We need to find Damon and then retake the bridge." Damon Becker was the only one with a direct line to the US government, because he had a separate comms system in his room. His innate knowledge would be invaluable to Donovan if he got to the liaison first. "But first," House added, squelching any rebuttal out of his daughter, "I need to make a call."

Gianna looked at him quizzically. "Who you gonna call?"

House refrained from making a Ghostbusters joke, knowing it wasn't the right time or place. Instead, he told her exactly what he was going to do.

Gianna's eyes opened wide. "You're kidding me, right?"

17

Marcus Malone had been called a lot of things in his long life. Asshole, uncaring, unworthy, sometimes even worse—the worst thing a black man could be called... But he was also called, *buddy*. It stuck as a nickname after a year of his commanding officer not being able to remember his name. Instead of calling him Malone, he was christened "Buddy."

Growing up in the fifties and sixties, he, like a lot of young African Americans, had it rough. He'd have loved to have just been called *buddy* back in those days and not some of the awful, hateful words people had used instead. It would've saved the childhood version of himself a lot of tears. His young adult self would've saved a good amount of knuckle skin too. Fights were frequent, whether you had a shot at winning them or not.

Even after he graduated from the Naval Academy and had been given a position aboard his first carrier, he continued to hear the rumblings. No matter what he did, no one would give him the time of day.

His past experiences hardened his heart for years to come and had built a wall no one could tear down. Buddy never married or had children. Instead, he dedicated his entire being to the United States Navy and her floating command centers. Decades later, he met a young, brash sailor named Sebastian House. Buddy instantaneously become enamored with the man.

"You remind me of a younger me," he once told House.

"Is that a compliment?" House replied, getting a chuckle out of Buddy.

"Damn right it is!"

The memory made Buddy smile, but his current circumstances shook him to the core. His boat had been shanghaied by a bunch of freaks, chasing him out of his workstation like he was back in the third grade. Buddy was the smallest kid on the block and was continuously picked on for nothing more than being the "runt of the litter."

Sooner or later, they stopped picking on him...after he broke the largest bully's nose...and after he bloodied his own fist on the boy's front teeth, knocking two of them out. He went on to joke that he was the scrappiest SOB on the ocean.

Now, he couldn't get his comms unit to work. Since the system had been updated, Buddy could never seem to remember how to activate the damn thing. Now, he screamed obscenities at it while ducking and dodging...

Monsters, he thought, still not believing it. *Unbe-fucking-lievable. Real-life monsters!*

Nova had saved his life earlier. For some reason, whoever was leading the attack was looking for Buddy, specifically. His assistant grabbed the much smaller Buddy and literally tossed him into the one-way elevator down to the engine room, guarding the closing doors with his hulking frame.

"George..." Buddy said, breathing hard. "No! Come with me!"

His imposing friend smiled at him and responded with a simple nod of his head. Then, he hurled himself at three of his fellow crewmen, fists balled, shouting like a Norse Berserker warrior.

"Captain House?" Buddy asked as the doors closed, trying desperately to make a call. It didn't connect. He tapped his earpiece like he always had. Then, he looked down at the contraption on his wrist, unsure of how to use it.

"Dammit, Sebastian, answer me!" Buddy pounded on the WiMP's green, glowing screen with the bottom of his clenched fist, not noticing the small telephone logo in the corner of it. His eyesight up close wasn't what it used to be, and his reading glasses were somewhere on his desk back in the mayhem.

Buddy was frustrated—and scared for his life. He wasn't the fighter he used to be, weighed down by piss and vinegar now, instead of being fueled by it. He could still talk the talk, but those close to him knew the only thing Buddy wanted was peace—peace and his engines.

He teared up at the thought of losing everything. "Damn you, Sebastian, answer me..."

* * *

Trip's headaches were getting worse by the minute. The sunglasses had helped initially, but over the last twenty-or-so minutes, nothing seemed to work except keeping his eyes closed. The amount of light penetrating his corneas didn't matter. "Any" was too much.

He needed rest, but regrettably, he didn't get much.

Gianna received a frantic call from Sam and went running off to find her father. At first, Trip offered to go with her, considering the danger everyone seemed to be in. She refused his offer and shoved him back down on the bed to "rest."

Even though I had to get back up and lock the door.

He was willing to follow her, but if he was being honest with himself, he was happy that she told him to stay. His head really was killing him. Even the cold compress that was laying across his forehead wasn't doing much of anything. It was also too early to pop another pair of painkillers unless he wanted to melt his stomach lining.

"Go away, you bitch," he groaned, rubbing his eyebrows with both palms.

Somewhere off in the distance, he heard a soft *ding* but thought nothing of it. The walls between the cabins weren't as thick as Trip would've liked. The loudest of noises from room-to-room were easily heard. Thankfully, they came out as nothing more than untranslatable muffles. Living near people you didn't get along with was awkward enough. Having them inadvertently listen in on your private conversations was even worse.

He heard the ding again and opened his eyes, wanting nothing better than to bang on his neighbor's wall and curse them out. When he heard the tone for the third time, Trip's pulsating mind finally did the math, and he realized what the sound was.

He pawed at his right ear and popped his earpiece back in, groaning when the minuscule device was back in place. In his current state, it felt like a bull elephant just sat on his head. Blinking away some of the discomfort, he answered the call and almost blacked out at the volume of the speaker's voice.

"Trip!" Gianna's high-pitched voice stabbed at his brain.

He went to turn down the volume but stopped, realizing that it wasn't his earpiece's level, it was the caller's. Gianna was screaming, and she was breathing heavily.

Running?

Trip sat blot-upright, shoving aside the pain to the best of his ability. His pregnant girlfriend was scared and on the run. His own pain could wait for a moment while he listened to her panicked voice.

"Oh, my God, Trip! Where are you?"

"Uh..." he replied, unsure of what else to say. "I'm right where you left me, remember?" Answering her question with one of his own seemed off, but he didn't know what else he could say. She had severely caught him off guard, and his brain was still trying to reboot.

"Oh, right," she said, saying something to someone else. "Can you meet us?"

Trip threw his legs over the edge of the bed and quickly stood, feeling the room spin. He stumbled and shook his head. "No," he said, "I don't think it's a good idea for me to be gallivanting around a rocking tanker right now."

"Shit," Gianna said. "The headaches are that bad?"

He nodded to no one. "Worse than before."

She, once more, spoke to someone off-mic, and when he heard her call the other person, "Dad," Trip understood who was with her.

"You didn't tell him, did you?"

"What—no!"

"No, what?" House asked, close enough to Gianna for his voice to come through clear as day.

Trip froze and waited for Gianna to respond.

"Um, nothing important. Trip was just trying to be funny and failed miserably."

Rolling his eyes, Trip was thankful that Gianna was good at thinking on her feet. Still...

"What's going on?"

"In a word," Gianna replied, "death."

"Excuse me?" Trip asked. "Death? Who died?"

He was stunned when she laughed at his question, snickering nervously. "Quite a few people, actually. Plus, the whole brainwashing thing happened too."

"Wait..." Trip said, pausing as he pulled on his pants, "I'm confused."

"Don't worry, Trip, we're all confused." He hefted a heavy breath as she continued. "That's what Dad says anyway, and you know, it's my dad, and he usually doesn't make this kind of shit up." That was most definitely true. House was as honest a guy as Trip had ever met. "Plus," she added, "I saw it with my own eyes."

"You did?" he asked, stumbling as he slipped into his sneakers.

"Well, I saw the bodies..."

"Bodies?" he asked, shocked. "As in plural?"

"Yes, bodies—more than one. Look... A lot has happened since I left your room. Trust me, will ya?"

He calmed and got both shoes on. "Of course, I trust you."

House was shouting at her to get down and stay quiet. Trip pressed his earpiece firmly against his head as if doing so would make it louder. He could've simply turned its volume up and saved himself the discomfort of pancaking the plastic device against his ear.

Trip heard someone roar—presumably House—and then Gianna shriek in fright.

"Where are you?" Trip asked, yanking open his room's door.

When she didn't reply, he freaked out.

"Gianna!"

"What?" she hissed, voice low. "Calm down, Trip. Dad told me to be quiet, remember?"

Right... He thought, feeling silly. His head swam from the sudden movement. *Ugh.*

Trip stepped into the hallway and was tackled to the floor. He freaked out, swinging wildly at his attacker, relishing in hearing him/her/it grunt when his right elbow made solid contact. Leaping to his feet, Trip balled both of his fists tight, and raised them, instantly feeling terrible for what he'd just done.

"Dammit, Triplett!" Sam shouted, holding his right eye with both hands. "What the hell was that!"

"XO Ferguson?" He cringed. "Sorry about that, sir."

"Ferguson?" Gianna asked. "Sam's there?"

"Yeah, sorta," Trip helped his superior off the floor, "and I, uh, may have just given him a black eye."

* * *

Donovan should've been standing proudly, overlooking his subjects. He visualized himself, resembling a conquering warlord. Instead, he stood and gritted his teeth in anger. House wasn't in the wheelhouse. The one person he needed to make his plan work, and *he* wasn't present when Donovan attacked the bridge.

As bad as that was, the combined failures of joining with XO Ferguson, Chief Engineer Malone, and Liaison Becker were worse. The latter would be a more significant catch than Donovan had initially predicted. Both he and House needed approval from Becker to do anything outside of the Endeavor. It was a part of their onboard checks-and-balances. Then, with House's agreement and Becker's endorsement, Donovan could set his people free upon the world.

He picked out one of Buddy's men two stories below his feet.

"What's our fuel situation?" he asked as if the man was simply standing next to him. He thought about trying to make it to New Zealand and forego a return to McMurdo altogether. Just the thought spurred a question that the engineer was already checking on.

Donovan waited impatiently for the sailor to reply, hearing him clack away at a keyboard. When he did answer, Donovan despised what the engineer had to say.

"Not good. There's no way we can make it to New Zealand.

McMurdo is the only option."

Donovan gripped the top bar of the third-floor guardrail making the fortified steel creak in protest. McMurdo Station was a cold and desolate place. But New Zealand, and its nearly five million inhabitants...

It's a start.

Donovan smiled at the thought of having so many people connected to him. It was too much to comprehend. Even now, with thirty-six minds connected to his own, he basked in the data that he'd gained.

But there were still so many more out there.

His ultimate plan, however, would have to be put on hold, for now. He sneered at the thought. They'd, indeed, have to return to McMurdo. Taking the station wouldn't be an easy undertaking, either. The Endeavor required one room to operate successfully, and only a handful of skilled minds to do it. Overrunning an entire research station that contained over a thousand people was a completely different task, and if they failed in their first attempt, Donovan wasn't sure they'd get another try.

We need to target their security team first.

Everyone agreed.

Donovan hoped that McMurdo would send out a distress call mid-invasion too. He needed a response—a rescue attempt—to come south. They'd wait for it and then commandeer that vessel, and take it, and its crew back north.

Donovan grinned.

He required House and Becker to be joined to him regardless. None of it mattered if that didn't happen. If the Endeavor arrived unannounced, and without approval from McMurdo Command, those on the ground would know something was wrong. They'd have a better chance of defending themselves as well. Worst-case scenario, the McMurdo would be put on high alert, making Donovan and the others' jobs infinitely harder.

The next thing that ensued caught Donovan off guard. He'd been communicating mentally for a few hours now and had forgotten that it wasn't the only way to reach him.

"Call from: Sebastian House," announced the device's automated receptionist.

The captain was calling him through the Endeavor's comms system.

Can we trace the call?

A technician silently shook her head, no. Growling, Donovan tapped his wrist unit, opening the line, but he didn't verbally say a word.

"Hello, Seth."

Donovan frowned. House already knew what was going on, to a point. Why waste time with pleasantries?

"Sebastian," he said, unable to hide his disappointment, "you're sounding well."

"Unlike your people, you sick bastard," House replied, likewise getting down to it. "I know what you're doing to them. I've seen the things you put inside them, and it's disgusting."

Donovan still felt the lingering gut punch that was Grigson's "signal" dropping. It saddened him, but she did her job. She aided in supplying Donovan with an army.

His mind wandered.

Was Jennifer Grigson really gone, though? *Hmmm.* Was there a way to bring them back with another dose of his lifeblood? Morals and ethics were out the window anyway. Plus, the Seth Donovan of the past didn't have any of those ideals entrenched inside of him to begin with, so why start now?

"So," Donovan said, standing tall, "you're the one who killed Jennifer?"

House burst out in laughter. "Still putting the blame on someone else...just like the Seth I knew. You never could take responsibility for your own actions." His tone got serious. "Sorry, but you're the one who ended her life. What I put down wasn't Jennifer Grigson anymore. *That* was an abomination from Hell created by a despicable creature from the same zip code."

Fuming in anger, Donovan squeezed the guardrail harder and crushed it with a screech of crying metal.

"So," House said, "besides being a genetically modified freak, what exactly are you now?"

What are we? Donovan thought.

His collective mind gave him an answer, digging through decades of learning—school and life knowledge combined. One of the men in Navigation, his father was an English teacher somewhere in South Florida. The sailor had, apparently, picked up on his father's love for the subject, supplying Donovan and the others with their new name—their new identity.

They all said it aloud together. "We are Coalesce."

"Hmmm," House replied, "fitting, I suppose. So, what, you control these things with your thoughts, like some ridiculous *SyFy Channel* movie?"

Donovan shrugged. "In a way, yes. I'm their antenna, if you will. They are willingly following me—"

"Cut the bullshit, Seth!" House roared. "You murdered them and raped them of their free will." He sighed. "You realize you're a monster, right?"

Find him! Seth ordered.

Six members of the newly dubbed *Coalesce* rushed off, including the one that could take down House without breaking a sweat—not that the deceased could perspire. The beast of the ship was Donovan's consolation prize.

House and Becker, Donovan thought, sending out another set of orders, *I need those two alive. The rest...* He smiled, knowing it would go against his goal. But there were so many others out there. The handful of humans still left aboard the Endeavor didn't much matter without the two he sought now.

"Either join with them..." he said aloud, feeling better as he verbally voiced the words, "or kill them. I don't care which."

18

Before he became the Endeavor's line of communication to both the US Navy and DARPA, Damon Becker had been a very successful attorney on the outskirts of Washington DC. He lived a lavish lifestyle with friends in even higher places than him. Some of those friends were in the government—a retired admiral.

After one of Becker's partners stole millions from him and the others in the firm, Becker got out before it was too late, retiring from the "strenuous" profession. Six months later, the firm collapsed because of the incident, and since Becker was truly innocent of any wrongdoing, he was free to take on another job and decided on one far away from the courts.

With the retired admiral's blessing, Becker was brought in as a third-party to help oversee a project centering on a state-of-the-art research vessel, a boat he had no intention of ever stepping foot on. It was a section of the fine print he, unfortunately, neglected to look over. His inner lawyer was embarrassed. His weak stomach was furious.

Damon Becker hated the water—all of it. He excelled in mental warfare. Put it simply, he wasn't a physical pugilist and definitely wasn't one while out at sea where he was regularly nauseous. The strong gusts kept his comb-over standing at attention too.

Now, Becker staggered through the bowels of the Endeavor, bleeding heavily from a laceration to his left arm and side. A cook had attacked him, successfully opening his skin with a knife.

"House..." he rasped, his vision dancing. "Where are you?"

*　　*　　*

Sitting in the back corner of the room, Becker liked to keep everything in front of him so he could see anyone—and everyone. He'd personally known police officers who did the same, ever watchful of the front door to anywhere they entered.

Becker's reasoning wasn't the same, though.

He was a nervous person when he wasn't in control, uncomfortable with his surroundings aboard the Endeavor, and even more uncomfortable with the people he'd been sharing a home with for the last three months. No one here was wealthy, well, not like him. He wanted to gush about the vacations he'd taken—Nepal, Australia, Peru, Norway—and the handful of classic cars he owned but was smart enough to know when to keep his mouth shut. He had nothing in common with anyone and was mostly hated by the whole of the Endeavor except for Captain House.

Becker knew House didn't like him, but the man was respectful of the office he reported to, including Becker himself. In turn, he didn't hound House for results. He let the capable sailor do his job without breathing down his neck or continually looking over his shoulder.

Something inside of Becker wanted House to like him. The man's demeanor was intoxicating—always in control and always, *always* esteemed and reverent. Plus, the captain of the ship wasn't under the same type of scrutiny as Seth Donovan's science team. They were the real reason any of them were there. House's job was to keep them afloat—literally. But Donovan...he was under immense pressure to deliver promised, world-altering results.

Hence the brash attitude, Becker had thought after his first meeting with the young man.

Halfway done with his meatloaf and mashed potatoes, something he ate separately much to the dismay of most onboard, Becker was startled when one of the crewmen came barging in through the mess hall's double doors. With six tables between him and the man, Becker initially thought nothing of it and returned to his meal. The "Home Cooking" themed dinner wasn't half-bad either. Maybe it was just the tilting floor that had stumbled the sailor into, and through, the now swinging doors, making it look and sound worse than it really was?

Regrettably, that wasn't the case.

The crewmember leaped atop the nearest table and charged straight for the government liaison, his electric blue eyes flashing wildly. *What the hell?* Becker froze, fork in his mouth. He had no idea what to do. Luckily, he wasn't the only person enjoying a meal right then. A sailor jumped up from his seat and confronted the attacker, but was quickly thrown aside, tossed headfirst into a nearby wall. Another man swiftly burst through the door leading back into the kitchen, knife in hand and joined the fray, taking the downed man's position between Becker and—

"Taylor!" The cook shouted, identifying the aggressor.

Taylor didn't respond.

"Dammit, Taylor, what's gotten into—"

Taylor bowled into the chef, spilling them both to the floor. They fought and clawed at one another, rolling beneath the table just in front of the still seated Becker. He heard his rescuer scream and then gag on something. To Becker, it sounded like he was being choked.

Being the noncombatant that he was, Becker slid off the bench and cautiously stepped toward the double doors. Unfortunately, someone else pushed through them before he could make it another foot. Like the first man, Taylor, this one had the same killer look in his eyes.

Eyes, Becker thought, once more seeing the otherworldly blue pulse. Taylor's were the same. *What's wrong with their eyes?*

Instead of confronting the second man, Becker took off for the kitchen door, quickly shouldering through it and locking it behind him. Not a second later, it was rammed into from the other side. He jumped back and grabbed the first thing he could find to use as a weapon. The heavily serrated bread knife looked ultra-sharp and would have to do. Becker had once cut his thumb with a similar blade years ago, remembering how much it bled.

Holding it out in front of him like a sword, Becker knew he looked ridiculous, but how else was he supposed to look? He wasn't one of King Arthur's famous knights. They didn't even have circular dinner tables aboard the Endeavor. Theirs were rectangles and the metal, floor-bolted benches incredibly uncomfortable.

The kitchen door was struck again, but it held firm. Becker's bladder, however, was about to burst.

The door took another blow, softer this time, allowing Becker to catch his breath. His face was flushed, and he was sweating like crazy. Believing the barrier would hold, Becker laughed a sigh of relief just as the door was blown off its hinges and thrown right into him.

He tried to hit the deck before it hit him but failed and was taken off his feet by the impact. There, shaking beneath the mangled door, Becker silently waited, hoping he could do what he'd seen in the movies, and play dead. Still, he prepared for anything, gripping the handle of his knife harder. He was lucky to not drop it, or worse, impale himself.

One of the men stepped inside, and just the one man. In the stillness of the kitchen, the person's footfalls sounded like cracks of lightning. Becker didn't know which man it was either. It seemed that his rescuer, the cook, was dead, or at the very least, incapacitated and unable to aid him a second time. If it was the chef, Becker figured he wouldn't be moving so slowly.

Damon Becker was on his own, which scared him to death.

Becker took his attention off his pursuer just long enough to not notice him step up behind him. The twisted door was flung away, and Becker responded by blindly swinging his blade around, thrilled to feel the knife connect with his attacker. But when the person didn't react to the injury, Becker looked up, staggering to his feet in abject fear.

He wounded his defender, the cook, except this wasn't the same person as before. Now, there was something wrong with his eyes too.

They're the same as Taylor's!

"What...?" Becker said, stumbling back into the stove, unsure if he was being exposed to some fast-moving contagion or a bioweapon of some kind. Did one of the crewmen sneak a deadly prototype aboard and set it off?

Hitting the stove hard, he felt a drop of boiling water spit onto his exposed skin. It was a small amount, but he reacted as if it was the whole pot.

His overreaction saved his life.

The cook hacked at him with his own blade, and Becker stupidly lifted his arms in fright. The butcher's knife cleaved into the meat of his forearm, opening a cut that bled like a stuck pig. Then, he sustained an equally deep wound to the gut. In terrible pain, but aware enough to defend himself, Becker returned the favor and landed a solid blow into the meat of the sailor's shoulder.

Neither it nor the cut on his leg bled.

He asked the same question again. "What...?"

The cook leaped at him, but Becker ducked beneath his outstretched arms and dodged the attempt. As he did, the cook stepped on Becker's foot and rolled his ankle, sending him face first into the boiling pot of water. The sailor shrieked loudly and grabbed at his eyes. It was then that Becker had seen something wriggling inside the man's mouth. It too was thrashing, having been similarly scalded.

Holding back his bile and holding his wounded arm to his equally injured side, Becker ran for the ruined kitchen entrance, grateful to find the mess hall void of life.

* * *

Since his life-threatening ordeal, Becker ducked into whatever room he could find and waited out the unidentifiable, nearby sounds. Then, he'd move again. The worse part about it all was that he'd lost his earpiece somewhere back in the kitchen. There was no way for him to contact anyone. The only thing he knew was that they were definitely under some kind of attack. It appeared that a group of crazed—possibly drugged—crewmen staged a mutiny, and Becker couldn't warn anyone.

His head was swimming from a loss of blood. If he became too weak to move, his knowledge of what was happening would die along with him.

But why? he thought, sliding around a corner.

Becker wasn't a fool. His connections to the American government, along with that of New Zealand via McMurdo Station's partnership was vital to everything they did here. He was an essential person, one a gang of "Antarctic pirates" could use as a bargaining chip.

If he couldn't find House, the only other person to look for was Donovan. Even though he was a petulant man, Becker doubted he had the balls to pull off such a deadly stunt as this. If he weren't in such agony, Becker would've laughed at the thought of Donovan sporting an eyepatch and a hook for a hand.

"Yeah, right..."

* * *

A moan forced Trip and Sam down the hall. They tried every door they could before finally finding one that was unlocked. Both were shaking with fright. Neither really hurt the other when they collided, not counting the blow Trip had delivered to his superior officer. Both were still terrified, however, well aware that it could've been much worse than two friendlies running into one another.

Trip eased the door shut and checked on his XO. He wasn't all that buddy-buddy with Sam, didn't even try to call him "Sam" to his face. Like House, Sam was easy to get along with if you gave him the respect his station deserved.

The XO blinked away the tears in his right eye and shook his head. "That was a nice one," he said, laughing it off. "Like Bones Jones himself."

"Yeah, sure..." Trip replied, having no idea who Bones Jones was. "Sorry about that, sir."

Sam shrugged. "It's fine, Triplett, I'd have done the same, considering."

Trip stuck out his hand. "Call me Trip—everyone else does. I don't think we have to be so professional at a time like this."

Sam smiled. "I was thinking the same thing." He shook Trip's extended hand. "Call me Sam."

"Right, Sam..." he said, leaning up against the room's owner's desk. "So, what's happening out there?"

Sam gave Trip the rundown, and he was happy to hear that it fit with what Gianna told him. It wasn't that Trip didn't trust his XO, it's that he didn't have confidence in the man's mind if he'd been infected like the others. Trip shook his head, floored that he missed all the action while he had been bedridden.

As a sci-fi geek, everything going on was awesome!

But as a real-life human who was currently in a murderous creature's sights, it wasn't the greatest of news. People were dying for real, unlike in the comics or movies. He knew no one would be dramatically charging through a portal like at the end of Marvel's *Endgame*. If someone thought you were dead, there was a good chance you were.

Gianna described Abbott's fate to him before hanging up, and it was horrifying for Trip to even imagine. He couldn't fathom what Gianna felt upon seeing it with her own eyes.

And in her current condition.

"What do we do?" Trip asked, looking to the person in charge for advice.

Sam scratched his head. "Do what we can from here."

"What?" Trip asked, appalled that Sam didn't want to go out and find House and Gianna. Trip needed to get her, regardless of knowing whether her father was with her, or not. It wasn't right that Trip was safely hiding out while his eight-week pregnant girlfriend was risking hers and the baby's lives.

Sam raised a hand, cutting off Trip. "And, yes, we're going to help. But we need to help in a different kind of way." He smiled. "Two smaller teams can get around the ship easier than a single, larger one."

That made sense to Trip...sort of. Sam was the strategist, not him. He'd have to trust the XO on this one.

I mean, he thought, *if I trust House, then I can trust Sam, right?*

Trip nodded. "What do you have in mind?"

Sam's eyes snapped to the door. "Donovan's room... We'll start there. It's back down the hall a bit." He looked at Trip. "Shouldn't be a problem getting there."

"Shouldn't be?" Trip asked,

Sam looked as unsure as Trip felt.

Trip had yet to see any of the creatures, but Sam had. He was going to have to follow the guy's lead for now. This wasn't a movie. If Trip fouled up too badly, he'd die.

"Let's go," Sam said, slowly opening the door.

They stepped out as one and glanced down the hall in both directions. From where they stood, they couldn't see anyone. Donovan's room was near Trip's, some thirty feet back toward the front of the ship. It didn't feel like an insurmountable distance to traverse, but with everything going on, it might be closer to crossing the Antarctic mainland.

Sam turned right and stopped when something creaked behind them. Trip, who hadn't followed just yet, saw a strange blue strobe light down the hall. It was far away, and even with his protective sunglasses on, his eyes were still in too bad a shape to make anything of it.

But Sam did.

"Come on!" the XO hissed, yanking on Trip's arm.

He followed Sam, moving quickly, yet quietly. Seconds later, they slid into Donovan's room. The door was wide open, eerily inviting in a way. Just as they entered, a growl reverberated down the hall, originating back the way they'd come.

Cringing when Donovan's door squeaked as it shut, Sam bit his lip and engaged the deadbolt. Then, he cautiously backed away from it, mumbling something incoherently to himself. Trip didn't pay attention to the nervous man's words. Instead, he focused on the feral noises back in the corridor.

They grew louder and more frenetic with every passing heartbeat. Then, just outside of the room, the thing on the other side shrieked into the air. Sam was still talking to himself, and it took Trip until he was almost finished speaking to realize that he was in the middle of a phone call.

"Yes, sir," Sam said, obviously conversing with Captain House. "Good luck to you too."

"Yes?" Sam asked in response to a question.

Trip really hated not hearing the other end of the conversation.

Sam laughed and glanced at Trip. "Will do—"

BOOM!

Trip and Sam's entry into Donovan's cabin hadn't gone unnoticed. Both men rushed to the thin metal door and held it in place as it was rammed over and over again.

Looking to the XO for courage in a trying time, Trip's stomach dropped when Sam's face was full of fear, instead of overflowing with the steadfast strength he was hoping to see.

19

House and Gianna desperately looked for Damon Becker. Both of them tried multiple times to contact him through their comms but were unsuccessful. Either he was already dead, or worse, dead and a part of Coalesce.

"You know, maybe he just lost his earpiece, and he's okay," Gianna suggested. "You almost lost yours back there too."

House knew she was right. There was a chance, no matter how slim it felt, that Becker was alive and only missing his earpiece. Unfortunately, he was also the least likely candidate to survive alone on a ship full of mind-controlled monsters.

He glanced at his daughter. "Keep trying him either way."

She nodded and spoke softly into her own unit, barely above a whisper. While she did that, House focused on keeping them alive. Doing so would be easier if there were more of his men around. So, he called Sam and went over things.

"Negative, sir," Sam replied, keeping his voice down. "Trip and I are fine for now. We're going to do a little recon before meeting up with you."

House didn't like it, but he didn't have a better option. Knowledge was power right now. The more they knew about their enemy—Donovan and the rest of Coalesce—the better.

"Alright," he said, still not liking it, "stay safe. I'll call you back in thirty minutes. I don't care what you've found by then. You two are meeting up with us, is that understood?"

"Yes, sir," Sam replied. "Good luck to you too."

House added more to the conversation before hanging up. "Oh, Sam?"

"Yes?"

"Tell Trip that if he dies, Gianna is going to kill him."

Sam laughed. "Will do—"

His voice was interrupted by a loud bang on the other end. House stopped in place and listened carefully, hearing both Sam and Trip grunt in protest. Then, he overheard a second impact—then, a third. Whoever it was that found them, they were trying to force their way into Donovan's cabin.

"Shit..." House said, seeing the worry in his daughter's eyes. "We may have to switch courses."

She squinted at him, not being able to hear the struggle for herself. The only thing she knew was that something was wrong.

House's face said as much.

"What do you mean?"

"Trip and Sam are having some...issues."

Her eyes got serious. "What kind of issues?"

He sighed. "Blue ones."

Gianna spun on a heel and headed back the other way, to the nearest staircase. They were two levels above the guys and half the length of the ship away. Knowing he wasn't going to talk her out of going, House quickly caught up to her and led the way. Not only was the ADS pilot someone special to his own flesh-and-blood, but Cole Triplett and Sam Ferguson were both damn good men—House's men to boot.

The floor beneath them contained mostly offices and smaller, lightly used labs and workshops, but it also held the ship's gym and heated swimming pool. When House was told that these fitness items were aboard the ship, he snorted a laugh and said, "Seems like an awful waste of space."

Becker shrugged, not understanding what was so bad about having either on board. House wasn't at all surprised by his reaction. Then again, House wasn't so sure how much say Becker had in anything at all.

Becker, like House, was a stooge at the end of the day. If Uncle Sam wanted a swimming pool on a ship, then he got his damn swimming pool—plain and simple.

Still, even after the initial disagreement about the pool and gym, House found himself using the latter frequently. The pool, however, very few, including himself, gave it the time of day. Something about swimming in water while being afloat on the water didn't feel right to most of the crew.

It felt dumb.

The Houses snuck past the first two offices, finding them locked. Softly, House rapped on the first one's door and called out Becker's name. Gianna left his side and knocked on the door of the office across the hall. As soon as her knuckle found the smooth, hard surface of the metal door, it was thrown off its hinges by something huge.

Gianna was struck in the head and slammed right into House's back. The force of her hitting him pounded his own skull against the opposite door and knocked him for a loop. Not out of it entirely, but slightly dazed, House felt his daughter go limp and quickly caught her under the armpits. From there, he immediately began dragging her further down the hall and into the onboard gym. It had no door, allowing them unperturbed access to the large, forty-by-thirty room.

Ducking inside the gym, House saw the man that had been waiting for them, at least, that's what House figured he was doing. Then, he heard multiple sets of footsteps follow the giant out of the door.

House cursed under his breath. *Nova, and he turned more of them.*

The man called Nova wasn't simply hiding, he was adding bodies to the Coalesce army—to Donovan's ranks. Whoever was on the other side of that door was either dead, or worse, joined. House saw two more people from Donovan's science team, and if Nova had been successfully turned...

Buddy, no!

Throughout his and Gianna's retreat, House tried multiple times to raise the old fool but was unsuccessful. He knew Buddy hated the system, especially the latest update that had added the WiMP into the fold. Even without the newest addition, Buddy rarely answered it anyway. House didn't necessarily like it either, but he couldn't deny the convenience it provided them.

He hurried them both down the gym's center aisle, between a half-dozen weight machines. The free weights were in the rear of the room. Those are the ones that House, himself, preferred. Even having free weights on board was a surprise considering the damage they could do if they came loose during a storm.

"Experimentation with no consequences." It's how House described the thinking behind the ship's designers. If something terrible happened as a result of the experimental changes, it wouldn't physically affect any of them, only being left to deal with the results. Those outcomes would lead to nothing more than a stack of paperwork, which was ludicrous to House.

Sliding Gianna's unconscious, bleeding body behind a rack of thick, rubber weights, House ducked down beside her and waited. She'd taken a blow to the forehead and was bleeding from the cut just beneath her hairline. Peeking between two thirty-pound plates, House witnessed the blood-splattered Nova step into the room and stop just inside the arched entryway. From the looks of it, a few of the people he'd tried to turn fought back with gusto.

And probably died for their efforts. House closed his eyes and sighed.

He was losing men left and right. Those that didn't take to the joining, as Donovan called it, died. And those that successfully bonded with him also died but were reborn as one of Satan's spawn.

Gianna began to rouse awake, moaning in pain. House called Sam and whispered their predicament.

"You sure, sir?" Sam asked.

"Yes," he replied, "forget about staying apart and get your asses over here now!" The *now* was a little too loud. Nova's head snapped toward their hiding spot. With the extra-large engineer blocking their exit, and with Gianna's moans turning into increasing groans, House needed to buy the two men some time until they arrived.

Right, he thought, *my noncombative XO and my kid's geeky twig-of-a-boyfriend as our only backup.* He stood, balling his fists. *This should go well.*

To those that didn't know him, George Novacek was just a big, dumb ox, unable to properly communicate with the average human being. There were even rumors that he had a learning disability of some kind, but House could never find anything in his file to confirm as much.

House didn't care, though. Put Nova in front of an engine block, or any other mechanized piece of equipment, for that matter, and the man spoke its language perfectly. He loved being an engineer aboard the Endeavor. What he didn't like were the other humans around him.

None of them.

Except for Buddy. Somehow, out of all the people in the world, Nova got along with Buddy Malone—another person that wasn't well-liked. *Two peas in a pod.*

Nova's glowing eyes pulsated wildly upon seeing House. He stepped forward, sporting a bloodied pair of grey coveralls. House tried desperately to delay the man any way he could. First, he attempted to reason with the already unreasonable behemoth. Few people ever got through to him. House doubted that even Buddy, the only man that had, could remind the brainwashed corpse-of-a-man that he was usually one of the good guys.

"Easy there, George," he said softly, raising his hands. "It's me, Sebastian House."

No reaction at all. Nova didn't recognize him as anything besides his next target.

Slowly moving away from the weights, and Gianna, House needed the beefy addition to Coalesce to keep his attention on him and not his vulnerable daughter. Even healthy, Gianna was no match for the rage-machine. House doubted that even he could've ever bested the man one on one on an average day.

"Come on, Sam..." House mumbled, eyes shifting toward the

entrance. He was hoping he'd see both Sam and Trip tackle Nova from behind, one going high, and the other taking out his knees. Instead, he only saw the monstrous beast step forward again, inching closer, but limping.

Interesting...

House still had his axe in hand. He also had Grigson's pistol and knife. Everything inside him told him to draw the gun and put two in the creature's head. Unlike the movies, however, this was actually happening, and House wasn't a badass marksman with perfect aim. He couldn't even remember the last time he fired a gun! He'd probably wind up missing the lug's melon with most of the rounds, wasting them on the wall behind him instead.

Axe it is, he thought, gripping it tighter.

Even a man of House's physical size and customary in-control demeanor staggered back when Nova backhanded an entire weight machine out of his way. The larger man could've just as easily taken a step to his left, but didn't, opting for the straight-line approach instead.

House winced when the bones in Nova's hand cracked and shifted back into place. It was both impressive and disgusting.

Then why not his leg? he thought. *Unless the injury occurred pre-joining?*

House didn't wait to see what Nova would do to him. If he let the massive *man* attack first, the fight would be over even before it got started. So, he launched his own assault and swung the axe in a long-swooping arch, aiming for the Engineer Assistant's gut. He didn't care if the dead felt pain or not, disembowelment should still be enough of a debilitating injury to allow House and Gianna to get away relatively unscathed.

Nova's left hand caught the blade, the steel head cutting him deep. But the powerful strike did little else. Staring at the axe head, Nova's furious, swirling eyes slowly panned from it over to House's sweat-soaked face. The captain was doing everything he could to continue the axe on its intended path, through the infected sailor's hand.

Come on...

House gritted his teeth and leaned into the axe handle. For his part, Nova slowly balled his right hand into the biggest fist House had ever seen. Not only was the mechanic huge, but so were his thick, meaty paws. About to slug House with the force of a sledgehammer, the axe gratefully tore through Nova's fingers and plunged deep into his left side.

The sudden movement startled House. He was stunned with the

ease that Nova lost four of his fingers. It made no sense.

The stuff? he thought. *Are they weaker in some ways now?*

Before he could comprehend what it truly meant, he was tossed away, scrambling backward as soon as he hit the floor. In horror, he watched as the base of Nova's missing fingers spewed the same blue plasma that covered House during his fight with Agent Grigson. But, almost immediately after the injury, the firehose-like spray halted, and the goo began to solidify into what reminded House of tiny cobalt traffic cones.

"Damn," House mumbled, dread washing over his body. His victory, no matter how small it was in the first place, was too good to be true.

Nova was growing back missing fingers.

Unable to move or turn away, House could only watch in fascinating disgust as the jelly continued to harden. Then, within the pulsing, mostly see-through ooze, he witnessed bones quickly reanimate beneath the forming skin. The entity residing inside Nova was reacting like an octopus would've when facing the same situation.

Regeneration was one of the many talents the species possessed. In this case, Nova, along with the rest of Coalesce, owned that ability too. Grigson's missing hand didn't start growing back before her parasite died, but House believed, without a shadow of a doubt, it would've eventually grown back, given more time.

Unless each creature is unique in their own way.

Standing, House was too dumbfounded to block Nova as he reached out and gripped his shirt. Then, House was thrown straight back, over the weight rack and his daughter. He smashed into the glass wall at the rear of the gym. The impact knocked the wind out of him, and his noisy arrival sufficiently stirred Gianna awake.

She shot to her feet and screamed in horror when she saw Nova. Woozy, she tried desperately to pull her father up, but failed in her attempt, too discombobulated to do so. House groaned in pain, but quickly shook the cobwebs free and staggered to his feet just before Nova could advance his assault further. With the rack between them, House took a moment to collect himself.

Just then, Sam and Trip came into view at the gym entrance. Hearing them, Nova glanced over his shoulder and sneered. Then, he turned toward the new, healthier threat, his left hand nearly intact. House's eyes darted back and forth from his people to the creature in the middle of them all.

"Oh no..." he said, knowing what was about to happen. House's personal fight with the undead engineer wasn't over. The battle would ensue once Nova was finished with Sam and Trip.

The beast turned and stomped toward the two unarmed men. House needed to stop him before his people were either killed or joined. It was hard enough for House to fight Nova, someone he had an above-average rapport with. If he was forced to take down Sam, Trip, or God forbid, Gianna, he knew it would break him. His skin broke out in goosebumps just thinking about it.

Knowing what needed to be done, House planted a hand on the weight rack and vaulted over it, charging after the imposing mechanic as soon as his feet hit the ground.

20

House's shoulder met the small of Nova's back just as the bigger man stepped back into the corridor outside of the gym. Mid-impact, Sam and Trip dove to either side, allowing the two combatants to stumble through unperturbed. Unable to turn around in time, Nova was thrown off balance and couldn't stop House from driving him forward into the room across the hall.

The floor disappeared beneath their feet just as House reached for his combat knife. They fell two feet before plunging into the warm water of the indoor pool. The eight-foot-deep pool was only filled with six feet of water, which House had thought was odd, but he was told it was so the water could slosh around and not spill out while the Endeavor was at sea.

The rim was two feet taller than House. The only easy way out would be the ladders on either side of it. But he had bigger fish to fry first before even thinking of exiting.

As soon as they went underwater, House felt Nova's body convulse and then, just as quickly, the man relaxed and went limp. The guy had been rigid and on edge since stepping foot into the gym. Now, beneath the soothing, comforting water, Nova seemed more at ease.

House thought the water felt amazing. The air aboard the Endeavor, though warmer than outside, still carried with it a permanent, sometimes uncomfortable chill. Being a southerner, House naturally preferred "front porch weather," the kind that consisted of a warm sunset and a cold drink.

Unsure of what Nova would do next, House was about to let go and stand. He didn't, though, holding on with all his might just as Nova's back arched. Next, blue gunk grossly spewed out of his mouth, diluting as it mixed with the chlorinated pool water. Even beneath the surface, House heard Nova's jaw unhinge. He looked on in horror as the creature squirmed its way free with a second pop, wiggling out of his mouth and throat.

Nova's body went limp again. Without the life-sustaining effects of the entity, the dead man was actually dead.

Wanting nothing more than to surface and jump from the water like a frightened seal, House instead, remained below and stayed perfectly still. Remarkably, the tubular, three-foot-long parasite did nothing else except jet around the pool like a dolphin, twisting and spinning, seemingly loving life. It didn't seem to notice that

House was there too.

It looked happy.

House was more astonished at how big it was.

Man, they grow quick.

Across the length of the pool, eighteen feet or so away, it suddenly turned and stopped. Facing House, its "tail" pumped side-to-side like a shark's, propelling itself directly toward House's face. He watched in disgust as a circular opening, its mouth presumably, opened and began drooling blue goo.

Letting it get in close, House dodged its advancement by merely tilting his head to the right and ducking, kicking deeper. He spun, planted his feet on the bottom of the pool, and shoved. House broke the surface and took in a much-needed breath. Not wanting the thing to sneak up on him, he begrudgingly ducked back beneath the water.

The parasite was right on top of him.

Startled, House grabbed its sausage-like body with both hands, giving him an up-close look at what it had to offer, physically. Its tiny mouth opened and shut violently. Naturally, its body pulsed in different shades of blue. The thing had no eyes to speak of, but House felt as if it was making eye contact with him, nonetheless.

Honestly, House wasn't a hundred percent sure he was looking at its head. From his vantage point, he couldn't see the other end well enough to make an accurate enough hypothesis—and this was the end it attacked with too. When it started pumping blue jelly from the orifice's opening once more, he prayed that it really was the creature's mouth and not its ass.

Like Nova, the thing reared its head up and arched its back. But unlike Nova, the parasite acted like it wanted to get away from House, not beat his head in. So, House let go and was stunned to see it zoom straight for Nova's floating corpse. Then, it forced its way back into the inert man's mouth, disappearing back down his throat with a spurt of lubricating slime. Surfacing, House witnessed Nova's body twitch to life.

Oh, no... he thought, shocked.

It had the ability to reanimate a corpse multiple times. That also meant that Grigson wasn't dead for good—none of those that died were. The realization that even a man like Abbott could get brought back made the situation even worse.

Seth Donovan presently held a blade to Death's throat.

Paddling to the edge, House reached two feet over his head and snagged the lip of the pool. Soaked to the bone, and weightier than usual, he paused his ascent and moved to the closest ladder.

Quickly, he shimmied up it, still struggling to pull his fully clothed frame out of the water. Moving slower than he'd like to be, he cried out in pain as something wrapped itself around his ankle.

He looked back and found the six-foot-five Nova standing behind him in only six feet of water. His right hand was locked around House's ankle, squeezing it like a vice. If the thickly built man applied any more pressure, House was sure the bones would snap.

He couldn't let that happen.

Flipping onto his back, House lashed out and kicked Nova square in the face twice while the larger man scaled the ladder. The second kick busted the giant's nose. Injuring him had no effect, though—not now. House needed to kill the parasite inside of him, just like the one that had been inside of Agent Grigson. At least, for the time being, it would wholly disable the former engineer.

But how? he thought, kicking at Nova's face again.

He doubted he could get close enough to use Grigson's knife, and he really didn't want to use his gun. There were too many of these things on board now, and every bullet was precious.

They won't be so precious if you're dead, Sebastian.

Drawing the pistol, Nova reacted to seeing the weapon by squeezing House's ankle harder, making it difficult for the captain to accurately aim it. About to pull the trigger, he was surprised when a figure stepped into view beside him, bringing the axe head down on Nova's outstretched arm as if he was hacking at a downed log.

The first blow loosened Nova's grip, cutting precious tendon and muscle. The second and third hack removed the lower half of the man's arm from his body. Unlike his fingers, his stump-of-an-arm didn't begin to heal immediately—but it tried! Blue plasma spewed and spit from the stump beneath his elbow, solidifying in seconds. Kicking away the detached limb, House slipped and slid on the wet tile, dropping his gun.

Now free of Nova's embrace, House scurried away from the emerging monster, unable to reacquire the pistol without getting back inside Nova's reach. House was still unable to process that this thing used to be George Novacek—and just like the stories associated with the brute—Nova wasn't going down without a fight. House knew the Coalesce version didn't need both arms to do the job.

I got lucky.

Gianna bolted forward, snagged the pistol, and promptly pulled the trigger just as House fully emerged from the water. Point-blank, the bullet entered and exited Nova's skull with a splatter of bone, grey matter, and goop.

It didn't stop him, though.

Even with pieces of his head missing, the dead man kept coming. At a complete loss, House couldn't come up with another plan before the monster fully emerged from the pool. With his mechanic's jumpsuit waterlogged, Nova's exit was slow and clumsy.

The few extra seconds gave someone else time to act.

Trip rushed forward and wound up. Then, as if he was a professional baseball player, he swung the axe like a Louisville Slugger, grunting hard from the effort. The already tainted blade connected with Nova's open mouth. More importantly, it connected with the creature protruding from it. The front half of the entity was cleaved right down the middle in an explosion of slime.

The axe head's forward momentum quickly passed through the parasite and sliced into Nova's cheeks like they were made of butter. Only when metal found bone did it stop, wedging itself in deep between Nova's upper and lower jaws.

House's lower body was showered in the awful smelling plasma. Seeing Trip move in for another go, he quickly backpedaled away, still in a somewhat seated position. If he didn't move, the infectious fluid might get on his face or, worse yet, in his mouth.

House wasn't sure what it took to turn into one of the creatures. Either way, he wasn't planning on finding out.

Nova's twice-reanimated corpse flailed, pawing at the wounded entity with a hand and a stump. His reaction wasn't any different than Grigson's when she was stabbed in the neck. Both host and parasite had freaked out. House was hoping that, like Grigson, Nova would suffer a quick death.

But instead of laying into Nova again, like House assumed he would, Trip grabbed him under the left armpit and helped drag him away to a safer distance. Sam was doing the same on House's right side. Gianna still held the pistol but hadn't loosed another round. Her eyes were wide, terrified that the headshot had done nothing.

House didn't have an answer for the failed headshot until Trip had explicitly targeted the entity itself. Damaging the creature's vessel—the people it killed and brought back to life—was a waste of time and energy. They would need to impair the pilot of the vessel for anything destructive to occur.

Trip and Sam helped House to his feet, steadying him while he tested his ankle. Patting both men on the back, House stepped away, limping slightly. The injury wasn't serious, but it would be sore for a couple of days. They'd seriously averted disaster. Everyone's quick thinking saved his leg...and his life.

"Thank you," House said, looking at the three of them individually, panning back and forth between them all. "I'd be a goner if you hadn't acted as fast as you did."

21

Gianna threw herself into her father's arms and cried softly. They didn't sound like tears of sadness, though. She was crying because she was happy that her dad was okay. House rubbed her back softly.

"It's alright, G. I'm fine." He tilted her chin up to look her in the eyes. "You're doing that a lot lately, you know?"

She averted her eyes and stepped away. "I know," she said, glancing at Trip. "I'm... I'm good. Haven't been feeling well with everything happening to us."

House studied the couple before settling on the sweaty face of his XO. "What's the news?"

"Besides that?" Sam asked, thumbing over at the inert, beached form of George Novacek. The thing in his mouth had finally stopped wiggling and shriveled up in the same manner as the entity that had taken over Grigson's body.

"Well," House said, "at least we know how to kill them."

"But..." Trip said, looking sad, "they're our friends."

Somber, House glanced at Nova. "Believe me, I know." He turned. "From now on, we stick together and watch each other's asses as if our lives depend on it—because they do."

He turned to Trip. "You knew how to kill it, how?"

Trip cowered, shrinking in on himself. He looked mortified. "I, uh, don't know anything. I, um...I missed."

"You missed?" Sam asked, pointing at Nova. "That doesn't look like *missing* to me."

Trip handed the axe back to House and almost stepped entirely behind Gianna, trying to hide from everyone. "I was going for his neck."

House chuckled, then sighed. "Well, either way, we know what to do now."

"What are they exactly?" Trip asked.

House recalled his conversation with Donovan—with Coalesce. He recounted the discussion's finer details, filling the others in.

"To come together. Unity in one mass," Sam said, still staring at Nova. "That's what 'coalesce' means."

Trip snorted. "Nerd." He grinned and winked at Sam.

The XO rolled his eyes. "Says the guy wearing sunglasses indoors. Who are you, Corey Hart?"

Trip frowned, raising his voice. House wasn't even sure Trip knew who Corey Hart was. "It just so happens..." He retorted, before getting shushed by Gianna. He calmed a little. "It just so happens that I'm suffering from some really bad headaches!"

Sam smiled, but his mood darkened. House understood his change in emotion. It was hard to be jovial about anything considering their surroundings. If there was anyone that could appreciate that, it was his own XO, a man who was put in some difficult situations since coming aboard.

The science trip wasn't going to be recognized as a way to get a leg up or to get your name noticed. Sam didn't know this, but House knew there had been several sailors turn down the job that Sam jumped at. The fact that House was brought in, a man who never commanded his own ship before, didn't help either. No one wanted to work for the recently un-retired Sebastian House. It wasn't until the rest of the crew joined him that they understood how good of a boss House was.

The fact was that House was a good person. He treated everyone the same, regardless of race, beliefs, gender, or sexual orientation. It started with his upbringing. He had grown up in a Christian home and his family taught him to love everyone because Jesus loved everyone—even his enemies. As an adult, House had strayed away from the Church, but deep down, he still possessed some of its core beliefs. It's what made him the man he was today.

Not that he ever acted like he was "above" anyone.

If you did your job to the best of your abilities, you'd get nothing but praise from the captain. There was never a time when House didn't give one of his crewmen the time of day. If someone needed to say something, he made an effort to hear them out. Nothing was off the table, even if he didn't agree with their point of view.

"How's the ankle?" Gianna asked, heading for the entrance.

House shrugged. "Sore, but fine. Could've been worse." She looked worried. "Why do you ask?"

"Because," she replied, head tilted to the side in thought, "I think I hear more of them coming."

House rushed forward, pushing aside the discomfort, and turned the corner out into the corridor. Two more of Donovan's minions stood before him. One was a member of his science team. The second person was someone House knew well. She was the ship's medical specialist, Dr. Lisa Bowen.

"Lisa," House muttered, gritting his teeth. "Damn you, Seth."

"Lisa?" Gianna asked, hurrying into the hallway.

When she saw Bowen, her footing faltered, and she stumbled back, lips quivering. She looked like she was about to faint. House wasn't sure why Gianna was so upset over the woman being turned, besides her caring for someone else's well-being. As far as he knew, the two ladies only knew each other casually.

Bowen turned her attention to Gianna but spoke to House. "She hasn't told you, has she?" Her left eyebrow raised, amused.

House's armor cracked, and he looked over his shoulder at his distraught daughter. "What's she talking about?"

Both of Gianna's hands went to her mouth and she shook her head wildly, eyes locked on the doctor. Whatever Bowen was talking about, the subject petrified Gianna.

With no reply from Gianna, House turned his attention back to Bowen. "What hasn't she told me, Seth?" House asked, knowing who he was *really* talking to.

"Your child," Bowen gently caressed her own stomach, "is *with* child." She smiled wide, amused with House's ignorance. "With him."

House followed her outstretched index finger over his right shoulder and found a cowering Cole Triplett. Under everyone's gaze, he shrank back, half-hiding in the doorway to the pool, looking away from the irate and betrayed captain. House was mad, yes, but he was also aware that Donovan was trying to drive a wedge into their group. Mistrust was a dagger in a situation like this.

Divide and conquer, he thought.

Taking a deep breath, House asked, "This true?" He didn't take his eyes off of Bowen for a second. So far, the man that had accompanied her had said, and done nothing. Neither of them advanced, seemingly here to do nothing more than to deliver the shocking news.

"Uh..." Trip replied, stepping forward a little. "Yes, sir... It is."

House glanced over his left shoulder this time and found Gianna's tear-filled eyes. She was obviously mortified that he had found out this way. Hands in his pockets, and shoulders slouched, Trip fully emerged from his hiding spot and nervously stepped up next to Gianna.

"I'm sorry we didn't tell you sooner, sir. It wasn't our intention to hide anything from you. But with everything going on..."

This wasn't the place for a conversation like this, but House wasn't sure when he'd be able to have it again. So, he asked the one question that needed asking.

"Do you care for my daughter, Trip?"

Trip glanced at her and then met House's eyes with a stern look. "Yes, sir. She means the world to me." As Trip spoke those words, he and Gianna locked eyes and smiled at one another.

Nodding, House turned back to Bowen, glad to hear Trip confess his love—even happier that his daughter was able to hear it.

"Thank you, Seth," House said. This was the boost he needed.

The Bowen-creature was visibly confused. "Thank you? Thank you for wh—"

Uncaring what Bowen had to say in response, he tossed the axe back to Trip. "Take care of them!"

House charged the two members of Coalesce, roaring into the air like a feral animal. He unsheathed Grigson's combat knife and took a page out of her book. Leaping into the air, House drove the blade deep into Bowen's chest. His body weight and downward momentum drove her into the ground hard. He quickly yanked the knife free and jammed it right back into her, specifically the soft tissue beneath her lower jaw.

Bowen gagged, swallowing hard. House had no doubt he punctured the entity within but didn't stick around to make sure. Yanking the blade free, he turned his attention to the other member of Coalesce.

The science team member put up a better effort than Bowen did, taking two slashes to his forearms before House buried the blade in his abdomen. Like the stab wound to Bowen's chest, it wasn't a killer blow. It served its purpose though, bending him forward at the waist. House met the man's face halfway with a savage, rising knee strike.

Teetering back, Donovan's assistant regained his composure and stood tall, his nose crushed and bent sideways. Next, he did what House figured, and he freed the creature within. Like the others, the *bug* didn't make the scientist a more capable foe. It only made him fearless. It also made him predictable. An adversary that knew fear—an average person—would show a certain measure of caution for his, or her, own life. Coalesce didn't display such concern. It gave House a sizeable advantage. He knew they'd go for gold every time they attacked him.

Like this one now, he thought, getting ready.

The man's jaw popped and unhinged, but House reacted instantaneously bringing the knife up, and in one, skyward arch, cut the thing in half. What was left of the creature jerked upward and coated the ceiling in blue plasma. As the scientist collapsed, more and more of the goo sprayed, equally covering the walls and floor—Bowen's body too.

With the enemy dead, House grunted, bent down and wiped the

blade clean on the scientist's shirt. Then, he stood, felt his lower back pop, and breathed a sigh of relief. Turning to his party, he slid the weapon back into the sheath on his hip.

House eyed Gianna and Trip. "Pregnant, huh?"

22

Donovan was losing pieces left and right. House had personally slain a number of them too, which enraged him that much more. Even some of the captain's people were joining in on the rebellion. But with Coalesce's numbers slowly growing, more than half of the crew now, Donovan was still confident that House would be joining him soon enough.

Regrettably, it was taking longer than he'd first thought.

Patience, Seth. Patience...

Donovan had no idea if House was combat trained or not. Nevertheless, he witnessed first-hand that the captain could handle himself in a fight.

Four days after setting sail, two sailors got into it with one another over something nonessential and trivial. To break up the skirmish, House simply stepped into the room—the mess hall. Physically, the only thing the captain did to intimidate the duo was fold his arms and deepen his scowl.

His presence spoke volumes.

Donovan didn't understand it at the time. The sailors directly beneath House's station did. If his title of "Captain" didn't beat you into submission, his fists surely would.

From the start of his naval career to the end, House's resume contained that of the average man-at-sea, nothing more. Donovan growled, knowing he'd severely underestimated the man's abilities.

Maybe I should go after him myself?

Donovan understood the gifts he now possessed, those that served him, didn't. They were more like mindless drones than anything else. While more confident in himself, regardless of the man he used to be, Donovan wasn't sure what would happen if his life was lost in battle.

Would Coalesce go on without him, or would his efforts perish with his own death? Leaning toward the latter, he decided to stay put in the wheelhouse, surrounded by a dozen of his underlings. Plus, he wanted to know more, and he needed to be alive for that to happen.

Stepping away from his own thoughts, he tapped into those of his people in pursuit of House and the others. He witnessed the captain's savagery for himself, through the eyes of Dr. Bowen and Jeff Cohen, the man that accompanied her below decks. If Coalesce's death toll continued to rise, Donovan was going to have to put all his cards on the table and give in and send a mass of his people House's way. The captain showed the ability to take out one or two at a time, but what about twenty?

Strength in numbers, he told the others, reaffirming their mission. *I require more.*

Once he figured out what House was up to, he'd send an overwhelming force to collect him. Initially, Donovan figured that the captain would charge into battle and attempt to retake the Endeavor. That didn't happen, however. But until it did, Donovan needed to concentrate on growing Coalesce as large as *humanly* possible.

The word "humanly" rang out loudly in his head.

Donovan knew he wasn't one of them any longer—but he still didn't quite know what he'd become after melding with the octopus' plasma. His people had orders: Collect Sebastian House and Damon Becker alive. He wanted to personally join with them both, not trusting anyone else to do it. If one of his own fouled up and killed the two men instead...

"No," he said, grinding his teeth, projecting his feelings, "they're mine."

He smiled when he felt all of Coalesce quiver in fear.

Becker... No one had seen hide nor hair of the man since he escaped the mess hall. *One at a time, Seth. House first.*

Turning around, Donovan walked over to the captain's immovable chair and sat. Instead of waking the monitor to his left and scrolling through the sailor's reports, Donovan did something he hadn't tried yet. Taking a deep breath, he closed his eyes and willed a line of communication to open between him and the thing living inside of him.

So far, all he'd heard was his own thoughts and ideas. He understood that they'd been planted in his head by the creature— the microbes deeper within the organism. This time, Donovan intended to speak directly with it, not be influenced by it.

He quieted his mind and concentrated.

"Hello?"

It almost felt as if he was praying to God. Some people said they heard the Almighty's voice in their head. Never being a man of faith, Donovan had honestly never tried to talk to God.

His inquiry was met by silence, agitating the already restless man. Donovan's mind wanted sleep. His regenerative capabilities fixed that, however. Donovan no longer required rest.

"Answer me, beast."

"We are here," boomed a voice.

He spoke with his own lips.

"Who...who are you?" Donovan stammered, stunned that they actually responded.

"We are you, Seth," he replied. "We sound like you, don't we?"

Never one to beat around the bush, he got straight to it. "Where did you come from?"

"Ah, I see, yes. You want to know our origin."

The voice—his voice—went silent.

Donovan grew frustrated. "Hello?"

"We are still here. We are formulating an answer to the best of our ability—one you will comprehend."

That was a fancy way of saying that they didn't know, which upset Donovan even more.

"How do you not know where you're from?" he asked.

"Put it like this... How do you know where you're from?"

Seth's reaction was one of confusion. He'd never really thought about it like that. He knew where he was from because he was told where he came from—he was imparted with that knowledge by another. People that were part of modern civilization all understood where they came from.

Conception. Birth. Life. Death. Every living thing's cycle.

"Yes," the voice said. "You are right. We do not know how we were conceived because we were never privy to the information. We are here because, well, we are. But what we do know is *how* we were born."

"How?" Donovan asked, at the edge of his seat.

"Of fire."

"You were birthed from *fire*?" It sounded preposterous.

"Yes. Some time ago, we came to be because of what you would call, 'fire.'"

"But," Donovan said, trying to work it out, "you—the animal we found you in—were discovered at the bottom of the Southern Ocean—off the coast of Antarctica."

"The cold..." it replied, causing Donovan's body to shiver.

Donovan explained. "The water around here is the coldest in the world."

"Yes," it said, "we know that now. We have gained your knowledge, remember."

"Then why can't you use that to tell me what you are?"

Donovan felt his own shoulders shrug. "Because no one on Earth does. Because of that, we cannot know either."

Still confused, Donovan decided to move on. "But you're here now, right?"

"Yes, we are with you because of our first host's sacrifice."

"The octopus?" Donovan asked.

"Yes, that's what you call them."

Donovan did the math, per se, and put together the pieces. He was infected because of a random accident. The others within Coalesce were joined because Donovan made it happen. His eyes snapped open, and he accessed House's computer while still staying connected to the voice within. He didn't even notice that he'd successfully stayed connected while going about another task.

The new species of octopus was first seen about ten years ago, give or take. If Donovan could find something in House's files relating to around that timeframe, maybe he could fill in a few of the missing holes himself. It took him five minutes to find what he needed, in a classified document, one he shouldn't have been able to access. The password came to him like it was in his own memory, but he knew the memory belonged to someone else.

"A decade ago, a meteor splashed down just outside of McMurdo Station," Donovan's eyes went wide when he read the coordinates, "right where we found you..." He shook his head. "The report was eventually handed in but seen as nothing overly important."

"Why would it be?" they asked while Donovan continued to scan the file. "Why would the government care about another object falling from space?"

"You're an alien?"

The voice caused Donovan to shrug again. "That's what your kind would call us, yes. We are a living organism, not of your world. Neil Armstrong was an alien himself during the moon landing."

Donovan sat back, taking it all in. "I've been infected by an alien parasite."

"Parasite," they defined. "An organism that lives in, or on, an organism of another species—its host—and benefits by deriving nutrients at the other's expense."

Donovan was taken aback by the definition, repeating the portion of it that hit him. "...and benefits by deriving nutrients at the other's expense."

"Is this a problem?"

Donovan shook his head. "Absolutely not. You've given me a wonderful gift—a chance at unlimited knowledge." They smiled together. "We will change the world."

Donovan kept silent for a few minutes, relishing in his newfound understanding. But he needed to know more. He *had* to know more.

"Tell me more about you—physically."

"Very well..." Donovan felt his brain kick in, similar to how a hard drive spins to life. "We stay mostly dormant in cold weather. Space, as you've named it, is no different than the waters surrounding us now. But when we were brought on board, and our cores were warmed to a more agreeable temperature, we quickly made up for lost time. The specimen you collected... Its home was the seabed beneath. As a result, it was our home too."

"You sound so normal," Donovan said, sitting back.

"Seth, we are not talking to you. We, as a species, do not talk at all. This is just our minds melding and interacting with one another. We are conversing as you would with anyone else. We do not have language like you humans do. We adapt and communicate as our hosts do. *Homo sapiens* have a complex verbal language, and that's what we're using now. We are speaking to one another."

"So," Donovan said, "I'm talking to myself right now?"

"For the most part, yes," they replied, "but we are feeding you the answers you are searching for via thoughts and ideas. Again, we do not have a language."

Feeding.

"You really are a parasite then."

"I suppose, that's what you describe our kind as, yes. We do not know what that is, but we do, in fact, do the same things as your world's parasitic entities."

"Do you have a name?" Donovan asked.

"No, we are just 'We.' There is no 'I' here. We are one, as the two of us are now."

"You're—we're—an organism with multiple consciousnesses, but with a unified, singular purpose."

"Two, actually," it corrected. "Advancement and—"

"And what?" Donovan asked. He was given the answer immediately following the question. Everyone within Coalesce smiled again. "Yes... Advancement and assimilation."

He stood. "We are Coalesce," Donovan said, speaking to everyone connected to him, "and we will become even greater."

As soon as the words were uttered, Donovan collapsed in on himself, experiencing a pain he never thought possible. His chest and stomach were on fire, and so was the inside of his skull. Synapses fired...and he felt them all. Unlike the others, Donovan was still technically alive. For whatever reason, he was spared the same fate he'd bestowed unto the rest.

Since his bonding, the only pain he'd felt came from within.

He fell to the ground, his vision blurred. But through the haze, he saw the blood vessels in his hands pulse an even darker shade of blue—like the depths of the sea. The rhythm matched his heartbeat. Both were at an all-time high.

"What's...happening?"

The nearest sailor turned her blank expression away from a monitor and looked down at him and spoke, matching his own voice. "You are experiencing the next stage of your joining, Seth. Stay calm, and you will soon see everything."

Everything?

Donovan heeded his own advice, unsure of why he hadn't thought the words instead. It was the first time he received a verbal message from himself, through another member of Coalesce, one that he didn't see coming.

"Argh!" he shouted, feeling as if he was being torn apart, fractured into a million pieces.

Those connected to him shouted in agony as well, but they didn't seem to be feeling the same pain as him. Every shout came from inside of him as he was repeatedly ripped away from himself. Each reaction was his, yet, separate and disconnected.

Not knowing what to do, and unable to move, Donovan did as "he" said, and he waited. What would become of him, he had no idea, but he knew one thing... If he was forced to do it all over again, he might have actually taken House's advice and halted the dissection for another time.

"No..." he said, feeling something deep within him glue back together. "We are better this way." Then, another piece, and another. His entire being became stronger with every shard reassembled.

Donovan slowly opened his eyes, seeing through the eyes of everyone joined to him. It reminded him of the way an insect saw the world, but the variety of lenses before him were all unique images—live videos—not copies of the same thing.

He grinned, knowing he'd be able to do so much more now that he saw everything they did, not just in his mind, but through their eyes.

Sluggishly, Donovan stood, and in unison, everyone tied to him said, "We are better together."

23

Everyone followed House out of the pool area and headed left, further into a part of the ship no one ever went. It wasn't that the area was forbidden, few places were labeled as such, it was that there wasn't much there except the ship's servers and other electrical equipment.

It was the warmest section of the Endeavor because of the servers, and right now, House needed that warmth. He'd never admit it, but Trip knew the captain was freezing his ass off. He was still soaking wet and cold, plus, his nerves were fried—everyone's were. They needed a place to recover and regroup.

"Should we try and call someone with these?" Trip asked, tapping his earpiece. "I mean, there still have to be others like us, right?"

"We can try," Sam replied, sitting on the floor, just inside the door to the server room. He said he was going to listen for anyone coming, but in reality, Trip figured he wanted to sit down, so he didn't nervously pace the room. "Who do we try first?"

House joined his daughter at the server's main terminal. For her to hack into the mainframe without Donovan knowing about it, she was going to need her father's security clearance, thumbprint, and nine-digit passcode.

Instead of sitting on the floor like Sam, Trip decided to lay on it. He was also near the door, but unlike the XO, that's where he dropped to rest and nothing more. His head was killing him, and he needed to lay down and close his eyes. That was fifteen minutes ago, and he was still moaning like an injured animal.

"So, what happened again?" Sam asked, not hearing the entire story yet.

"I..." Trip replied, wincing as he opened his eyes to look at him, "got flashed point-blank by the squid we brought up from below."

"Squid?" Sam asked. "I thought it was—"

"An octopus," Trip interrupted, "yeah..." he chuckled softly. "We called it a squid to piss off Donovan." He smiled. "Driving that guy crazy should be America's greatest pastime, not baseball." Blinking hard against the discomfort, Trip sat up and propped himself against the wall on the other side of the door opposite of Sam. "Anywho... I guess the thing cooked something up here." He gently tapped his right temple and sighed. "I've been dealing with these godawful migraines ever since."

"That bad?" Sam asked, looking sad.

Trip nodded. "Like someone driving an icepick into my brain."

"You take anything?"

Trip nodded. "Everything I could."

"Drink anything?"

Trip laughed. "No, but I could use one right about now—the captain too!"

"Water, Trip," Sam said, smiling. "I mean, have you had any water lately?"

"Oh," Trip replied, shrugging, "with the pills, sure, but we've been a little busy since then."

Sam nodded. "Tell me about it... Anyways, get as much water in your system as you can. Sometimes the headaches can get worse because of dehydration."

"Sure thing, *Doc*," Trip said, saluting his XO.

Sam's eyes left Trip and found Gianna. "So, a father, huh?"

Trip shrugged and slipped his sunglasses back on. "Wasn't exactly planned, you know? Regardless, she's the best." He glanced back at Sam. "We'll make it work."

He noticed that Sam wasn't really staring at Gianna—he wasn't looking at anything. Sam was staring off into space, thinking of something else.

Someone else? Trip thought.

"What's really on your mind?" he asked.

When Sam looked back at Trip, his eyes were wet. The tears had yet to fall, but the sorrow in them was real. Trip had no idea why his XO was so upset, besides the obvious.

"I..." Sam said, getting choked up, "may have lost someone I cared about today—and..." he wiped his eyes before the salty liquid ran down his face, "I'm not sure what to do. I can't contact them either. It's not safe for anyone. What if I call them and they're one of Donovan's people now?"

Them? Trip thought. *Why didn't he say 'her?'*

Then, it dawned on him. It was because Sam wasn't referring to a *her*, he was referring to a *him*. Trip didn't care if his XO was gay or not, and he wasn't going to force him to spill the beans. He'd support the guy no matter what. At the end of the day, it was going to be Sam's decision to officially "come out."

"My friend..." Sam said, choosing his words carefully.

"What about *them*?" Trip asked, keeping the codeword going.

"Their father is a retired English teacher, and it rubbed off on them. We'd stay up late and do word games and puzzles for fun. Dorky, I know... It's how I knew the definition of coalesce so easily." He frowned. "Didn't realize how much they rubbed off on me."

"You seem to know them well."

Sam shrugged. "Two years is a long time to get to know someone, even if it's in the shadows of the public eye."

Sam was most definitely gay.

Wait... Two years?

"You knew them before boarding the Endeavor?"

Sam blushed but answered. "It was the main reason I jumped at the chance to be House's XO. But the other main reason is that I like House as a boss. Both reasons made it an easy choice for me." He looked at Trip. "He's a good guy."

Trip nodded his approval.

Blinking out of his stupor, he smiled at Sam. "We'll find your friend," Trip said, "okay?" He held out his hand and was happy to see Sam quickly clutch it and squeeze. There wasn't anything behind the act besides being a friend in a time of need. They all needed to have each other's backs. If any of them let down their guard, it could be over for them all.

Sam smiled, let go, and patted Trip's shoulder.

"You boys alright?"

Both Trip and Sam snapped their attention to Gianna who was looking back at them with a raised eyebrow. Right at that moment, Sam was still gripping Trip's shoulder, and both men were smiling at one another.

Trip reached over and grabbed Sam's shoulder, squeezing him back. "Sure are, but we'd appreciate it if you didn't interrupt our bro moments."

"Uh—yeah!" Sam added, glancing back and forth between Trip and Gianna. He gave Trip a curt nod and turned back to Gianna. "We were having a great bro moment before you said something."

Trip and Gianna broke out in laughter. The way Sam said it was so awkward that Trip couldn't help himself—Gianna either. The only one that wasn't laughing was House who was deep in thought, going through the files that Gianna had gathered on her tablet.

"This isn't good."

Everyone's smiles faded, and they quieted their laughter. House stepped away from Gianna and tapped the screen a few times. Then, he growled and handed the device back to her, looking very frustrated.

"What's wrong?" Trip asked.

"The Endeavor," Gianna replied, "we were hoping to disable it or, at the very least, turn it away from McMurdo."

Sam shook his head and got to his feet, stretching as he spoke. "Not possible from here." He continued. "We built in a safety protocol to keep someone from hijacking the boat from anywhere but the bridge."

House nodded. "I know, Sam. I was hoping we unknowingly left a backdoor open." He sighed. "The only other option besides an outright attack on Command is the engine room."

"At the other end of the ship," Sam said, about to flop back down on the ground.

"We need Buddy," House said. "He'd know how to stop the engines without damaging them beyond repair."

"Still need Becker too," Gianna added.

After a moment of silence, House stepped toward the door. "Right... Let's get to it then."

"Dad?" Gianna asked, looking scared.

"Stay here, G." He smiled softly. "Keep my grandson safe."

"Your granddaughter, you mean. Sure."

Trip looked back and forth between House and Gianna. He knew he needed to help his baby's grandfather. But the man was also his captain and someone he respected.

"Go," Gianna mouthed. And with Sam being a little under the weather mentally, Trip knew it would be the perfect opportunity for him and House to be alone together.

"Sam?" Trip asked. The XO looked at him. "Keep an eye on her for me?"

He nodded vigorously and stepped away from the door.

Gianna drew her pistol and held it out for her father, but he shook his head.

"Keep it... Just in case."

Gianna hugged both men, tears falling. "Please, be careful."

House winked at her. "Always."

"We'll see if we can come up with anything from here," Sam said, placing a reassuring hand on Gianna's shoulder. "Maybe there's something we haven't thought of yet?"

Trip and Gianna embraced next. House gave them some space and headed for the door. Gripping the lock with his left hand, he unsheathed his knife with his right. Then, Trip stepped up next to him, axe in both hands. He was nervous but was holding it together better than even he thought possible.

"We'll be in contact," House said, looking over his shoulder at Gianna one more time.

She grinned. "Take care of each other. You're family now."

The corner of House's mouth turned upward in the smallest of smiles. Then, it disappeared, and he flipped the deadbolt and slowly opened the steel door. Being newly built, it swung open without a sound. If they were back on the *Harry S. Truman*, it would've screeched in protest. The two men stepped through and gave Gianna and Sam one last look before closing it. The lock immediately reengaged.

Trip looked left and then right down the bisecting corridor, thankfully finding no one around them. He and House were alone. If they were fortunate, they'd be by themselves the whole way to the engine room.

House activated his comms, placing a group call. "Testing..." he said softly. "You hear me, G? How 'bout you, Sam? Trip?"

"I've got you, Dad," she replied. "Miss me already?"

"I hear you, sir," Sam replied.

Trip silently nodded his confirmation, his attention still focused on the hallway.

House grinned. "Always, honey." Then, he frowned. "But we should only use the radios if it's an emergency."

"Agreed," Gianna said. "Talk to you two in a few."

Hanging up, Trip and House heard something groan further down the corridor. Next, the lights above them winked out and cast the passage in darkness. Three seconds after the overhead lights went out, a set of foreboding, red emergency lights came to life. And standing directly beneath a set of those lights was a lone figure.

Trip didn't think one person would be much of a challenge for him and House. Together, they stepped toward the woman, stopping mid-stride when two more of the former crewmen appeared from within the gloom behind the first. Then, two more.

The seven of them all looked up at Trip and House, their eyes pulsing furiously.

"Um..." Trip said, stepping back toward the server room.

"No," House whispered, reaching for his arm. Grabbing his left elbow, House pulled him left. "We don't want to lead them to Gianna and Sam."

Trip eyed the mob before looking House in the eyes and nodded. "You're right." Then, he did something no one could've expected. "Hey, uglies," he shouted, waving an arm high, "come and get us!"

House shoved Trip to the left, down the perpendicular hallway. "Dammit, Trip. That's not what I meant!"

24

Feet pounded behind House and Trip. The footfalls were heard even before the monstrous horde appeared from around the corner. House watched as every single one of them bypassed the server room...and his daughter.

Even though Gianna was armed, House knew it wouldn't matter much if the mob made it inside the bedroom-sized space. Unless she landed a killing shot directly to the parasite, they'd just keep on coming. Plus, there were six of the creatures, not one or two. And if Coalesce did, indeed, get inside the room, there'd be no way he and Trip could hack their way back inside before she and Sam were overrun and killed, or worse, turned.

House didn't know what he'd do if Gianna became one of them. His grandchild would ultimately suffer the same fate as well. Death.

The men's path ended at a door labeled "Records," but it didn't dead-end... This way headed right, following the rectangular shape of the ship, taking the duo back toward the rear section. With any luck, they'd continue unperturbed and take a direct route to the engine room. It was on the same floor they were on now and they'd be able to access the space through its usually sealed backdoor.

Truthfully, it wasn't really a backdoor at all. It was the front door. They called it a 'backdoor' because it was never used unless the elevator was disabled.

House wasn't sure whether the elevators were out of order or not, but he assumed they were. Even if they did work, he and Trip would avoid using them at all costs. Donovan was sure to have people stationed outside each one in case they, or any of the remaining human crew, showed their faces.

The lights going out worried House, mostly because their communications array required power to operate.

Telepathy? House asked himself. *Is that how they communicate?*

He assumed so—a variation of it anyway.

Donovan could speak to, and through, all of his people. House witnessed it several times already. It was a considerable advantage when coordinating a large team in the field, or in this case, the different levels beneath the Endeavor's skin. All House and his remaining crewmembers possessed were their earpieces. Luckily, they still worked, even with the ship out of their control.

"Call from Gianna House."

"Uh, Dad?"

Breathing hard, House answered. "G... I'm a little busy."

"I know," she replied. "Sam and I could hear them on the other side of the door." She got to it. "Anyways, really quick—"

"Explain faster!" House yelled, looking back. The mob had grown since he last checked on them. Now, the line was nine or so deep.

"I am!" she responded, shouting back at him. "I was going to say that Donovan is trying to disable the Endeavor—the power—everything!"

"All of it, why?" he asked, glancing at Trip. He shrugged, apparently in on the conversation too.

"I think he's trying to reset the ship's systems back to their default settings—and if he does—he'll have access to everything, even without the passcodes from you and Damon."

"He can do that?" House asked, shocked. "He can take over my boat, just like that?"

She snorted. "I said he was *trying* to... He can't get dick done with me on the other end." She laughed. "I'm killing every opportunity from here, but eventually he'll get wise to us and come have a look."

House was proud of her, but he was, likewise, scared for her. "Fine," he replied, knowing there wasn't much else he could say or do. "Just hang tight and keep doing what you're doing. Trip and I'll be back as soon as we can."

The call ended, and Trip yanked on House's arm, pulling him into an opening to their right. They bounded over storage containers of all shapes and sizes. These held mostly electronic equipment for their various cameras, which were of the handheld and undersea robotic variety. Hearing someone coming up behind them, House slid to a stop, grabbed the nearest case, and heaved it back into the doorway.

The timing was perfect, and just as one of Donovan's people entered, the twenty-or-so-pound hard-shelled case connected with the person's face, driving them backward into the others behind him. With no time to celebrate, House scampered out of the room and slammed the door shut. Trip headed left and entered another room further down the hall, frantically waving House forward.

House dove in just as Trip closed the door, locking it and quietly stepping back. If things went as he hoped, their pursuers would have no idea where they went. Side-by-side and weapons brandished, House and Trip stood in silence and waited. Seconds went by before they heard a door back down the corridor open. It was the one House shut before following Trip into the room they found themselves in now.

Multiple sets of footsteps approached. Their door handle jiggled but was released after two attempts to get inside. House expected the door to be beaten down any minute. Luckily, it wasn't, and he breathed a sigh of relief when their pursuers headed off. Regrettably, it was because of a scream. Apparently, they found something else to chase.

Dammit, House thought, stepping forward. He and Trip successfully evaded the wave of Coalesce minions, but it was at the expense of someone else's life.

He stepped toward the door again but paused when Trip grabbed his arm and shook his head. With a free hand, Trip motioned to his stomach, rubbing it as if he were pregnant. He was telling him that Gianna was back there waiting for him. Unhappy about leaving anyone out there alone, House nodded and was released. He'd do as Trip asked and stay put.

For Gianna.

Despite feeling an uncomfortable twinge in his ankle, House glided across the floor and put his ear up to the door. Holding his breath, he closed his eyes and listened. For all he knew, a few of the things were still outside their hiding spot, waiting for them to give their position away. It was impossible to tell just how many of them took off in pursuit of the other person.

Regardless, he and Trip needed to stay quiet and stay hidden for a little while. Maybe if they paused their trek for long enough, Donovan would order his people to leave the floor altogether.

A squeak and a crash behind House startled him.

So much for staying quiet.

"Um, Captain?" Trip asked, thankfully keeping his voice down.

House turned around, planning on berating Trip for making so much noise. But he never got the chance... Trip was on the ground, having slipped and gone down. The younger man's attention wasn't even on House, it was on the pool of blood beneath him.

House gimped over. "You're injured?" As far as he knew, neither one of them had been touched.

Trip shook his head, got to his feet, then shrugged. "Besides my brain, no. This..." he motioned to his bloodied arms and clothes, sneering hard, "this isn't mine."

"It's mine..."

The voice croaked, calling out from the shadows behind Trip. Both men jumped back and, once more, brought up their weapons.

House lowered his as soon as Trip moved out of the way. The voice's owner wasn't a threat. He was dying.

"Damon, no..."

Becker wasn't alone either. Two others were with him. Both of them were a part of Donovan's science team, one woman, and one man. House didn't know their names. Then again, he didn't know a lot of the people on that side of the fence.

"We found him like this," the female scientist said. Her clothes, like the man's, and now Trip's, were stained with blood.

Becker's blood.

The male scientist shook House's extended hand. "He's in bad shape, sir."

House could see that. Becker's side was drenched in blood, as was his left arm. The government liaison hadn't been turned like the others. He'd been attacked.

"Sebastian..." Becker's voice sounded far off.

His ordinarily pale complexion looked almost translucent from blood loss. It seemed that Becker had fallen down in the middle of the room, then was dragged into the corner of the space and hidden behind a desk. The room itself was one of their little-used workplaces—an office. In fact, the last time House stepped foot in the room was before they departed.

The woman flicked on a small penlight and handed it to House. He nodded his thanks and began inspecting Becker's injuries. Something, or someone, had done a number on the man.

"Knife wounds," Becker explained, reading House's thoughts.

"From who?"

"One...of them," Becker replied, coughing hard. "Came at me...with a knife...down...down in the mess hall."

"You fought them off?" House asked, impressed. He would've never thought, not in a million years, that Becker could fight his way out of a conflict with an enemy like Coalesce. Very few in the world could.

Becker grinned and nodded. "I'm a lot tougher...then I look." He hacked into his hand, and it came away coated with blood. Before Becker could get another word out, he broke into a fit of uncontrollable, agonizing coughs, each worse than the one before.

"You'll be alright, Damon," House assured, not believing his own words.

Becker softly laughed. "You're a terrible liar, Sebastian. Just awful." He grimaced in pain, shaking hard. But he kept himself from coughing again. "Stick to what you're good at."

House smiled. "And that is...?"

Becker looked at him hard. "Being a damned fine captain." He held up a gunmetal-colored keycard attached to a lanyard. "Save," his eyes rolled back in his head, "as many...as you ca..."

House dipped his head as Becker faded away. When he did, he spotted the lanyard and keycard clutched in the dead man's hand. House had an identical one—as did Donovan. Only, unlike his and Donovan's variations, Becker's contained *all* of their private passcodes as well as Becker's even more secretive ones. With it, House would be able to bypass everything Coalesce had done to the Endeavor and call the United States government directly.

We can call for help! His shoulders fell. *If we can get a call out.*

That was still an issue. Donovan still had control of the bridge, and therefore the Endeavor itself. Having Becker's top-secret information only meant so much if you didn't have a way to use it.

Becker's room? It's where he made all of his calls from. If they could find Becker's laptop...

"Sir?" The man asked. "What are we going to do?"

House stood and faced Trip and the others, focusing on the newcomers while Trip wiped Becker's blood off his own hands and arms with a random towel.

"What are your names?" he asked.

"Kimberly Montez."

"Gregg Shields."

House nodded. "Okay, Montez and Shields, got it." He activated his comms unit. "G, Sam, you there?"

"Yes, sir," Sam replied.

"Always," Gianna answered. "What's up, Dad?"

House sighed. "We found Damon."

"You did?" she asked, sounding hopeful. "How is he?"

House glanced down at the body. "He's dead."

"Dammit..." Sam said, cursing softly. "Donovan's doing?"

"Sort of," House said, relaying everything that had occurred since they left the server room, and what Becker had told him.

"Okay, Dad," Gianna said, sniffing, no doubt crying again, "have Montez and Shields head this way and Sam and I will take care of them until you get back."

House beamed with pride. "Good girl."

Ending the call, he and Trip tip-toed up to the door and listened carefully. Hearing nothing, House opened it slowly and checked both ways down the hall. The good news was that nothing leaped out at him. Satisfied that they were truly alone, House turned back to the two scientists.

"The server room, you know where it is?"

Only Shields nodded.

"Good," House said, turning his full attention on him. "I have two people there waiting for your arrival. Do yourselves a favor and don't dawdle."

Both Montez and Shields swallowed hard.

He shut the door, keeping a hand on it for a moment longer.

I'm sorry, Damon...

Parting there, House and Trip headed toward the engine room. They'd just lost a valuable ally in Damon Becker but at least gained access to his personal domain. Obviously, having him alive and well would've been preferable, but his death wasn't a complete loss. His resilience and eventual sacrifice may have saved them all.

Whoever's left, anyway.

"Come on," House said, ushering Trip along. The younger man was still somewhat slathered in Becker's blood, but had, more or less, cleaned himself up. Still, it must've been hard on the *greener*, more inexperienced man to have that much of another person's blood on him.

The closer they got to the engine room, via the ship's starboard side corridor, the more House's mind turned to Buddy. Hopefully, they'd find him along the way.

And in better shape than Becker.

I'll find you, you old coot, House promised, smiling at a wave of memories. *I'll find you...*

25

Getting moving again wasn't easy for Buddy Malone—but at least he wasn't alone anymore. While dodging monsters, he stumbled across a pair of sailors hiding for the exact same reason.

If only I found someone who'd be useful in a fight, he thought, glancing behind him.

The person over his right shoulder was a data analyst from the bridge, a lady named Shannon Kyle. She was one of the few, besides Buddy, to make it out of there with their lives. Buddy wasn't sure of anyone else. The two that mattered most were Sam and Dominik Lucas. The pair, along with Buddy and House, could safely operate the Endeavor with little, to no, help.

The man stumbling next to Shannon was hardly a man at all. He was a shell of himself, at least, that's what Buddy took away from their initial conversation. Joshua Peck had yet to stop shaking since Buddy found him holed up inside the handicap stall of the fourth-floor restroom. Apparently, the lab rat had been there since the first sign of trouble. In fact, he still had dried snot caked on his upper lip from his ugly crying.

He was doing that when Buddy found him.

Peck had also wet his pants.

The man was more than a mess and was currently out of it to the point that Shannon was forced to drag him alongside her while they both followed Buddy. They were heading for the engine room with the idea of shutting it down. Buddy had a few tricks up his sleeves. If they could get the boat to be completely dead in the water, then McMurdo would know something was wrong. As of now, they were still steadily making their way back to port.

Buddy checked his watch and groaned. They still had quite a while before the storm was supposed to let up enough for them to start their official arrival sequence. As of now, they were just moving into position, still safely inside of their buffer zone.

Buddy had no idea what would happen if Donovan ordered the Endeavor through the barrier. He doubted McMurdo would open fire on them. It's not like they had the firepower to do so either way. It was a research station after all, not a battle station.

But they could call in for help from a nearby carrier group.

Then, boom...

The reason you followed base command's orders were for A) safety, and B) because, if you didn't, you'd be in big, big trouble.

Donovan had no such fear anymore. He'd led a brutally successful mutiny and had done it with a pack of horrible beasts—beasts that used to be Buddy's shipmates.

They were only fifty feet from the seldom-used engine room door. They'd taken the port-side hallway, thankful to find it mostly empty. Even Buddy hardly accessed his domain this way. Having reached the age he was at, he found creature comforts, like elevators, useful. Usually, he'd forego such things, calling them a "lazy way to live." Now, in his seventies, he'd gladly use one, if only to keep his energy up for something else later.

On the Endeavor, for instance, he used the elevator rather than the stairs so he wouldn't look winded in front of his peers. Then, he'd use that saved energy to rip into anyone who gave him a sideways glance.

People didn't like Buddy much.

Buddy stumbled forward. His knees and back were killing him from having to use the stairs so much recently. Placing a shaky hand against the left wall, he signaled for Shannon and Peck to stop. Without argument, the pair fell in line next to him and took a breather, staying silent, and still.

Besides the natural creaks here and there, all was well around them minus the blood smear on the floor directly in front of them. The streak ended around the next corner, heading toward the center of the boat. Whoever the slick belonged to, they'd been brutally murdered and dragged away. The victim's foot was still visible. For all their sanities, he hoped the rest of the person was still attached.

Buddy said a quick prayer for the poor bastard's soul and then shoved away from the wall. He turned to his two partners and told them what was going to happen next.

"Okay," he started, glancing over his shoulder when he heard a sound behind him. But it was nothing, and he continued his briefing. "Stay close and follow me."

"How do you know there won't be any of them inside?" Shannon asked.

Buddy shook his head. "I don't, but this boat is fully automated. You only need a skeleton crew down here if somethin' goes haywire." He lifted his left wrist, showing her the display. "My doohickey here says all is well. Plus," he added, pulling a four-inch, metallic object out of his back pocket, "I have this."

He quickly slid a small piece of metal up the item's side, getting a *sheenk* and a yelp in response. The latter was Shannon putting a hand to her mouth in fright when the blade of Buddy's tactical OTF

(Out the Front) knife sprang to life. OTF stood for the action of the switchblade.

"You'd use that on someone?" she asked, calming.

Buddy looked away from her. "If I have to, yes."

The lowest level of the research vessel was the most utilitarian of them all. Everything was in shades of grey, and the hallway floor was nothing more than a metal catwalk. The ship cost an ungodly amount of money to build, so naturally, the designers cut costs wherever they could. Buddy couldn't care less too.

Could've been dirt floors for all he cared.

Bypassing the dead body on their left, Buddy continued toward the rear of the ship but stopped when the engine room door unlocked and swung open. One of Buddy's men greeted them with a sneer and a pulse of his crackling, electric blue eyes. When the engineer spoke, it gave him the chills.

"Hello, Buddy."

"Seth," he simply replied, more confirming the man's identity than anything else.

"Yes, it is me, or should I say, I am him." The engineer, Ned Frohm, smiled and held out his hands, inspecting them.

The only positive thing that Buddy took away from the eerie interaction was that Frohm was alone. Knife still in hand, he stepped forward and stood tall, pushing aside the discomfort of his aching lower half.

"Can you do it, Chief Malone? Can you really kill one of your own?"

Buddy frowned at the use of his official title, knowing Donovan was using it to put his and Frohm's relationship at the forefront of the conflict. Buddy was the man's direct superior, and someone the sailor was supposed to trust. Frohm was a good kid, barely into his twenties.

Buddy snarled. "You did all the killin' yourself, Seth. You're the monster here, not me." He sighed. "If anythin', I'll be givin' Ned's soul some much-needed peace."

Donovan laughed through Frohm, which enraged Buddy further.

"You sick bastard!" he shouted, tearing up. "Shut your fuckin' mouth!"

"Come now, you really think there are souls at play here—that there's an afterlife for Ned to go to?" Frohm's arms opened wide, and he looked up at the ceiling. "Look what I've done—my abilities!" He smiled, relishing in himself. "I am Alpha and Omega, the first and the last, the beginning and the end. I am—"

"You," Buddy interrupted, getting Donovan's attention back on the moment and off of himself, "no matter how much you think you are...you're nothin' more than a delusional abomination from deep inside the Devil's ass crack. You ain't no god, Seth. You're a monster—a parasite—a disease! Nothin' more." Buddy took another step forward. "You're nothin'."

"Well then, Chief Malone," Donovan cooed, "prove it. Prove that I am not what I say I am and snuff me out." He grinned. "Do it."

"Chief?" Shannon whispered. "Why is he so eager for you to kill him?"

"Because, Ms. Kyle," Buddy replied, "he wants to break me, make me put this here blade in my own man's belly."

"What are you going to do?"

Buddy turned his focus squarely on the Frohm puppet. "I'm gonna put my boy to rest."

* * *

Frohm met Buddy halfway. Donovan tried a half a dozen times to secure the old man, but the elder engineer proved scrappy and elusive. While using one of Buddy's own men to guard the engine room felt like the right thing to do, Donovan was starting to second guess the notion. No one in Coalesce was worth a damn, they had no combat training. He was on a research vessel, after all.

His reasoning for placing Frohm where he did was sound enough. He had wanted Malone to arrive first. Then, he'd break his will—weaken him mentally—before joining with him physically.

The lack of fighting ability with just about everyone on board was frustrating Donovan to no end. The one *superpower* he gave those of Coalesce was the inability to feel pain and the gift of regeneration. But during a fight, his people were as meek as ever. Numbers were his strength, but not quite yet.

He needed to balance the odds of what would happen first. If they landed at McMurdo with only fifty or sixty people joined to him, he calculated that they'd be defeated. And if he sent all of his force to apprehend Captain House and lost even more of his men, well, then...

Not good, he thought, unsure of what to do next.

Buddy hacked and stabbed at Frohm, catching the sailor across the wrist. It was the fourth such injury the younger man had sustained while fighting with his boss. But Buddy was rapidly tiring. His face was already covered in sweat, and he was breathing hard.

"Finish this," Donovan said, uncaring how it ended. Frohm gave him little information that he didn't already have. While never one to throw any member of Coalesce to the wolves, Donovan knew this fight was a taxing one—for him too.

His head pounded from the effort. Being able to see everything his people saw was hard work—painful even—but his evolution into a better being was worth it. He knew he'd transmute again with time. *That* was the biggest reason he stayed put in the wheelhouse. He needed to see what happened next.

Forhm overpowered Buddy, taking the blade to the stomach as he tackled him to the floor. Now atop him, all Donovan had to do was order his minion to lean forward and begin the joining process.

But he never got to give the go-ahead.

Frohm was tackled by one of Buddy's people, taken off his feet by the woman, Data Analyst Shannon Kyle. Chief Lucas had worked closely with her. She was a whiz with computers, specifically the onboard systems she helped develop from Day 1, a few years back. Lucas knew she had begged to be on the Endeavor to see her creation in action. So, here she was.

"Her," Donovan said. "I want her instead."

Frohm grabbed Shannon's shirt sleeves and rolled on top of her, focusing on the person with the more pertinent information. Buddy's joining was vital, yes, but there was nothing his mind possessed that Donovan truly needed. What Donovan really wanted from Buddy was his body. He wished to own it so he could antagonize House—to break him emotionally like he had attempted to do to Buddy with Frohm. House and Malone were close, Donovan knew that, and he wanted to use their relationship as a weapon.

Smiling, Donovan forced the entity that had quickly grown inside Frohm's stomach from the man's throat. He urged it to slither forward and reveal itself. When it appeared, it got the expected reaction out of the woman. Shannon shrieked in terror and thrashed beneath his grasp.

Twelve inches of it wriggled into the space between him and Shannon. Just three more inches and it would be close enough to strike. Like all the other joinings, Donovan shook with anticipation.

"No!"

Frohm and the parasite were driven back, not by Buddy, but by someone else. The person who tackled Frohm wasn't the boat's chief engineer.

It was the third person in Malone's party: Joshua Peck.

"Leave her alone!" he cried, feebly beating Frohm with a flurry of weak, uninspiring punches.

"Aw…" Donovan snickered, happily taking each of the closed fists to Frohm's face. The sailor was dead, and wouldn't be bruising, swelling, or bleeding from the assault. "You like her, don't you?"

In between blows, Donovan observed Buddy dragging Shannon away from the action, and if he couldn't have the analyst for himself, then he'd make her suffer until he could. As Peck's vigor waned, Frohm's right hand shot up and latched onto the slighter man's throat, momentarily pausing the attack. In that time, Frohm sat up and drove the creature straight into Peck's mouth with enough force to detonate the back of his skull.

A stew of gore burst forth as if they were ejected by a shotgun blast. The miasma splattered the hallway with the type of carnage few people ever witnessed. Buddy and Shannon both cried out in fear and disgust, scampering further and further away.

Shannon was terrified, verbally expressing her feelings.

Buddy did nothing but stare, locked in fright.

Donovan may have lost this round, but the battle waged on. He failed to join with Buddy, but the look of horror on his prey's face had most definitely driven a stake into the old man's heart. He took solace in knowing that he had severely weakened the man's spirit.

26

Gregg Shields wasn't brave, in fact, he openly joked that he was one of the biggest cowards anyone would ever meet. In reality, he was just being honest with himself, unlike those who talked themselves up into being something they weren't.

Nope, not Gregg Shields.

Though, he wasn't a "warrior," Shields would definitely classify himself as a survivor. At just over five feet in height, he was easily the smallest man on the Endeavor, barely taller than only one other person. Even then, he was only an inch taller than the petite Latina he now walked with.

Kimberly Montez.

They currently clutched each other's hands and quietly made their way back to the server room. When everything happened, the first person Shields went to check on was Montez. They'd bonded and laughed as one over the last couple of months, but it never went any further than being close friends. Both were contracted by DARPA, put in offices on opposite sides of the country. As of now, they'd keep it platonic and not promise anything neither could follow through with.

It was taking forever to get to the server room. They were forced to backtrack several times, wanting to skip anything that Shields perceived to be an obstacle. Like he stated several times, "I'm a fleer, not a fighter."

Like most of the levels within the belly of the Endeavor, this one also had three major hallways running the length of the entire ship—until you got to the launch bay and engine room. The rear of the floor was one enormous space filled with machines Shields couldn't imagine trying to operate.

A *clunk* reverberated through the empty corridor before them, grinding the two to a halt. They ducked into the next bisecting hallway, pausing and listening for anything. After thirty seconds of silence, Shields moved off but stopped again. His hand was still intertwined with Montez's, but she, for some reason, wasn't following him. They should've been moving as one.

"Kim, we—"

His voice got caught in his throat. There, further down the hall was a set of glowing eyes. Until then, they had yet to be spotted, only seeing shadows moving about in the dim, red emergency lights. So, instead of continuing forward, they both retreated and ran back the way they'd come, weaving in and out of open offices, laboratories, and other intersecting corridors.

Barley being able to breathe, Shields slowed them down, once more, this time, staying inside an office filled with nothing but filing cabinets. But it was quiet, and they were alone. Locking the port-side door, the pair of frightened geneticists huddled together in the corner. Montez sobbed into Shields' shirt, using his body to muffle her cries.

"Shh, shh, shh..." Shields soothed, stroking her short, black hair. It was cut into a bob, which was terrific for him. He loved women with shorter hair. Plus, she was an expert in the same field as him.

She's perfect, he thought, rolling his eyes at the absurdness of where his mind had gone. *Stop it, Gregg! We need to live before we get into each other's pants.*

"I...I'm okay," she said softly, raising her face high enough to give him a soft kiss on the cheek. When her lips made contact, she gagged and laughed.

"What?" he asked, embarrassed that the girl he cared for cringed when kissing him.

"No, it's not you—well—I guess it sort of is." She grinned in the low light. "You're filthy, Gregg. It tastes like I just kissed a sweaty trashcan."

He smiled. "And you'd know how that tastes, because...?"

She playfully slapped his shoulder, earning a fake groan of agony from him. For just a moment, Montez thought she'd actually harmed him. But he couldn't hide his grin. They stood and stayed quiet, lost in the other's eyes. Their transfixion didn't last, though. A thud at the office's entrance got them moving again.

Exiting via the starboard-side door, Shields carefully closed it and they headed left. Still in the far-right hallway, it was a straight shot to the server room and Gianna House and XO Ferguson.

Not much further now, Shields thought, controlling the upswell of emotion. They were so close to being safe. He didn't believe in luck, but if he did, this would be the moment it would come crashing down if he got too ahead of himself.

Two more intersections passed by before they heard anything other than the shuffle of their own footfalls. A set of eyes burned at them to their left, just as they crossed through another intersection. A hand reached out for Shields but caught the trailing Montez instead.

Shields' flight-not-fight mentality ushered him onward, but his feelings for Montez forced him into action. He grabbed the person's arm and somehow pulled the attacker off her. Before he could celebrate the fact that he successfully freed her from her killer's bonds, Shields himself was apprehended and dragged away, kicking and screaming.

He couldn't get a good look at his assailant except that it was a man. The emergency lights weren't bright enough, and his awkward, upward angle shrouded the person's face in darkness.

Seconds later, his screams turned into a gagging, choking sound as something forcibly entered his mouth and snaked its way down his throat. Then, searing hot pain, which was followed shortly by blissful darkness.

* * *

Now, more than ever, Buddy needed to make a call. And now, more than ever, he despised the Endeavor's finicky comms system. Putting a finger to his ear, he held it there for two seconds and waited for the infrared scanner built into the casing to pick it up and activate.

"Piece of junk," he said, ripping the device from his ear. He wiped the scanner on his shirt, hoping that cleaning it would do the trick. It didn't work before, but eventually, he hoped it would. He stopped mid-wipe and sighed when he saw that he was, in fact, smearing it through a streak of blood and grime.

Fantastic, he thought, finding a much-less soiled piece of fabric to use instead.

"Um, Chief Malone?"

"What?" he asked, snapping at Shannon. He gave her an apologetic smile and calmed. "What is it, Ms. Kyle?"

"You have a WiMP on, sir," she replied, pointing at his left wrist.

He lifted the arm that held the piece of equipment. "And?"

"Anyone who uses a WiMP has their calls dial directly through it now, not your earpiece. Gianna and I installed a rather hefty update last week per DARPA brass. They wanted to give it a field test before we were done in the Antarctic." Her eyebrows scrunched in confusion. "You should've gotten an email about the changes. It came with instructions on how to properly operate it."

Buddy was enraged, and with a deep inhalation, he kept his skyrocketing blood pressure from launching him into oblivion. Then, he expelled the air slowly and evenly, reveling in how the exercise made him feel.

Almost normal.

"Email, right..." he said, grumbling under his breath. "Must've missed the memo."

Re-securing the earpiece in his right ear, he looked over his WiMP and squinted hard, spying a small, glowing, green icon in the corner of the two-by-four inch screen. It looked an-awful-lot like a telephone. Biting his lip and shaking his head in disbelief, he tapped it, hearing the familiar chime in his ear.

"Captain House," he said, voice dialing the man he needed to hear from.

After three seconds, he heard the same tone ding back, followed by, "Buddy! Thank God!"

As much as the old man wanted to continue with the pleasantries, he knew he needed to relay everything he saw, just in case he and House didn't get to speak again for a while. Without emotion, Buddy retold the events of the last few hours—even before the ship was overrun by monsters.

"You're not alone, old friend," House replied, likewise filling Buddy in with his escapades. They even included some more recent events, like the pair of scientists the captain had sent to the server room to meet Gianna and Sam. "Good to see you finally figured out how to use the new call system."

Buddy blushed, his eyes darting to Shannon. "Yes, well, I had some help with that."

His eyes locked on hers. "I watched one of my own men murder another human bein' in cold blood, Sebastian."

"Yeah..." House replied. "I've seen some terrible things too, Bud. Seth said that the joining process doesn't always take. Deaths occur instead of them, um, dying. Sorry, it's hard to explain."

Buddy recalled watching Peck get the back of his head blown out.

"No, Sebastian. Peck's murder was meant to do nothin' more than to fuck with me!" His voice caught. "I...I saw it with my own eyes. Frohm...Seth...eyed me the whole time. He wanted me to see my man die at his hands."

"Hmmm," House mumbled deep in thought.

Buddy knew House better than most. He was thinking hard, probably rubbing his salt and pepper stubbled chin too.

"This isn't good."

Buddy laughed. "No shit, 'Seabass.'"

House grumbled again. Buddy knew House expected to be addressed formally when in the presence of other crew members. Buddy never minded being casual with his own crew, but he always crossed the line with House.

"What I mean is...this is a new reaction on Seth's part." House continued. "From what I can tell, he's been more interested in collecting bodies, more minions to control. The fact that he'd willingly sacrifice someone just to get a message across doesn't feel like the new Seth—the one I've come to expect."

"He's desperate," Buddy said, trying to put the pieces together.

"Maybe," House replied, "but I think it's more that he's changing. He's evolving his thought process."

"You seem to know an awful lot about this, Sebastian." Buddy started to pace, needing to make sure the man on the other end was still the boy from Albany, Georgia. "I'm still talkin' to the scrawny little punk from Athens, right?"

House laughed. "Albany, but yes." He laughed again, sounding tired. "I see what you did there, Bud. Good try, but if I weren't myself, I'd still know where I'm from. Seth gains all the knowledge and memories of the person he joins with. It's the reason we haven't tried to make contact with any of the crew besides who we've already found in person."

Buddy had no clue what do to next since it was only him and Shannon. Hopefully, House did, though.

"What's next?"

"Well," House replied, "now with you back in the fold, I was hoping we could shut down the engines. We can't make port, Buddy. Under no circumstances can we make port."

Buddy nodded to himself, understanding the implications if they did. Donovan was able to take over half of the crew in a matters of hours. While the major players on board, besides Donovan himself, had yet to be turned, they'd still lost some key sailors.

Including George, Buddy thought, wishing Nova was around to help. Then, he remembered that he'd already done more than Buddy could've asked for. Nova sacrificed his own life to make sure Buddy got away.

Buddy nodded again, agreeing with House. "Seems to me that we need to draw Seth out of his nest somehow."

The line went silent, and Buddy thought he dropped the call. "Sebastian? You—"

"Yeah, I'm still here..." He sighed. "And I think I know how to get Seth to personally come to us."

"How?" Buddy asked, optimistic.

"Me."

"You?" Buddy had no idea what that meant, but he hated it. "Why you?"

"Because," House replied, "he needs me and Damon's info to

pull off a successful docking sequence. He needs to make it look like nothing is out of the ordinary."

"I thought we couldn't let him do that."

"We can't," House answered, "but if he thinks I'm willing to cooperate and play his game..."

"He might bite and agree."

House went silent once more, but Buddy could hear someone else speaking to him off-microphone, waiting to be filled in.

"That might just work," House said.

"What will?" Buddy asked, not hearing the proposed plan.

"Hang on, Bud." He heard another tone, then House spoke. "Add Cole Triplett to call."

An identical tone confirmed that Trip had been successfully added to the call. It was another feature of the new system that Buddy hadn't been aware of. "How you doing, Chief?"

"Better than most," he replied. "So, what's up?"

"Right," Trip said, "what I was explaining to the captain was that I think I know a place to make a stand against Donovan."

Buddy's eyebrows knit in thought. "You do, where?"

Trip's plan was insane!

"He won't go for that," Buddy retorted, scoffing at the notion.

"Says who?" House replied. "Seth isn't exactly the greatest of strategists, neither is anyone else on board, for that matter."

"And you're really going to meet him alone?"

"Hell no!" House laughed. "I'm not an idiot, but Seth will assume I'm being truthful when I give him a reason to believe me."

"And that is?" Buddy asked, becoming more and more hopeful by the second.

"I'll do something that he'll never expect." Buddy could almost hear House grinning on the other end. "I'm going to lie my ass off."

Buddy wasn't sure it would work, but if there was something House never did, it was lie to his people. It's one of the things that made him such a great captain.

"What do you need from me?" Buddy asked.

House's reply was serious and straight to the point. "Save as many as you can and bring them to our rendezvous point. We're going to need all hands on deck on this one."

27

For the next hour, House and the others did nothing else except search for survivors. With a plan in place, and most of the key officers still on the side of normalcy, the humans gathered as much intel on Coalesce as they could.

It was time to fight back!

Gianna went as far as setting up a private group chat that only her father could invite people to. Not even she wanted to know the password to get in. Just in case... The name of the group: ReVengeance. House thought the name was ridiculous, but everyone else loved it. They all wanted payback for those they lost.

And of course, Captain House led the uprising himself.

But not before placing another call to Donovan.

"That's right, Seth," he said, laying it on thick. "I'll surrender myself over to you if you keep your word that no one else aboard our boat gets hurt—including being added to your new...*family*."

It took a lot for House to say the last word. Donovan and the others weren't a family. If anything, they were a walking disease with several moving parts across multiple locations. The major problem with Coalesce was that they were all connected to one hive mind. If even one of them saw House's team and lived to "notify" Donovan, they'd be screwed.

The first person they came across wasn't a monster at all. It was someone House just saw only hours before. Kimberly Montez was alone this time, however, and it saddened him when she recounted what happened to her friend, Gregg Shields.

"He saved me," she said, sniffing. "One of the things grabbed me on the way to the server room. He..." her voice caught, "Gregg died protecting me."

As the ReVengeance found survivors, they took it upon themselves to escort each and every one of them below decks. Sometimes they'd have a small cluster of people to watch over, like a dirty, blood-splattered flock of sheep. House was the shepherd, along with Trip and Sam.

The three men were required to take down a handful of their own crewmen along the way too—but it was House who delivered the killing blow to each and every one of them. Gratefully, there weren't many. House only had to put three out of their miseries.

Unfortunately, one of them was Chief Navigational Officer Dominik Lucas.

On one of the lower levels, House ushered Trip and Sam up to the lone Coalesce segment, unsure of who it was. The emergency lights made it too difficult to tell. So did the torn uniform and smeared blood. Even from behind, he was easy to identify as friend or foe. His eyes strobed wildly, giving away the side he was on.

In reality, House didn't want to know who he was. House just wanted the man to stay put and not turn around. Then, he'd slide up behind him, jab the blade of his knife into the person's throat, and it'd be all she wrote.

After signaling Trip and Sam to stay back, House slowly crept up behind the unidentified sailor. Then, he silently stood, reached out, and wrapped a hand around his target's mouth. The blade was next, and like the others he killed so far, the reaction to having the parasite mortally wounded was instantaneous.

House hid inside the nearest doorway and waited for the inhuman to stop thrashing. When he did, it wasn't the captain who was the first to identify him...it was Sam.

"Dominik?" he sobbed. "No!"

House usually had a good read on people, but he had no idea that Sam and Chief Lucas were close. It saddened him immensely to lose a man of Lucas' talents and leadership. Even more, he was a good guy, and someone House had trusted.

Trip put a soft hand on the kneeling Sam and looked back toward House. The sorrow displayed on Trip's face told House all he needed to know, and it crushed him to see that Sam had lost someone he cared about.

Not knowing what to say, House kept his mouth shut and gave his XO the time he needed. He hated that Sam wouldn't be afforded the appropriate time to mourn until, well, maybe never. It certainly wouldn't be any time soon.

Donovan was expecting House in two hours. That was the deal. They'd meet alone in the launch bay. He figured Donovan would go back on his word—but so would House. Every able-bodied human crewmember was to report to the same bay for one specific purpose. They were to be a barrier against the incoming horde of Coalesce cronies.

The launch bay only had two entrances/exits. One was a floor above the bowl-shaped room, the one House had used earlier that day. The second door was directly beneath the first, and it led to one of the three elevators aboard the Endeavor. House bet that Donovan was going to use the above door which would allow him to enter unperturbed.

Plus, Gianna planned on shutting down the elevator remotely

using her tablet and genius knowhow. If Donovan really wanted to get to House, he was going to have to use the entrance of their choosing.

Once Donovan was inside, the remainder of the human crew was going to seal the entrance until he was taken down for good. Then, hopefully, Coalesce would go into a panic—or die—without their leader. House prayed it was death. This was uncharted waters for everyone aboard. No one knew exactly what to do or what would happen.

"Come on, Sam," Trip said, coaxing the XO to his feet.

Sam wiped away his tears and faced his captain. The only thing House could do was place a reassuring hand on his loyal number two's shoulder, matching Trip's earlier gesture. Trip added his own hand, once more, and the two men's strength seemed to energize Sam's spirit.

He stood tall, ready for action. House admired Sam's courage but doubted he'd display much of it in a fight. He knew of Sam's past, being a collegiate long-distance runner, and recognized that he was in incredible shape. He frequented the gym every morning. Being a runner, could he kill a man if he had to? Would his titanium-plated moral compass allow him to do so?

House could do it.

House had done it.

And he'd do it again.

The other issue with Sam being so quick on his feet is that he *knew* he was fast. Runners ran. He'd probably take off at the first sign of trouble. His station as the ship's XO kept him from ever having to put his run-first response to the test, though. No one ever crossed him...that is...unless they also wanted to cross the captain.

No, House thought. *Sam is stronger than that. He won't run.*

He berated himself for thinking poorly of Sam. If there was something he wasn't, it was weak. He was one of the youngest XO's in naval history for a reason.

Because no one else wanted the gig.

House needed to stop thinking poorly of himself too.

He hated to give himself credit for anything. Both his father and Buddy taught him to work for it and never be self-complimentary. The moment you started to do so was the moment you became an egotistical prick like Seth Donovan. The old Seth Donovan... House would give anything for the DARPA scientist to return to normal. That would be the easiest victory of his life.

Even after successfully "freeing" a handful of Donovan's people, House wasn't sure of their true capabilities as a whole—as an army.

He pictured tens-of-thousands of them rolling over a city, consuming everything, and everyone, in their paths. The death toll would be catastrophic, including those assimilated into Coalesce.

He gave Sam a few more minutes to recover. Then, the trio headed off again. Level by level, they cleared the floors the best they could. Along the way, Sam found one of the ship's pilots, Bill Johnston. As far as they knew, Sam was the only one who made it out of Command alive. When they approached Seaman Johnston, their estimation was, indeed, correct.

Sam leaped away from the injured man as he snarled and swiped at him. Johnston's legs were bent horribly, broken from a nasty fall. Broken before he was turned. He couldn't stand, but that didn't mean he wasn't a dangerous threat. Without a second thought, House stepped forward and drove his knife into Johnston's throat with two quick strikes.

They left the man to die on his own, not needing to witness another of their crewmen's demise.

* * *

After watching five of his own fall to Captain House, including Bill Johnston just now, Donovan finally emerged from the wheelhouse. He was scheduled to meet House in thirty minutes but needed to try something he'd been contemplating for some time now.

Accompanying him was a squad of a dozen Coalesce members. Until he understood more about his own potential demise, he'd protect himself better than the President of the United States did.

He stepped into the office of the Endeavor Security Detail and spotted his first and most special, Agent Jennifer Grigson. If he had known then what he knew now, he would've kept her close by his side up in Command. His connection to her was incredible for the short amount of time she was with him.

I'm sorry...

The room was empty. Donovan told the others to wait for him outside. He wanted some alone time with Grigson. The concept of being alone felt foreign to him now, though. He knew the meaning of the word but couldn't entirely remember the feeling it caused. All he did recall was hating it vehemently.

Kneeling, he stroked Grigson's pale, sunken-in cheek. Bodies didn't usually decompose this fast. Somehow Donovan knew why. It was the stress of her joining. Grigson's body was a shell of itself, a corpse that had aged tenfold in less than a day.

Unhinging his jaw, Donovan brought forth his own entity. It

snaked its way out of his mouth, exposing three feet of its six-foot length. As it came forth, he stroked it gently, like a dog owner did to his pet.

Carefully, Donovan ushered it back into Grigson's mouth and began to pump. The plasma pulsed, some of it seeping through a hole in her neck, though the majority of it entered her body. It was easy to see it do so through her nearly translucent skin.

Nothing happened.

Panicking, Donovan sent more and more of it into her body, mentally willing her to wake.

I give you life.

Still nothing.

He forced as much of the plasma from his body as he could. His vision blurred and darkened. It was the closest to death he'd ever felt. His breath caught, and his heart stopped—but he kept going.

Then, only slightly, Grigson's body twitched.

Donovan fell away, quickly started to feel like himself again. His hands shook and looked withered and old. His luminescent blood dimmed some too.

Grigson's eyes flickered, and her ashen skin flushed with color. She still looked like death, but his attempt at bringing the dead back to life... It succeeded. Slowly, she picked herself off the floor and stood as upright as possible. Hunched and ghoulish, Grigson turned and faced him with a blank, lost expression. In passing, she didn't remember him.

So, Donovan did the only thing he could think of. He closed his eyes and searched his incredibly deep memory bank, picking out everything he had on her. He focused on their relationship the most but also her training as a soldier and an ESD agent. Other, more personal, things like her home life and family before they became connected, he left out. The only family she'd know from now on was Coalesce.

He opened his eyes and was pleased to find Grigson's gaunt face attempting to smile. Only half of it succeeded. Excited, he ordered those not stationed outside his door to abandon their hunt for the captain, instead, focusing on something even more prominent. He'd take care of House himself.

The rest of Coalesce was shouldered with the responsibility of continuing the construction of his army. Everyone that had died, whether at the hands of a failed joining, or not, would get another chance at being a part of something better.

Spinning on a heel, Donovan laughed aloud. Resurrecting the dead added another dimension to his already out-of-control psychosis. He truly believed himself to be, without a shadow of a doubt, a god.

"We are better together." He grinned. "I am better."

Grigson shambled along behind him as he sought out his next rejoining. The only other sailor he truly desired to have back in the fold was the largest of them all. With Nova's life restored, Donovan knew he'd be successful in overtaking the remainder of the Endeavor's crew. Just seeing the behemoth alive again, and in the same ghastly physical state as Grigson, would be even more terrifying than before.

Chief Lucas was next, followed closely by Dr. Bowen. He'd also try to bring back Damon Becker if they could even find the man or his body. Donovan would target those closest to House's people first. Like he did to Buddy, through Frohm, Donovan wanted to tear down the survivor's lingering emotional barricades.

28

"How many?" House asked, exhausted.

He, Trip, and Sam backtracked up and down the stairs and back and forth from bow to stern more times than he could count. With every sailor found and returned to the launch bay, Gianna called out the number to everyone in their group chat.

"Nineteen," she replied after their last time out. "We have nineteen survivors, including ourselves."

Out of a possible eighty, House thought, shaking his head. He knew deep down that he and the others had done the same math. If they had decided to just sit tight in the server room and not go out looking for anyone, their numbers would've stayed stagnant at four.

But it also meant that three-quarters of the crew either turned into monsters or outright died at the hands of those same monsters.

Sixty-one souls lost in a matter of hours... The death toll was mindboggling. *Sixty. One.*

A tear slowly made its way down House's right cheek. It was the first time he displayed this level of emotion in some time, especially since taking the helm as the Endeavor's captain. Luckily, there wasn't anyone within earshot of him—no one close enough to see it. He currently stood alone by the launch pool, staring intensely at the surface-lit Antarctic waters. Everyone else was either resting or getting ready. Their story's climax was about to come.

Hopefully, it'll end better than 'Where the Red Fern Grows,' House thought, recalling the tearjerker. He read it back in school, and both hated it and loved it. The demise of both Big Dan and Little Ann hit him hard.

Typically, the pool was surrounded by all kinds of machinery and other equipment. It had all been moved out of the way while he was gone. Gianna supervised the "redesign," lining most of it up near the center of the room instead. The hope was for House to lead Donovan into the trap set back at the launch pool.

"Get him off our boat by any means necessary," he said earlier, eyeing his daughter. "By any means necessary..." He let the finality of his words linger before turning and heading for the shimmering circle in the floor.

If this was to go the way he wanted, Donovan needed to be

restrained and forced underwater by someone or something.

Trip suggested tranquilizing Donovan with the same sedative the team used on the octopus. Then, they'd toss him inside the ADS and sink it. While, in a way, it was doable to a normal human being, their enemy wouldn't be manhandled so easily. No one had seen Donovan in a fight since he transformed into the creature he was now. House doubted he was as feeble as he was before. No, he'd be even more ferocious than his underlings.

And that scares the hell out of me.

House wasn't sure if it was the frigid temperature of the bay or the thought of facing Donovan one on one that made him shiver. He'd foregone adorning a coat before entering the space. So far, since taking a dip with Nova, all he did was sweat. Ducking and dodging Coalesce was tough work. Feeling the brisk air on his skin felt good, reinvigorating him some. It also reminded House of why he was initially out on Antarctica's sea.

It reminded him that he was still alive and kicking too.

The dead don't feel.

He was an explorer, not a battle-hardened soldier. Obviously, House could hold his own in a brawl, but that's not what he wanted to do and it wasn't who he was. He loved the ocean because of its endless possibilities, it's infinite escapes and its multitude of wonders.

Regrettably, it wasn't this planet's marvels that caused the mess they were in. It was another world that was at fault. Donovan said as much before House inevitably hung up on him.

"So, you're a god now?"

Donovan laughed. "You tell me? Who decides who lives and who dies? Who came from above, only to unselfishly descend and unite his people? Who holds the power of creation in the palm of their hand? Who—"

"Call ended," the automated voice said. House had nearly broken his WiMP's screen when he jammed his finger down on the ultrasensitive display.

Who came from above? House thought. Above, in this context, meant Heaven. *Space? Maybe...*

The organisms had to come from somewhere. All over the world, new creatures, big and small, were being discovered. House refused to believe that a threat like this was Earth-made. He believed everything Donovan told him so far—but he didn't buy the deity thing. Why would the man lie about any of it? It didn't matter whether Donovan was telling the truth or not. Plus, House kind of figured Donovan loved talking about his new self. He wasn't exactly a creative person either. There was no way he made everything up just to mess with House.

Movement to House's left alerted him to someone's presence. He didn't speak to the visitor, however. After what they'd been through, he honestly had nothing else to say to his daughter.

"The camera down the hall is up and running," she said, speaking first. "It wasn't easy, but we'll be able to see Seth coming a mile away."

House glanced at her, happy that she was still with him. Her eyes were also transfixed on the water beneath their feet. He could tell she was getting lost in it, like the effect the glow of a flickering fireplace had on a person. Something about shimmering water could do that to House—Gianna too, apparently. It made the corner of his mouth rise slightly.

She must've noticed the attention. "What's that look for?" she asked, left eyebrow high.

He shrugged. "Nothing. I'm just happy you're okay."

Gianna snorted out a laugh. "Don't get too cheery, yet. We aren't out of the woods by a long shot."

His smirk grew to a broad, beaming smile. He was proud of the woman his little girl has grown into. But it was time to get down to business. Narrowing his eyes, House turned away from the pool and faced her, placing a firm hand on her jacketed shoulder. The pleasantries they were exchanging were wonderful. He wished they could last all night long.

"Look, G... If anything happens to me, I—"

"Don't!" she growled, stepping away from him. "Don't you start with that shit." She hurriedly stepped back up to him and slid into his arms. "I'm not getting off of this boat without you."

Releasing her father, she tried to step around him, but House grabbed her arm and pulled her in. Only this time, he didn't hug her.

"If anything happens to me, I need you to look after everyone. They'll be in some serious need of leadership, and I need you to step up and take my place."

Teary-eyed, she laughed. "You're kidding me, right?" She motioned at the room. "There are plenty of better candidates than me—Sam for one. Buddy too."

"No." House shook his head. "It has to be you."

"Why?"

"Because..." he said, crying now, "if you're leading them, then that means you're safe. It means you've survived."

Gianna started to cry too. "If I'm leading the crew, then it means you're dead, and you won't know if I'm alive or not."

House smiled softly. "I'll know." He took a deep breath. "I'll know..."

"How—how will you know?" Gianna shouted, her voice echoing.

Not wanting to get into a theological debate, House stepped away and got back to his captain duties. "Are we ready?" he asked, yelling the question as loud as he could. He got a mixture of "yes, sirs" and "aye-ayes" in return and went and checked on everyone else that was involved.

Five of the nineteen survivors they'd found were unfit for battle, suffering a variety of debilitating injuries—both physically and mentally. The stuff they had all seen was enough to freak anyone out. No one aboard this boat had signed up for open conflict, war or otherwise. It was a research vessel, and it was staffed accordingly.

That left him with only fourteen able-bodied men and women. Trip volunteered to look after the wounded. House quickly shot the proposal down, though.

"No, I need you on the frontlines with me." He lowered his voice. "Look... I trust you, Trip. I need people I can trust to watch my back if anything bad happens."

"Like what?"

House unclipped the sheath from his hip and handed it and the combat knife to Trip. The message was loud and clear. If House became one of the monsters, Trip was ordered to put him down.

"I will not be one of them," House said, ending the discussion.

That left him with the fire axe, which Trip handed over with a curt nod. Gianna still had the gun holstered on her belt, but was, so far, unwilling to draw it since she shot Nova in the head.

Per Gianna's instructions, Sam had disabled both entrances' keypads. No one would be entering or leaving via the upstairs hatch or the elevator without Gianna's assistance. House's eyes flicked toward the pool again. Once Donovan was inside, the master of Coalesce wouldn't be leaving in any conventional method.

*　　*　　*

The trauma Donovan sustained while resurrecting Grigson forced his body into another evolutionary modification. When he stepped out of the ESD office, four of the ten joined accompanying him detonated in a quartet of fiery blue explosions. For his part, Donovan collapsed and blacked out.

In his vulnerable, motionless state, he heard the cries of everyone he amalgamated with. Each of his victims screamed, echoing with both pain and fear, and all of them were ricocheting around inside his head like a game of Pong on fast-forward.

"Help!" Dr. Bowen shrieked. "Please, God, help me!"

"What..." Chief Lucas asked, cowering in the corner of a room that didn't exist, "What's going on? Sam, are you there?"

"Hello?" Grigson asked, her voice resonating as if she was standing at the bottom of a deep, rocky chasm. "Is there anyone there?"

"Jennifer?" Donovan asked.

"Who's there?" she replied, shrinking away from his nonmaterial presence.

"It's Seth," he explained. "Don't you remember me—remember us?

"Seth?" she asked. "There is no 'us' you creep! What have you done to me? Why can't I feel my body? Why won't I wake up from this terrible nightmare?"

Grigson's lack of understanding confused Donovan. He'd spoken with her several times about his goals, and she'd been nothing but supportive. She wanted the same as him. She wanted knowledge and partnership. She didn't want to be alone.

"I saved you, Jennifer," he said, keeping his voice calm.

"Saved me?" she looked appalled. "Saved me from what?"

"From life," Donovan replied. "You are with me now. You are better, Jennifer. You are free."

Her hands went to her mouth and tears flowed. "You... No... You killed me? But—but why am I here? Why is it so dark and cold? Why!"

Donovan was disturbed by this revelation. Were the voices in his head still alive or was it just his overstimulated mind playing tricks on him while he recovered, attempting to decipher what was real and what was, as Grigson put it, a nightmare?

Back outside the ESD office, Grigson's shell stepped up behind Donovan's inert body and looked down at him, giving Donovan a view of his physical form's current self. In response to the episode, he unknowingly tucked himself into a ball. There, he shook uncontrollably with his knees tucked into his chest. Whatever was happening to him, it was so painful that it sent him into a comatose state.

He could also see the results of what had happened to the four joined that were involved in the explosion. They were all missing their heads. Each one of them was missing their heads. Their necks, and the entity within them, were obliterated. Witnessing the discharge himself, Donovan compared it to an energy surge. Their remains were a horrible sight to behold. His severe reaction triggered something within them—something incredibly violent. As the center of Coalesce, it saddened him, but as a scientist, it intrigued him.

They're weapons? he thought, reaching out to the others.

He was stunned to discover that five more shared the fate of the four here. One painted the chart table up in Navigation with a cobalt smear. Another, the wall just outside the launch bay, where he was set to meet, and overrun, Captain House. Yet, another was one of two pilots up in Command. She'd only recently replaced Bill Johnston.

Faster, he told the remaining pilot. *Go faster!*

Instantaneously, the man "floored" the Endeavor, no doubt setting off some sort of alarm at McMurdo. The station would no doubt be tracking the ship's every move. Their sudden change in velocity wouldn't go unnoticed.

No matter. Plans change all the time. Now, he hoped they could reach McMurdo quicker than the station could be ready to receive them. Coalesce had shrunk significantly. The smaller force would have to storm the base before anyone knew what hit them.

Not that he was going to tell House that.

Regardless, nine more of his brethren were dead in the blink of an eye. Taking his mind off the carnage, Donovan turned Grigson's attention back to his physical form and she—he—studied his newest changes.

Slowly, and with every thump of his still-beating heart, Donovan's skin became more translucent until he could barely detect his own flesh. It was exactly how a vast populace of deep-sea wildlife looked. His innards were easy to spot. Everything was blue too—organs, muscles, tendons—and they pulsed with energy, all in different shades and rhythms. It was quite beautiful.

"Seth!"

He woke and shot straight to his feet. Not Coalesce, but the minds inside his own head shouted his name. It was enough of a jolt to startle him awake. All of them were full of vengeance.

Catching his breath, he fell into a nearby wall, eyes wide and in shock. The six survivors collectively gazed at him with blank, unmoving expressions. He was out of sorts, which meant that they were too.

"I'm..." he said, putting a hand to his forehead, "I'm fine."

"We are fine," they replied, standing at attention.

"Yes," he said, reaffirming himself, staggering off, "we are fine."

He didn't believe his own words. He was anything but fine. Even now, back in his body, he could still hear the cries of everyone that had been assimilated into Coalesce. No matter how hard he tried to quiet them, it didn't work.

And it drove him mad.

29

"Dad!" Gianna shouted, staring down at her iPad.

An explosion of some kind just erupted outside the launch bay door. She quickly dove into her pack and dug out her tablet to check it out. Waking it, she rolled back the footage and gasped.

The only image the iPad currently displayed was that of the newly installed camera down the hall from the second-floor entrance. So far, no one had tried to enter, but what she saw still troubled her. A dozen or so of Donovan's drones had sauntered by over the last forty minutes. Each of them seemed as *ordinary* as the next, except for a trio of them. They displayed some odd changes—even for anyone associated with Coalesce.

She turned the device so her father could see. Three of the joined jolted as if they were hit with a bolt of lightning. One of them was blown entirely off her feet with a blast of electric blue light. None of House's people knew what to expect from Coalesce in the first place, but this...

"That can't be good," House said, stroking his chin in concern.

She put the tablet to sleep after two more of them passed by and dropped, hit with the same strange... House didn't know what to call it. One didn't get up again. His demise looked horrible from behind the camera's lenses. In person? No thanks. The jolt was so powerful that it took the sailor's head right off his shoulders.

Gianna swallowed hard, disturbed.

"We could wait it out?" she asked, looking up at her father. "Maybe they'll all blow themselves up before we get to McMurdo."

House shook his head. "We can't take the chance." He lifted his WiMP, checked the time, and sighed. "Only thirty minutes till we get to port after our recent speed change."

Time stood still while waiting for Donovan to show himself. Everyone's nerves were cooked. Playing the waiting game had made everyone edgier than ever, twitchy, irritable even.

What have you been up to, Seth? House thought.

"Sebastian," Buddy said from across the room, "we're ready to roll."

"Right," House muttered to himself, "let's see what's been taking him so long."

He took one last look around the bay and then placed the call. Six rings later, no answer. Either Donovan had backed out of their deal, or he was having trouble with his communicator. After what they had just witnessed on Gianna's tablet, House was beginning to think that there was another option.

Maybe Donovan couldn't accept the call. Something could've gone wrong. Coalesce was connected directly to him, so it made sense that if they were *malfunctioning*, it would start with him and trickle down to the others.

Needing some advice, House relayed what he and Gianna saw to Buddy. Of course, Buddy said the exact opposite of what Gianna had suggested.

"Let's go after him." Both Houses rolled their eyes, infuriating the older man. "Well then," he snarled, "don't ask for my input if you don't wanna hear what I got to say!"

Buddy stormed off, leaving House and Gianna alone once more. Gripping his axe, House actually thought about doing what he suggested and take Donovan out while he was weak. It might be the only chance they had.

No, House thought, going with his gut. *Stick to the plan.*

He tried to contact Donovan twice more before finally giving up. With nothing else to do and nothing else to go on, House tasked Gianna and Sam with continuing to track the Endeavor's path while also trying to delay them any way they could. If they got close enough to McMurdo without hearing from Donovan, they'd have no choice but to take the fight to him.

Fifteen more minutes. Then, we go to war.

It seemed that Donovan was doing the exact same thing House was attempting to do. Apparently, drawing the enemy out of hiding wasn't that unique of an idea. Still, House was betting on Donovan not being himself anymore. At least, that's what he was hoping.

That didn't mean he wasn't just as dangerous. It might make him even more dangerous than before—more volatile and unpredictable. But as the minutes ticked away, House grew incredibly nervous.

"Now or never, Dad," Gianna said, holding out her tablet.

House took it and swiped through a series of windows. They all told the same story in a variety of ways. The storm had died down just as McMurdo said it would. As it did, the Endeavor turned and was moved into position, accelerating further.

"Doesn't make sense, though," Sam said, taking the offered tablet. "He can't initiate a successful docking sequence without the captain and Becker's codes."

"He doesn't need to," House said. "All he has to do is run the ship aground and storm the station."

"Run it aground?" Buddy snorted. "There is no ground! It's all ice out here!"

House rubbed his face. "You know what I mean, Bud... It'll give him away, but it won't stop—" He stopped mid-rub and swung his attention back to Gianna. "The intercoms!"

"What about 'em?" Buddy asked.

"Can you patch me through?"

Gianna shrugged. "Probably, but we've never tried." She tapped her ear. "Not with these things in use. That tech is ancient."

Trip appeared beside her, yawning. "What'd I miss?"

House had ordered him to lie down for a few minutes. The rest seemed to have freshened the young man up a bit.

No one backfilled Trip with an explanation. Instead, they continued at warp speed with what House wanted done.

"Get me on air ASAP. I need to get ahold of Seth now!"

"What are you gonna say to the loon?" Buddy asked, crossing his arms.

"Anything—everything!" House replied. "I need to irritate him as much as I can. We need him here where we can contain him."

Gianna looked worried.

"What?" House asked, seeing it plain as day.

"Sorry, Dad, but you aren't exactly the antagonizer of the group." She pointed at Buddy. "But he is."

Buddy smiled wide and cracked his knuckles. "Let me at 'em. I'll make his great-granny wince."

With no better plan, House agreed to have Buddy make the call instead of him. If he was honest, he was happy someone else was doing it. He was exhausted and wanted nothing better than to curl up on his couch back home in Georgia and fall asleep watching a movie or reading a book.

"Hey, Shannon, give me a hand, will ya?"

The analyst that had accompanied Buddy here waved back to Gianna, quickly finished her conversation with another crewman, and hustled over. Even before she stopped, House's daughter was already shouting out instructions. Shannon pulled out her own tablet and swiftly began typing away. It pleased him to see her happy and in her wheelhouse.

Wheelhouse.

The word saddened him. House had lost his boat, which to him was like losing his identity. The only people that knew "Sebastian" were Gianna and Buddy. One was family, the other was as close as it got without actually being a part of it. After them, he was just "Captain House" to everyone else. Without the Endeavor, he was nothing more than Sebastian from Albany, Georgia.

He squeezed his fists hard. *Stop selling yourself short.*

House glanced over his shoulder. Gianna, Buddy, and Shannon were conversing quietly, no doubt going over what they'd do next. The first two of the trio saw him as more than that, which was all House needed...Trip too, who was called over to help. He liked the guy. He was a good soul, and he obviously cared for Gianna immensely.

* * *

With a hodgepodge of equipment set up on a large metal crate near the elevator entrance, Buddy waited impatiently to get started. He had a lot to say to Donovan and couldn't wait to get it off his chest. He'd seen some awful things in his long life on Earth, but everything that had transpired in the last few hours topped it all.

He was surrounded by everyone that could walk. They were all in this together, but Buddy knew that the people gathered were more curious with what he was going to say than anything else. It honestly felt great to have the full support of the human crew, ReVengeance. Very little of what he did aboard the Endeavor was ever given this much attention.

Too old to shrink under their eyes, Buddy was signaled to place the call to Donovan. The system, however, was reprogrammed and the comms system connected to the overhead intercom. It ran through the entire ship, never used to this day. No one would be able to hide from his future berating.

Gianna nodded, telling him he was live.

It's go time, he thought, surprised at where his mind took him first. It wasn't down a road of unbridled rage. Buddy felt compassion for a man that had wandered down a dark path, whether on purpose or not. He wasn't an idiot. Buddy knew that Donovan was being influenced by an otherworldly evil.

* * *

"Seth Donovan!" a voice blared over the ship's loudspeakers. The speaker's tone was low and had a southern drawl baked into it. Its owner was someone Donovan loathed almost as much as House.

"Chief Engineer Buddy Malone here," the speaker said, confirming his identity. "I'm not sure what's happened to you, but I understand the pickle you find yourself in. You've made some terrible choices of late. I can't forgive you for that—no one can, nor should they. It..." his voice caught, "it's just not right."

Oh, please, Donovan thought. The last thing he needed was to receive a speech like this from Buddy, of all people. The man was rude and short with everyone he came across.

Yet, Donovan was forced to sit through the rhetoric. He couldn't disable the speaker system or even interrupt the man.

"You've taken the lives of dozens of good people, Seth. I know you think what you're doin' is some great achievement of science, but in reality, it's a wicked, wicked deed. I could never comprehend acting out such atrocities."

"Quiet!" Donovan shouted, making all of Coalesce slink back in fear. "Shut your fucking mouth, Malone!"

Halfway back up to the bridge, Donovan turned and bolted back the way he'd come, leaping from landing to landing, skipping the stairs between them entirely. He knew his rage was getting the best of him, but he didn't care. Now, he had one single focus, shutting Buddy up for good.

No, Seth, a voice said from within. *Don't do this.*

He staggered. The voice was Dr. Bowen's, and she was trying desperately to dilute his mania. Donovan had never felt so unhinged before. The power he gained was incredible, but his brain was having trouble processing it—controlling it.

Please, stop, Grigson begged.

"Quiet!" he roared, hands to his head. "Everyone be quiet!"

Now it wasn't just Bowen and Grigson trying to calm him down, it was everyone. He pleaded for them to stop. The noise itself was excruciatingly painful—like his head was about to explode.

If he couldn't mute the voices in his head, then Donovan would do the next best thing. He'd personally silence the world and kill every single last one of them. All of them. Assimilating the people of Earth meant nothing if he couldn't enjoy the fruits of his conquest. Knowledge meant very little to a broken mind.

He'd still conquer the world. Only, now, he'd do so, so he could be alone, to find peace, to rid himself of the nuisances that mankind carried with it.

Silence the world, Donovan thought, drooling a mixture of blue plasma and saliva down his chin and chest. As he charged forward, he tore away the rest of his clothing and marveled at what he'd become. He really was a monster from the deep.

And he loved it.

Discombobulated, he tripped and fell to his hands and knees. Breathing hard, he snapped his flashing eyes up and visualized his targets. When he spoke next, it sounded as if every voice in his head was conversing at once.

"We are not Coalesce... *I* am! And I will silence the world!" He sneered. "Starting with Buddy Malone and Sebastian House."

30

Eventually, Buddy's heartfelt speech turned into what everyone initially expected. House's long-dead grandmother had, no doubt, rolled over in her grave—twice! Still, even as nasty as his friend got while on the air, House couldn't really disagree with anything he said.

Once Buddy started talking about Donovan willingly getting anally probed with a telephone pole all in the name of science...and personal curiosity...that's when House did his best to tune the man out. Gianna and Shannon let Buddy rant as long as he could before he needed a break. Apparently, swearing while making horrible space-sex innuendo took a lot out of the old man.

All House could do was chuckle to himself.

"Bud has a way with words, huh?" Gianna asked, collapsing on the floor next to him.

The Houses sat together, on the opposite side of the launch pool. They reclined against one another next to Trip's ADS suit, away from any, and all, commotion. In her hand was her trusty tablet, and on its screen, where it had been since setting it up just outside the bay door, was an image of the empty hallway.

"Anything?" he asked, plainly seeing nothing but a lifeless corridor.

"No," she replied, "and we're scheduled to make landfall in ten minutes." She laid her head on his shoulder. "What are we going to do, Dad?"

"I'm not sure, baby, but—"

"Hang on, Dad," she sat bolt upright. "I think we've got... Oh, shit!"

House glanced down at the tablet long enough to see a figure come barreling towards the camera, passing beneath it in a strobing blur. Then, the door was impacted with the force of a small bomb. The door lock snapped, and it swung open, impacting the nearest, unsuspecting sailor. He was thrown off his feet and rolled to a stop where he didn't get up.

"Scatter!" House shouted, jumping to his feet and moving to intercept the bat-shit crazy scientist.

The feat of strength that Donovan just displayed was more than even Nova showed during his and House's skirmish. Whatever Donovan was now, he'd be even more of a challenge than the monstrous mechanic.

"Get that door shut!" Buddy shouted, helping three others. It protested with cries of screeching metal, but at least it was still operational.

And so was Donovan.

House slid to a stop in front of the pool, axe in hand, absolutely stunned at what he was seeing. Even with the chilling water at his back, he broke out in a sweat. Donovan ceased to be human long ago, but what he was now, well, House wasn't sure what to call him.

"Oh, my God, Seth," House said. "What have you become?"

On his stomach, Donovan craned his head up at an ungodly angle to make eye contact with him. Then, one by one, the broken vertebrae in his neck, back, and limbs mended together and popped back into place.

All while Donovan smiled at him.

"What..." he replied, in between cracks, "have I become?" He cackled uncontrollably and slowly climbed to his feet. "I'll tell you, Captain..." His naked body flashed and pulsed, precisely as the octopus had.

From here, House could see the parasite beneath his translucent skin. It was in Donovan's chest and abdomen, tearing apart his organs and flexing his sternum and ribs as it moved. The only thing beating in Donovan's chest now was the creature's heart, not the heart of the DARPA scientist.

Seth Donovan was dead.

"I," he rasped, his voice harmonizing with dozens of others, "am Coalesce."

"*You* are Coalesce?" House asked. "What about the others?"

"Shut up!" Donovan shouted, pounding on the side of his head. "I am in control, not you!" His eyes found House's. "I'm in control." He stepped toward House and twitched, his head turning slightly and his eyes squinting. Donovan was mumbling to himself too.

What the hell?

House wasn't a medical expert, but he knew Donovan was displaying a form of schizophrenia. He was talking to himself...or maybe he was talking to someone else?

Hmmm, House thought, raising his axe, *Maybe I can use that against him?*

"Who you talking to, Seth?"

"I am Coalesce!"

Donovan launched himself at House and unfurled the parasite within. It too had evolved into something else. The mouth opened and shut like an octopus, beak and all. It flailed around like an out-of-control firehouse, and just when House was about to catch it midair with the blade of his axe, it recoiled back into Donovan's body and the two men collided with one another.

Seeing the impact coming, House braced himself and met Donovan with his shoulder. He took Donovan off his feet but felt like he dislocated the joint. The former scientist was dense and powerful and acted with no fear of death—just like the others.

"Quiet!" Donovan yelled, stumbling when he tried to get back to his feet. His hands went back to his head.

"Who are you talking to, Seth?" House asked again, antagonizing his foe to the best of his ability. He needed Donovan to continue to act irrationally and violently.

Snickering, Donovan stood. "Me?" he laughed. "Oh, I'm talking to a couple of friends of yours."

House's bravado waned.

Donovan shivered but looked more in control. "Say hello to Lisa Bowen."

Donovan's face instantaneously morphed from one of rage to one of fear. It was the best acting job House had ever seen, except he didn't think the man was actually acting.

"Sebastian?"

House's shoulders fell. It even sounded like her.

"Lisa?"

Donovan laughed, his body pulsing with every loud guffaw.

Boom.

His attention turned to the door long enough for Donovan to do the same. Trip, Sam, Buddy, and Shannon had finally gotten it shut before something else got inside. The lock was decimated and wouldn't be getting fixed any time soon. For now, it would have to be held closed from their side.

Donovan turned toward them.

"Seth, no!" House yelled, stopping any advance.

"What will you do, Sebastian?" He peered over his shoulder and looked back at House. "What will you do?"

Donovan bolted straight for Buddy, letting loose the entity as he ran. House was too slow to catch the much faster man, but luckily for him, and Buddy, someone else cut Donovan off. If not, House's oldest and dearest friend wouldn't have stood a chance.

Trip unsheathed his knife and slashed at the whipping creature. Frozen into place, Buddy did the same and pulled out a blade of his own. The two men held it off until Sam and Shannon could get away—and until House could jump him from behind.

The captain buried the head of his axe into Donovan's back, aiming for his spine directly between his shoulder blades. Lodged deep, he was horrified to watch the flesh around the wound bubble and crust. Then, it began to heal and forcibly eject the axe, pushing the handle along with his hands away too.

Seconds later, it popped free with a horrible slurp. If House didn't know any better, he would've thought he'd missed with the lack of any kind of injury. There wasn't even a scar.

He backed away, unsure of what to do next. If he couldn't injure Coalesce—Donovan—then what could he do?

His eyes flicked toward Buddy.

Be Buddy...

"What did they say?" House asked, backing away. "What did all those good people say to you?"

Donovan snarled and twitched. He was both annoyed and bothered by the question. Whatever was going on inside his head, it was affecting him in this world as well.

As he got Donovan's attention back on him, Trip and Buddy slid away. And as they slipped away from the fight, the door above them was walloped from the other side. Four more of House's people scampered up the stairs to help the four that were already holding it closed. From his lower vantage point, the only thing House saw on the other side of the slightly ajar door was a wall of pulsating blue light.

Donovan had predictively gone against his word.

So did I...

"Lights!" he called out, happy when twin beams appeared on Donovan's face. Back to the pool, House was unaffected. The incredibly brilliant illumination should help hold back Donovan until House could think of something else.

"Containers!"

The storage crates to his and Donovan's left and right came rolling in. Usually, they'd be locked down or tethered to the walls. But not now. Now, they were currently being used as battering rams against a foe that wouldn't go down. Each one was shoved into the scientist with enough force to take a man, Nova-sized or not, off his feet.

Donovan did little else besides wobble and drool and seethe with rage.

Then, the man turned on the crew, bashing one of the containers away with an incredibly strong backhand.

"Seth!" House shouted. "You want this?"

Donovan faced him and smiled. House was holding up his and

Becker's keycards. Gratefully, the gesture took Donovan's attention off the people around them. Unfortunately, he zeroed in on House and House alone.

"Mine!" Donovan cried, leaping across the space with little difficulty. It was an impressive display of strength and agility, but it was also an easy maneuver to dodge, and House did it with no trouble at all.

Side-stepping the landing enemy, House swung the axe as hard as he could. Like before, the blade buried itself deep into Donovan's soft tissue, this time catching him in the left side just beneath his ribs.

House was swiftly tossed aside, sliding fifteen feet until he was merely inches away from the pool's edge. Being so close to the frigid water, House could feel the temperature nipping at his exposed flesh. He could also feel the warmth of his own blood as it ran down the right side of his face. Still on his hands and knees, House draped the two lanyards over his head where they settled around his neck.

Donovan lifted his bloodied hand and sniffed it. His eyes flickered excitedly, and he did the last thing House wanted to see. The parasite shot out and wiped itself through his blood. Then, it retracted back into Donovan's mouth, and the man smiled, pleased with House's *flavor*.

With nowhere to go but forward or into the freezing water, House stood his ground. Holding the axe like a baseball bat, he squeezed the handle hard and waited for Donovan to make his move. But he didn't... Instead, he grabbed his head and started shouting for the voices to stop talking.

The light show that accompanied the agony was brilliant in multiple ways. It bathed the launch bay in a multitude of shades of blue, but it was also so bright that House couldn't make direct eye contact with him.

"Brace for impact!" Gianna shouted from somewhere behind him.

The ground beneath House's feet shook violently, and he was thrown back toward the front of the room. Right into Donovan's waiting arms.

31

McMurdo Station was just hit by a ship. Technically, it wasn't the station itself that was hit, but its docking system that was destroyed, mangled beyond repair.

Commander Gavin Kirk stood over his radar technicians like a hawk, eyeing the screen that he personally sat behind a decade ago. At first, he hated his post, but after paying his dues, he moved up the ladder quickly, eventually accepting overseeing duties.

He'd seen everything Antarctica had to offer...until now.

The Endeavor had run aground, decimating their docks and wedging itself in tight. The bow was tilted slightly, but the ship was in no danger, from what he could tell, of capsizing.

"What the hell is going on?" he shouted, getting his people moving faster.

"I'm not sure, sir," Virgil Davidson replied, typing as fast as he could. "We still can't reach anyone on board."

Turning, Kirk stomped toward the door, grabbing his heavy jacket from a hook on the wall. Never in his time stationed at McMurdo had there been such a debacle. He'd no doubt get a talking to by someone back in the states.

"What are you gonna do, sir?" Davidson asked.

Kirk growled. "I'm going to tear House and Donovan a new one."

"Uh, sir...?"

Kirk was in no mood for any more questions. "What!"

"There are people out there."

Can't be, he thought. There was no way to disembark this quickly in the current setting and conditions—no way!

Kirk voiced as much. "Davidson, there can't—"

Yet, there they were. Members of the Endeavor's crew were leaping from the top deck, dropping five-plus stories to the ground, and walking away like it was nothing more than sliding out of an armchair.

Kirk rushed for the door, snagging his binoculars as he did. Shutting the hatch, he moved to the secondary entrance, a door designed to keep the interior one from freezing over and then pushed through it as well.

The Antarctic chill stung his face immensely like it always did. It didn't matter how long you were on Antarctica. There were certain things you never "got used to."

Having a direct line of sight to the Endeavor, Kirk put his binoculars up to his eyes and stumbled back at what he saw. The people coming toward him had little to no clothes on...and their bodies were illuminated in a bizarre blue light.

Radiation? he thought, holding a walkie-talkie up to his mouth.

"Davidson," he said, holding his binoculars in place with his other hand, "We, uh, have a situation..."

*　　*　　*

"Dad, no!"

House paid no attention to his daughter's cries. He was busy keeping Donovan's parasite at bay with the handle of his axe. It was sheer luck that the creature retracted back into its host when the ship stopped abruptly. Landing atop the scientist, House jammed the handle into Donovan's mouth, blocking the entity from emerging point-blank.

"What...are they saying?" House asked, grunting, putting all his weight into the axe. "Tell me!"

The second set of doors, those leading to the elevator, boomed. Something massive hit them from the other side. Then, it happened again.

"Barricade the doors!" Buddy shouted.

Sailors began piling up whatever equipment they could find, even rolling over a few of the huge containers they initially used to build the center aisle that House and Donovan were in now.

Donovan's naked, translucent body strobed chaotically, and he thrashed beneath House's thicker frame. Even if he wanted to tell him what the voices were saying, Donovan wouldn't have been able to utter a single understandable word. House was trying to keep him off-center mentally.

It worked.

Donovan hissed like a snake, spraying goo all over House's hands, arms, neck, and chest. The captain reflexively lifted his face up and away from the incoming splurt. Gagging at the smell, he held on and shouted for assistance as the elevator doors were hit once more.

"Help!"

"Comin'!" Buddy replied, hurrying over.

From when House looked up at the hobbling Buddy, to when he glanced back down into the menacing eyes of Donovan, he knew something dreadful was about to take place.

The fortified elevator doors burst open, throwing all kinds of equipment into the air. Out stomped the very-dead-looking, yet very-much-reanimated, George Novacek. His mutilated skull looked horrifying and his exposed brain pulsed in time with his eyes. He must've climbed down the empty shaft, traversed the short hall to the lower level doors, and then bashed his way through.

No...

A large plastic case hit Buddy in the back of the head, dropping him halfway in between House and Nova. He wanted nothing more than to get to his feet and aid his dear friend, but he couldn't let Donovan get up, nor could House afford to allow the man to set the creature loose within such close proximity to his face.

Buddy went down, but he never lost consciousness. His hand went to the back of his head and came away bloodied. Unarmed and woozy, the engineer staggered to his feet and beseeched his assistant to halt his rampage.

"George, listen to me," Buddy said. "This isn't you. You're better than this."

Nova stopped within a foot of his mentor. He looked like the Incredible Hulk next to Bruce Banner. The two men were incredibly different in stature but somehow got along exceptionally well with one another.

House was so transfixed on the scene taking place before him, that he neglected to notice that it was Donovan controlling Nova, not the bigger man thinking for himself. Nova reached his left hand out—the only hand he had—and gently placed it on Buddy's left shoulder. His right arm, below the elbow, was still missing. Then, his hand went to Buddy's face, and he stroked it like only someone close to the other would do.

What happened next shattered House's soul.

Nova opened his extra-large hand and closed it around Buddy's slight neck.

"George, wait..." Buddy croaked, clawing at Nova's hand.

Nova crushed Buddy's neck like it was a soda can being run over by a dump truck. All House could do in response was scream in anguish as his friend's lifeless body was nonchalantly tossed to the floor.

Donovan laughed.

Filled with rage, House jumped to his feet, raised the axe above his head—quickly getting kicked in the chest. He sailed five feet through the air and landed hard, rolling to a stop ten feet from the launch pool. With tears streaking down his face, House could barely contain himself, uncaring that he was openly weeping in front of everyone.

Nova, for his part, did nothing else except stand and watch. Then again, Donovan was in complete control of the situation and had since gotten to his feet. He looked very smug and as cocky as ever. He knew there was nothing on the Endeavor that could stop him.

House hoped there was but was shit out of ideas.

His eyes found Buddy's peaceful face, and he broke out in heartfelt sobs again. There, inside the Endeavor's launch bay, Sebastian House mourned for his murdered friend. The fact that it happened at the hands of a zombified Nova infuriated him beyond anything he ever felt before. House had never felt such anger in his life.

Not even when his wife was killed by that drunk driver. House was taught forgiveness at an early age, understanding that bad things happened to good people all the time. Karen's death wasn't anything he'd ever forget, but the twenty-two-year-old *kid* that was responsible was given his sentence and would, inevitably, pay his dues. House came to learn some months later that it was the driver's first ticketed incident on the road in his young life.

House wasn't in the mood for forgiveness.

He wanted revenge.

Climbing to his feet, House attacked Donovan, slashing the axe at Donovan's midsection. He caught him good, but it did very little damage, healing almost immediately. Donovan barely tried to dodge it. He knew House couldn't hurt him. Now, he was just toying with the distraught captain.

"Is that all?" Donovan asked, gloating. "Is that all the great Sebastian House can muster?" He grinned. "We are not amused."

"Argh!" House growled, again launching himself right at his foe.

Donovan, like a cat and a mouse, simply sidestepped him and let House fall back to the floor, landing between him and Nova. The giant didn't advance toward him any, but he did catch Gianna around the wrist as she ran over to help her father.

Gianna! House thought. *God, please, no...*

But neither Donovan, nor Nova acted against his daughter more than subduing her. It seemed that the former DARPA scientist wanted House, and most likely Gianna, all to himself.

"After I assimilate you..." Donovan looked up at a frightened Gianna, "I'm going to do the same to your little gir—"

Something exploded out of Donovan's chest. Looking down, it took House a moment to recognize what the object was. Then, it dawned on him. What he was looking at was the tip of a razor-sharp harpoon. Looking past Donovan, House was shocked to see Trip inside the suspended ADS suit. The harpoon gun that he talked about installing was, indeed, in place on Stay Puft's right forearm.

Donovan's incredible healing abilities took over and the wound sealed around the four-pronged harpoon blade, effectively gluing it in place. With a look of terror, Donovan realized what was about to happen.

Trip leaped out of the open suit and shimmied down a nearby ladder. Sam was there waiting for him, and in his hand was the controls for the crane that lowered the suit into the launch pool. Wasting no time, the XO depressed a large red button, releasing the crane's hold on the hefty ADS. The suit plunged into the icy waters and sank like a stone, dragging with it a screeching Seth Donovan.

His reaction made Nova release Gianna and shamble forward. House dove at the larger man's knees, tripping him up and sending him tumbling to the floor.

Donovan wasn't out of it yet, however.

He clung to the rim of the pool, strobing like mad. Both his hands and the parasite gripped the floor in front of House. Taking his time, House reached down and reacquired his axe, flipping the large weapon in the air as if he were Tom Cruise in *Cocktail*.

Now standing over Donovan, House thought of something witty to say to the man but decided to keep it to himself. Instead, he raised the axe high over his head and brought it down, slicing through the girthy, tubular entity that had caused so much pain.

With his "cord cut" Donovan released his grip, fell back, and was swiftly pulled beneath the surface. House didn't need to check whether or not he kept sinking. He knew the man was finally done for. Nova's eyes darkening was one clue—so was him puking up his parasite.

As Sam closed the pool's hatch, Trip rushed over, leaned out over the shimmering water. Smiling, he turned and found House's disheveled face. "Told you I was going fishing, didn't I?"

EPILOGUE

Without Donovan's ethereal connection, the remaining members of Coalesce dropped like flies. The things living within them were ejected, shriveled up, and died, just like the demise of Grigson back in the ESD office.

Commander Gavin Kirk was wrestling one of them off of his radar technician when the lady that had attacked them both simply let go and caved in on herself. McMurdo lost six people before that, having initially met the emerging Endeavor crew halfway to help. No one could've guessed that they'd become a band of murderous brutes.

After peace returned to McMurdo Station, more people were spotted climbing down from a lower exit. Through his cracked binoculars, the bloodied Kirk recognized at least one of the sailors.

"Captain," he said, shaking House's hand.

"Commander," House replied, looking, feeling, and smelling awful. He gripped Kirk's offered hand with his right hand while still gripping the plasma-covered axe in his left.

Kirk quickly looked over the unkempt lot in front of him. His face went from one of concern to anger. "Mind telling me what the hell happened just now, and why six of my people are dead?"

House glanced at the eighteen other survivors and shrugged. "Six...that's it?"

"That's it?" Kirk asked, fuming.

House nodded. "I lost nearly ten-times that."

Kirk's mouth opened. "This..." he said, unable to find his words, "you're telling me that this is all that's left of your eighty-man crew?"

House frowned. "It is. We lost a lot of good sailors out there."

Sam stepped up next to House. "I can vouch for the captain."

"Me too," Trip said, stepping up.

"And me," Gianna added, sliding under her dad's right arm.

Kirk didn't look like he wanted to argue. Everyone was cold, and they all needed to get indoors before the storm picked up again like it was supposed to. But there was one more question that Kirk needed an answer to before they got moving.

He looked House dead in the eyes. "What happened, Captain?"

House opened his mouth but shut it. He looked over his shoulder, to a boat that he loved, a boat he knew he'd never step foot on again. If it were up to him, the Endeavor would be dismantled and sold off for parts.

He returned Kirk's gaze with his own, still truly unsure of everything that had occurred. "Let's get inside first. I'm still trying to process it all."

Trip stepped up and in the most simplified way, gave Kirk a rundown of everything that occurred on board the Endeavor over the last few hours.

"Aliens. Meteor. Infection. Monsters. Blood. Pregnant. Death. Disgusting. Tired. Cold."

"Wait," Kirk said, remembering something from his past—something he himself saw splashdown in these very waters, "did you say 'meteor?'"

* * *

After a thorough, three-month-long investigation, Captain House and the surviving crewmembers of the Endeavor were finally cleared of any wrongdoing. While the concept of an alien invasion via parasitic octopus wasn't listed as the direct cause, the incident was officially blamed on an "unknown contagion." The ship was then quarantined and towed to an undisclosed location for "cleaning."

"It needs to be destroyed," House said, speaking to Damon Becker's replacement, a man he had no interest in getting to know.

House was done with the military for good—and so was Trip. Including Gianna, the three planned on moving into House's current home just south of Savannah, Georgia with the plans of raising Baby Boy Triplett together. Hearing of the career seaman's retirement, House was immediately given a job as Senior Director of the Port of Savannah, a leg of the Georgia Ports Authority.

Gianna and Trip would be working closely with the port's IT team to help increase productivity, while also introducing new, technical jobs to the GPA.

Sitting in his office, House read up on an article detailing the incident in the Southern Ocean. Because of the deaths, and the following lawsuit, the government was forced to release as much information as necessary to satiate the wolves of the media market.

But, like most disasters, not everything was included in the writeup. The identities of those on board were deemed classified, and House's record remained impeccable.

A knock at his door announced the arrival of his daughter, and she was starting to show. Her belly was protruding slightly, and she looked even more beautiful than usual. House's smile was apparent.

"What?" Gianna asked.

"*What*, what?" House asked back. "Why can't I smile at my little girl?"

She rubbed her belly and snorted. "Well, don't get used to it, cuz I'm not gonna be 'little' for much longer."

House laughed and looked out his window, out to the sea of shipping containers. Just past them was the Savannah River and further down it, the open ocean. His ocean. He missed it, but it wouldn't come between him and his family—not again. He missed too many of Gianna's birthdays and his share of anniversaries and Christmases. His goal was to be there for the rest of them until his time on this planet was over.

"Oh," Gianna said excitedly, "guess what?"

House blinked away a memory of him, Karen, and Gianna, and raised an eyebrow.

"We picked out a name!"

House sat up, excited to hear what she and Trip had picked out.

Her face softened. "His name will be Sebastian Marcus Triplett." Her eyes watered. "But," she sniffed, "he'll go by Buddy."

*   *   *

Slashing through the water like a thirteen-foot-long, eight-thousand-pound torpedo, the enormous bull southern elephant seal searched for its next meal. Typically, it would gladly snag a squid or fish, but today the seal wanted something bigger.

Being able to hold its breath for twenty minutes at a time gave the marine mammal a broad range to hunt, diving to depths exceeding three-thousand-feet. The southern elephant seal was the deepest diving, air-breathing, non-cetacean ever recorded and was a sight to see in the open water. Unfortunately, the seals' thick, clumsy build made them easy prey.

Nearly out of air, the bull turned to head for the surface but stopped, seeing something off to the south. Curious, it headed off, using its keen eyesight and sensitive facial whiskers to locate the potential snack. After three pumps of its muscular tail, it propelled forward with an intense burst of locomotion.

Just feet from its inert, floating prey, the seal opened its jaws and tore at the creature's neck. Thrashing back and forth, it ripped a chunk of flesh away and woofed it down, greedily going back for seconds until it had its fill. Admittedly, the meal tasted different than the others he'd had in his life.

It tasted better.

Slowly, the seal began its return trek to the surface, and to its colony of forty females. There, it would mate and slumber, digesting its latest catch until it was time to return to the ocean.

The bull blinked hard, feeling odd. Shaking it off, the seal continued onward, unknowingly digesting a small piece of a creature not of this world. As the chunk of tubular, hypothermic meat thawed within the warm-blooded mammal, it started on its next conquest. Slowly, it released a small amount of a strange, pulsating plasma before shriveling up and crumbling into a grey, ashen state.

But as quickly as the original piece decayed, a new one began to form. The microscopic organisms continued to spread, latching onto one another, merging into a single, stronger worm-like creature. They "assimilated" with one another, growing exponentially, quietly transmitting a message the seal would easily understand.

We are better together.

The End

CHECK OUT OTHER GREAT DEEP SEA THRILLERS

THE BREACH
by Edward J. McFadden III

A Category 4 hurricane punched a quarter mile hole in Fire Island, exposing the Great South Bay to the ferocity of the Atlantic Ocean, and the current pulled something terrible through the new breach. A monstrosity of the past mixed with the present has been disturbed and it's found its way into the sheltered waters of Long Island's southern sea.

Nate Tanner lives in Stones Throw, Long Island. A disgraced SCPD detective lieutenant put out to pasture in the marine division because of his Navy background and experience with aquatic crime scenes, Tanner is assigned to hunt the creeper in the bay. But he and his team soon discover they're the ones being hunted.

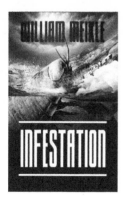

INFESTATION
by William Meikle

It was supposed to be a simple mission. A suspected Russian spy boat is in trouble in Canadian waters. Investigate and report are the orders.

But when Captain John Banks and his squad arrive, it is to find an empty vessel, and a scene of bloody mayhem.

Soon they are in a fight for their lives, for there are things in the icy seas off Baffin Island, scuttling, hungry things with a taste for human flesh.

They are swarming. And they are growing.

"Scotland's best Horror writer" - Ginger Nuts of Horror

"The premier storyteller of our time." - Famous Monsters of Filmland

CHECK OUT OTHER GREAT DEEP SEA THRILLERS

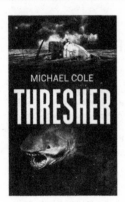

THRESHER
by **Michael Cole**

In the aftermath of a hurricane, a series of strange events plague the coastal waters off Florida. People go into the water and never return. Corpses of killer whales drift ashore, ravaged from enormous bite marks. A fishing trawler is found adrift, with a mysterious gash in its hull.

Transferred to the coastal town of Merit, police officer Leonard Riker uncovers the horrible reality of an enormous Thresher shark lurking off the coast. Forty feet in length, it has taken a territorial claim to the waters near the town harbor. Armed with three-inch teeth, a scythe-like caudal fin, and unmatched aggression, the beast seeks to kill anything sharing the waters.

THE GUILLOTINE
by **Lucas Pederson**

1,000 feet under the surface, Prehistoric Anthropologist, Ash Barrington, and his team are in the midst of a great archeological dig at the bottom of Lake Superior where they find a treasure trove of bones. Bones of dinosaurs that aren't supposed to be in this particular region. In their underwater facility, Infinity Moon, Ash and his team soon discover a series of underground tunnels. Upon exploring, they accidentally open an ice pocket, thawing the prehistoric creature trapped inside. Soon they are being attacked, the facility falling apart around them, by what Ash knows is a dunkleosteus and all those bones were from its prey. Now...Ash and his team are the prey and the creature will stop at nothing to get to them.